LOVE

calls the

SHOTS

D1526259

DEB GARDNER ALLARD

ST JOSEPH, MISSOURI USA

LOVE CALLS THE SHOTS
Copyright © 2022 Deb Gardner Allard

Paperback ISBN: 978-1-936501-68-7

All rights reserved. No part of this publication may be reproduced or transmitted in any form or by any means, electronic, mechanical, photocopying, recording, or otherwise, without written permission of the publisher. Published by CrossRiver Media Group, 4810 Gene Field Rd. #2, St. Joseph, MO 64506. CrossRiverMedia.com

This book is a work of fiction. Names, places, characters, and incidents are either products of the author's imagination or used fictitiously. Any similarity to actual people, organizations, or events is coincidental.

For more information on Deb Gardner Allard, visit DebGardnerAllard.com

Editor: Debra L. Butterfield
Cover Design: Tamara Clymer
Cover Image: office background, 80295260 © Siraphol | Dreamstime.com; female doctor 185688914 © Roman Samborskyi | Dreamstime.com
Printed in the United States of America

This book is dedicated to my heavenly Father who inspired and helped me to write this book.

And also to the publishing team at CrossRiver Media. Without them, my dreams would not have come true. Thank you, Tami, Deb, and DeeDee for being such fantastic cheerleaders who see your vision through. May God bless all that you do.

ONE

Saige Westbrook groaned as she lay sprawled over her apartment floor like a television crime scene victim. She'd made a scene all right, but thankfully, not a fatal one. "A fine display of professionalism, doctor. Now get up."

She gripped the wobbly coffee table then dragged herself upright. "Stand erect." She rolled back her shoulders, shook her arms at her sides, then exhaled an emerging bout of self-doubt. Failure was not an option. Head aligned with her spine, she moved her foot a few inches on the stick-thin heel.

Why had she listened to Darcy? Her roommate had assured her stilettos were the craze. "Not only that," Darcy added, "but they're the rage among the rich and famous of St. Anne's Landing."

Hmm. Exaggeration? More than likely Darcy had nothing to match Saige's gown except for the silver stilettos and overstated their worth.

Saige moved her foot a few more inches. "So far, so good." She'd never worn heels while growing up on the farm, but she'd conquer them now because millions of ladies had done so before her.

Step, crumple.

"Aagh!" More practice time—that's what she needed. If her cardiology patients at the university hospital hadn't consumed her life, maybe—

Wait a minute. How was it she could leap pigsties in a single bound, perform textbook-perfect heart procedures, and save dying patients' lives, yet she couldn't balance in worthless stilettos?

7

She gripped the sofa, pulled herself to standing, then reached for the living room wall…the hallway wall…the bedroom doorframe.

Frazzled, she arrived at her closet.

Taking hold of the knobs, she blew wayward hair strands from her eyes then opened the bifold doors. Flats, sneakers, slippers. Not a fancy shoe in sight. Wait a minute, didn't an actress wear sneakers to the Oscars a few years ago? Too bad Saige's old clunkers weren't stylish. Maybe a new fashion trend was in order—beige Crocs. Ugh. She had no choice but to risk her life in Darcy's killer heels.

She crumpled to the threadbare comforter on her bed. Massaging her sore ankles again, she groaned in pain. During tonight's invitation-only Christmas party, Dr. Edgar Addington planned to announce the cardiologist chosen by his team to work at his complex. If she were selected, she'd soar above her farm girl status. She'd become a city girl instead of a small-town bumpkin with credentials.

But how could she possibly fit into an office filled with city-bred specialists? She flopped back on the bed, arms over her head. Was it too late to chicken out? Her bedside clock showed two hours remained until the party. Would anyone notice if she didn't show? Over a hundred candidates had applied for the position, so her absence wouldn't make a ripple in the Addington's illustrious pond. But it might affect her standing with fellow medical school graduates. She'd forever be known as "the quitter."

She rose from the bed and fiddled with the updo piled on her head. The hairspray-wielding stylist at the salon had transformed her fawn-brown locks into an elegant creation, but between the heavy make-up and the updo, she didn't recognize herself in the dresser mirror. The real Saige looked nothing like the fancy woman before her. As she repositioned a sparkly hairpin to capture wayward hair strands, the bracelet on her wrist glistened in the overhead light.

Mom had gifted her with the keepsake a few months before she passed away. Diamonds lined the white gold top, but the inscription on the underside touched Saige's heart: "To my precious gem. You will conquer giants. Love, Mom."

Tears trickled down Saige's cheeks as she remembered what her mother had shared: "Giants don't always have two legs, dear one. Stand up to your fears and accomplish your dreams."

Wearing the bracelet, touching it, keeping it close reminded Saige of how much her mother loved her.

As she released the stiletto straps on her ankles, the clasp on the bracelet flicked open. Saige snapped it shut. The touchy mechanism worried her. Her busy internship and then the cardiology fellowship with Dr. Vanderwald hadn't left much time for her to take the bracelet to the jewelers for repair. But regardless of the delicate clasp, if she attended the event tonight, she'd wear the gift from her mother to calm her nerves, especially since she had to dance on the killer heels, face to face with fear.

A knock interrupted her thoughts. Saige hooked the stiletto straps with her fingers and hurried across the carpet in her bare feet. Through the door's peephole, she spotted the visitor—Aiden Littlefield, her faithful study partner/good friend/total nuisance and across the hall neighbor. Why did he have to show up at a time like this? She cracked the door. "I've only got two hours to get ready for an important event. You can't stay."

Aiden scratched his scalp near the man bun on his head, tapped his oval wire-rim glasses to their perch, then glanced at her wiggling toes. "Anything I can do to help?"

"No. Yeah…come to think of it, would you hold me steady while I practice walking in these ankle-breakers?" She dangled them for him to inspect.

Aiden shoved his hands deep in his jean pockets then slipped through the door crack in stiff penguin style. "Of course, Saige. What are friends for?"

TWO

Two hours later, Saige clutched her borrowed cashmere coat to her chin and tottered up the Addington mansion steps in the killer heels.

As "Deck the Halls" boomed inside the estate, light poured through the glass panels on both sides of the entrance. Did she dare steal a peek? She leaned in—

The door swung open.

A human nutcracker snapped to attention.

"Huh?" Saige shrieked as her ankles crumpled in the stilettos. The nutcracker dove for her hands and pulled her upright.

Where was she? Saige eyed the soldier's ruby red cheeks, painted lips, and matching uniform. The vivid combo accented the snow-white mustache and goatee on his pasty face. As he drew her over the threshold, a minty scent pricked her nose. Liniment? So, the old soldier had sore joints. Focus, Dr. Saige. His arthritis is the least of your worries. She turned her attention to the plight at hand. "Is this the Addington mansion?"

The nutcracker nodded. His knowing grin added a brief sparkle to his eyes. Had he caught her peeking through the glass?

"I was…uh, I didn't mean to—" Saige bit her tongue to stop the incessant blubbering.

The nutcracker removed his coal-black hat to reveal a shock of hair whiter than the snowbanks along the circular drive. With a bow, he swished the headpiece to his waist and bid her into the foyer.

Overhead, the walls ascended for what seemed like half a mile, creating an echo for each heel click on the marble tiles. "Sleigh Bells" suddenly erupted through the foyer as Saige inspected the surroundings. The pianist, wherever he was, livened the tune with fancy finger work, giving the song a twenty-first-century vibe.

The pretend soldier checked his wristwatch while she oohed and ahhed. After a few more seconds, he flicked lint from his uniform.

"I'm so sorry—" she began.

The nutcracker tipped his shiny hat, accepted her coat, then disappeared.

Calm down, Saige. Nausea had nagged her ever since the taxi ride through the busy St. Anne's streets. But the futile conversation with the stiff greeter wasn't much help either.

She tugged her fitted gown into place—the one she'd bought with her rent money. Darcy, her roommate, had agreed to cover their December payment as a going-away gift since this was most likely Saige's final month in their tiny, four-room apartment. After six weeks of interviews with Dr. Addington's team, Saige and the other selected candidates had received invitations for the doctor's grand announcement. She'd have to meet the esteemed doctor in person tonight, and first impressions counted.

Pull yourself together, Saige. No one will care if you grew up in a small country town. Professionals come from every corner of society. You can do this. It's your chance to move to the city and leave farm town life behind. She fiddled with her bracelet, making sure the clasp remained intact.

Seconds later, the nutcracker returned with an outstretched hand.

What did he want? Tilting her head, Saige waited for a clue. The rigid actor took her hand and draped it over the crook of his arm. Like a mechanical toy, he marched her past a narrow wall table adorned with flickering Christmas candles and holly sprigs. Saige's shoulders relaxed as the aroma of sweet Jonagolds and cinnamon sticks drifted her way. Apple cider had been a Christmas tradition on her family's farm for as long as she could remember.

Without warning, the nutcracker picked up his pace. He rounded the corner then led her, wobbling on her heels, past a majestic staircase as impressive as the ones in old movies. A man on the top landing, dressed in a tuxedo, played a baby grand like a concert pianist.

Oblivious to her mounting anxiety, the pretend nutcracker soldiered onward. The thought crossed Saige's mind to pinch him, to make sure he was flesh and blood, but instead, she folded her lips to stop a frown from taking hold.

A few yards later, the nutcracker paused before a crowded living room where people decked in what Saige imagined was Saks Fifth Avenue chatted around a blazing fireplace. Through pursed lips, they sipped from crystal mugs and fluted glasses. Here and there, Saige spotted pretentious pinkies extended with flair. In the far corner of the room, bright lights and golden bulbs with matching bows adorned the most beautiful Christmas tree she had ever seen.

The actor released her arm and stood at attention. Did he expect her to enter the party alone? No way would she give the unflinching stick man the pleasure of seeing her tremble. Instead, she repositioned her bracelet—diamonds up—squared her shoulders, then tilted her nose the way she'd seen a lady in pearls stroll through Neiman-Marcus, where she purchased her outfit. Ready, she took a step into the room.

Her left heel stem skidded sideways. This can't be happening to me! Her arms flailed. Her ankles folded. Like a clumsy bumpkin, she toppled across the sunken room.

Why hadn't the fake soldier warned her about the drop?

If not for an overstuffed chair nearby, she would've landed on the hard marble floor. Draped over the chair's arm with her nose buried deep in its pillowy cushion, she could barely breathe. But if she tried to wiggle free, she'd split her dress seams.

Never in thirty-four years had she ever been in such an embarrassing predicament. She struggled to release herself, frantically pedaling the air. Her lungs demanded more oxygen, but her gown was too tight. A muffled scream burst from her mouth. "Help!"

She didn't care what the well-bred people in the room thought. Fear clutched her throat; she couldn't escape. She let out a pitiful shriek again—high-pitched this time. "Help me, please!"

A whisper brushed her ear. "Calm down, miss. I'll assist you."

Strong arms wove around her torso before they lifted her to a broad chest. Saige wrapped her arms around the man's neck and settled her head on his tuxedo lapel to avoid the guests' shocked stares. He carried her from the room, past the formal grand staircase, and down an endless hallway lined with priceless artwork. From the corner of her eye, Saige stole glimpses of masterpieces by Van Gogh and Monet.

"Thank you for saving me from total embarrassment." She shifted her view to her hero's handsome dimpled chin.

"Glad you survived, miss." The servant's suave British accent caught Saige off guard.

Goosebumps traveled up her arms. What did he look like? Did she dare raise her head to inspect his face? Not a chance. What would he think if their eyes met?

"Is anything injured?" The man not only had a fascinating British accent, but he also had a caring heart!

Calm down, Saige. Between her shocking fall and his charming rescue, she felt woozy. "My dignity requires major surgery, but otherwise, I'll be fine." Who was he, and more importantly, where was he taking her?

Several yards down the hallway, he opened a door with her snugly in his arms and strode into a dimly lit room with a small fireplace. "I believe you'll be more comfortable freshening up in here. Please, rejoin the party when you've had time to pull yourself together."

"I appreciate your kindness, sir, but I doubt I'd ever fit in with these wealthy socialites."

"Perhaps not, but it wouldn't be because of your looks. Many of them, I dare say, live in pretentious worlds." The man gently placed her on a leather loveseat near the warm fire then turned to leave, his face cloaked by shadows.

Was he Dr. Addington's servant? He sounded like a British TV butler. From the backside, his perfect physique and dark wavy hair brand-

14

ed him a hunk of the highest order. She'd dreamed of someone like him many times—a romantic hero who would sweep her off her feet to a candlelight dinner then for a stroll along a fragrant lilac path.

Before she strung together a thank you, he exited the room.

Sighing, she removed the stilettos. The heels were beyond repair, broken, like her pride. Darcy had wanted her to look stylish, but too late for that now. She broke off the heel stems then slipped what remained of the shoes back on her feet.

Wood crackled in the fireplace as she walked across the room from the loveseat. A desk stacked wth books indicated the room's purpose, a study of some sort. She turned up the desk lamp, bathing the room in brighter light to evaluate her surroundings. Proving her hunch, built-in bookshelves filled with cardiac medical books lined the walls. She'd give her right thumb to skip the party and curl up on the loveseat with a good book on heart disease.

Blissful evenings aside, she returned her attention to the room. She'd seen a picture of Dr. Edgar Bridgemont Addington on the internet. His grim countenance was focused, even pompous. Medical school friends had whispered about finding the aged doctor challenging to approach. But many candidates flocked to apply for the prestigious spot on his team anyway.

Saige repositioned her gown over her hips then eased into a chair at the desk. Feeling her face and hair, she evaluated the damage. Runaway tendrils cascaded from her lopsided updo and mascara mixed with tears smudged her fingertips when she touched her face. How could she fix the makeup without a mirror? She was a mess, an utter, humiliating mess. Had she bungled everything—her first impression and her chance to work with the old curmudgeon? After falling, screaming, and ruining her makeup, she couldn't return to the party, not now—not ever. She seized the tissue box on the desk and sopped the goop from her face.

A thought crossed her mind. What if the famous doctor hadn't seen her? Could he have been the grim, silver-haired gentleman holding the smokeless pipe near the Christmas tree? Would he use words like "quite right" and "old chap this" and "old chap that"?

She didn't care. A position on his team would distinguish her in the cardiology field. A slim chance existed that he hadn't seen her mishap since the living room was more expansive than her entire apartment. Another nose blow and mascara dab with yet another tissue, then she straightened. Why had this whole awful nightmare happened?

She knew exactly why. The nutcracker. It was all his fault. He should have warned her about the step. Humph. It felt like a hundred-foot drop in the stilettos. She had a mind to tell him what she thought of him acting like an unfeeling mannequin. But she wouldn't. Her mother taught her that ladies never say unkind words. No matter the offense, no matter the situation, thoughts should remain just that—thoughts. "One can never take back words, my sweet one," Mom always said. "The less you say, the fewer your regrets."

Those words remained in the "Mother's advice" folder Saige kept in her memories ever since she turned sixteen, when Mom began teaching her about how to succeed in life. Saige searched her mind for her mother's words of wisdom often. The timeless counseling spared her from many sticky situations.

By now, her debut at the party was a full-blown scandal. Trying not to make a sound, she inched open the study door. The hallway was empty. She let loose the breath she'd been holding then considered asking God to help her out of this mess but immediately bit her lip as she remembered the past. God hadn't answered her prayers when her mother died, so what good would it do to ask Him for help now? She wiped her face one last time for missed smears then tiptoed into the hallway and headed to the foyer.

The nutcracker met her at the door with her coat draped over his arm. "I'm sorry for the mishap, miss. I took the liberty to retrieve your wrap in case you planned to step out for some fresh air."

Too bad the man hadn't loosened his tongue before she fell. Saige caught his drift, though. His offer was a pleasant way of allowing her to leave gracefully. "Thank you." Who in her right mind would return after creating such a scene?

The pretend soldier's mouth twisted into a sick grin, or was it a wrinkled attempt at remorse? Did he wish he'd broken character earlier to assist her like a gentleman? She sighed. We all play-act, a few of us more than others. She raised on her toes and pecked him on the cheek. "I appreciate your thoughtfulness."

Red blotches appeared on the nutcracker's unpainted neck as he opened the door for her. Attempting what little poise she could muster, she exited in the lopsided stiletto soles and wobbled down the icy steps toward a waiting cab. The nutcracker hadn't planned on her taking some air at all. He had provided her with a ride home!

She wouldn't let her humiliation get the best of her. At least she'd met the valiant dark-haired hero of her dreams, the man who would save her from a terrible fiasco. Tonight's unexpected fall certainly counted as a fiasco and more—an utter disgrace. Other partygoers had surely witnessed her fall, but the servant was the only one who came to her rescue. Even if she couldn't see his entire face, he had the cutest dimpled chin. And his kind heart and strong, safe build, not to mention his accent, charmed her in many ways. If only she could speak with him again, get to know him, learn if he was her soul mate. Halfway down the steps, she turned back to the nutcracker. "May I ask who carried me to the study?"

But, oblivious as usual, or maybe half deaf, the pretend soldier waved farewell and closed the door.

THREE

D r. Edgar Graybourne Addington, known as "Gray," searched the prominent guests for the rose-colored gown worn by the young lady he had carried to his study an hour ago. Lights and glass ornaments sparkled as he scanned every corner of the sunken room. Surely, the woman had plenty of time to compose herself and return by now. Amidst the laughter and boisterous chatter hemming him in, he spotted his faithful valet, the dignified nutcracker. "There you are, Fernsby. Have you seen the young lady I assisted?"

Acting every bit the stiff soldier Gray had coaxed him to portray, the old chap stood at attention, his arms at his sides. "I believe she left, sir. Must not have wanted to make a fuss."

"Her name?"

"Didn't get it, sir."

Gray swallowed his disappointment but it refused to go down smoothly. He had planned on spending time with the lady when she returned from the study. Something about her piqued his curiosity. What was it? Her gentle behavior? Maybe it was her frankness; she spoke naturally and from the heart. No one in his social circle would ever admit to not fitting in. Gray removed a sealed envelope from his tuxedo jacket, but instead of opening it, he shook his head and returned it to his pocket. "I believe I'll retire to my study."

"But sir, your guests—"

A familiar female in a shimmering evening gown apologized to the man on Gray's left before edging past him to sidle up to Gray. "Darling, you're not leaving the party yet, are you?" The woman slipped her hand through the crook of Gray's arm.

"I'm tired, Lilith." Gray glanced around the room again. Where was the young lady who fell?

Lilith smoothed her auburn updo before weaving her fingers through Gray's, the way she did when she persisted in getting her way. Even though she was nothing more than a friend, she had begun acting otherwise.

"I'd love for you to meet a friend of mine; someone I've known since childhood." Her not-so-gentle tug yanked him away from his valet.

Gray loosened his hand from hers as she pulled. "I'm retiring for the evening." He scanned the crowded room again. "Parties tire me. If it weren't for Father demanding I keep our traditions, I'd avoid this event altogether. Besides, I'd planned to announce the new appointee for our team."

"And you can't because?" Lilith paused as a servant outfitted in a tux strode by carrying a polished tray laden with fluted glasses. Extending her hand in the manner of a prima ballerina, she lifted a drink from the platter then stared at someone across the room.

"One of the candidates might have left." Gray spoke into thin air since Lilith had swiveled away from him. He frowned at the nutcracker. Was his valet the reason for the mystery woman's departure?

Squirming under the heat of Gray's stare, Fernsby interjected a dash of advice as he stood at attention. "Tomorrow, the candidates should receive the formal announcements in the mail, sir. Take comfort. Your team's appointee will know his or her fate before dinner."

"Thank you, old chap, but I wanted to see the reaction on the selectee's face. Too late for that now."

With theatrical flair, Lilith spun around to face Gray. "Such a pity, darling, but despite the unfortunate situation, you should become familiar with your neighbors in the community. As the host, you must introduce yourself and thank them for attending." She managed the tiniest sip from her glass. "Be a perfect host now and mingle. I'll stay by your side."

"I dare say, you've given me no choice."

"You could try enjoying yourself." Lilith looped her unoccupied arm in his before pivoting him to a group of partygoers by the fireplace. Glass in hand, she raised it in a grand gesture. "Everyone, please join me in a toast to our generous host, Dr. Edgar Graybourne Addington, the son of Dr. Edgar Bridgemont Addington. Here's to his continued success!"

"Cheers!" resounded from the attendees.

Gray shifted his balance in response. He was a cardiothoracic surgeon, not a social icon. Although he operated on hearts, strangely enough, he wondered if he even had one. Professors had advised him his IQ was absurd. Unfortunately, they forever added an afterthought: "The downside of brilliance is a lack of common sense."

Was that why his father took charge and ordered his affairs? The senior Dr. Addington had planned Gray's entire life. Gray merely obeyed like an automaton. But that would soon change. Gray would make sure of it.

Glasses clinked in unison.

Did they want a speech? Gray pursed his lips tighter than the surgically enhanced faces of the partygoers. "Thank you." The two words would have to suffice.

His mind drifted to the girl he had carried to his study. Who was she? The young lady acted the way he always felt. Lost. Would he ever see her again?

FOUR

The following morning, Saige awoke in her apartment bedroom and rubbed her bare wrist, daring to hope her loss had been a dream. After realizing the truth, she flooded her pillow with another round of tears. Wiping her eyes for the hundredth time, she strained to recall where she'd lost the keepsake. Was it when she fell? Maybe it dropped on the floor or in the chair cushions, or the study, or did it happen in the taxi? If it fell in the cab, she might never find it again. She gripped her covers to her chin for comfort.

Her mother had purchased the gift with the savings she stashed away for a romantic European anniversary trip with Pop before her final bout with cancer. They were the most loving, most romantic couple Saige had ever known. Despite sacrificing their trip, Mom's face glowed with excitement as she handed Saige the small velvet package topped with a bow.

"My greatest hope has been for you to graduate medical school and accomplish your dreams, Saige." Her eyes sparkled with joy. "When you're fearful or worry you won't succeed, reread the words engraved on the underside of the bracelet."

Heaviness crushed Saige. Blaming herself made it worse; she had to get out of bed or risk spending the entire day sobbing.

She checked the time on the nightstand digital. The mail would've been delivered by now. On Saturdays, she often received a letter from home. Comfort. That's what she needed.

Since Darcy was in Minnesota for Christmas, Saige intended to lounge around in pajamas for the day, but the hope of mail dragged her out of bed. After grabbing her keychain and wrapping her mid-calf puffy coat over her pj's, she hurried downstairs to the apartment foyer.

Bits of white lay inside the decorative slots on her mailbox. Excited, Saige unlocked Number 227 and withdrew a handful of envelopes. Under a cherished letter from home, she spotted a fancy white card with a gold seal and the return address of Addington Complex. She covered her mouth to keep from squealing. Pull yourself together, Saige. Looking both ways, she checked for nosy neighbors. What would they think if they caught Dr. Westbrook dancing around like an adolescent?

She relocked the mailbox then leaped up the steps to her apartment. After chucking her coat and the junk mail on the secondhand sofa, she hurried to her bedroom, plunked down on her twin bed, and crossed her legs with the fancy card on her lap. The postdate indicated the office had mailed it two days earlier. Quivering, she opened the envelope and withdrew the gold-edged card. She pressed it to her chest. Was it a notification of acceptance or rejection?

She turned it over.

Flopping back on her bed, she stifled a scream with her hand.

Congratulations! Dr. Saige Westbrook, you are invited to join the Addington cardiology team.

The job was hers. Stars floated before her eyes. She had won the opportunity to work with the best of the best.

A rap on the door made her jump. Who would knock at ten a.m.? She threw on her flannel robe, slipped the fancy card into the pocket, and tiptoed to the peephole. Aiden Littlefield from the apartment across the hall studied the doorknob while raking loose hair strands behind his ears. Saige had planned to rest today. Maybe if she ignored him, he'd go away.

The pounding started on the door again.

"Hey, sleepyhead. Can I borrow some pancake mix? Open up!" His shouts and thumps blasted through the closed door.

Saige reared back. The vibrations from his caterwauling would wake the entire building if she didn't make him stop. Despite her ratty bed hair, she tied her robe belt, released the bolt lock, and waved him inside. "Might as well come on in, before the neighbors call the apartment manager."

Clad in flannel pj bottoms paired with a long-sleeved tee displaying the words: "Doctors Call the Shots," Aiden slipped through the opening as though Saige might close it before his entrance. He tapped his oval wire rims in place then scratched his scalp between long disheveled hair strands escaping his man bun. "Sorry, I'm starving."

"When aren't you hungry?" Saige dug through every kitchen cupboard until she found the mix. "There you go. Help yourself." She set the box on the rickety table beside her lone Christmas decoration—a small poinsettia plant.

"You'd find things easier if you'd organize a little. You know, boxed goods on the bottom shelf, canned goods on the middle one."

When did she have time to organize anything between her studies and cardiology fellowship? "I've got a great idea! How about you do it for me in exchange for everything you borrow." She couldn't resist adding the sweet-natured jab.

"Sure. And speaking of borrowing, can I get two eggs and a cup of milk while I'm at it?"

Saige chuckled as she lifted the pancake box from his hand. Aiden always asked for the works. "I might as well fix them. Make yourself at home."

His quick scoot into a folding chair at her secondhand table proved this had been his intention all along. If he weren't such a great friend, she might not have fed him as often, but he created the best or maybe the corniest mnemonics for memorizing medical school material. After repeating them and laughing until she cried, Saige never forgot a single fact.

Aiden reminded her of Liam, her older brother. But Liam kept his short, mousy-brown hair trimmed, unlike Aiden's scraggly blond mop that he forever twisted into a knot on the back of his head. Both guys possessed a wicked sense of humor, though, and like Liam, Aiden teased her unmercifully. That was why Saige considered him friend material and nothing more—the continuing saga of her love life.

She wanted romance, someone to sweep her off her feet, like the mystery man who carried her to the study at the Addington mansion. Would she ever see him again? Why couldn't Aiden have a romantic side?

"Hey, you going to make those pancakes or just memorize the directions? If I remember right, there are only three steps—add ingredients to bowl, beat by hand, and spoon into hot pan. Some heart doctor you'll make."

Saige sent him a lopsided grin before opening the box. Several minutes later, she placed a stack of pancakes swimming in melted butter on the table. Maple syrup, a jug of orange juice, and two mismatched glasses completed the meal. After she took a seat, Aiden bowed his head. "Dear Lord, thank You for caring about us more than we can imagine. Help us to be blessings to You, and please use us to show others the love of Christ. In Jesus' name, amen.

When he finished, Saige propped her elbows on the table while chewing a bite until the Addington Complex flickered through her mind. She folded her hands under her chin and glanced at Aiden. "Can I ask you a question?"

He lowered his fork. "Sure, if I'm allowed to speak with my mouth full."

"Do you think I'd fit in—you know, in a distinguished cardiology group like the Addingtons? The place is crawling with wealthy St. Anne's Landing blue bloods."

"Wait. What? Whoa." Aiden raised his palms. "Were you selected?"

Saige hesitated before removing the acceptance card from her robe. She placed it on the table then slid it across to him.

The color drained from Aiden's face. He stared at the card for eons as though reading each syllable but not comprehending the words. "Congratulations." The word fell out of his mouth half-heartedly after he recovered from the initial shock. He lifted his foot to his seat and wrapped his arms around his shin. "You're obviously skilled at cardiology." He cleared his throat before proceeding. "But what I think and what's best for you aren't what you'll want to hear. I doubt you'll like my answer."

She shifted in her chair, bracing for his advice. "Okay, lay it on me."

"I think you should marry me, become a missionary, and forget about St. Anne's Landing. We'd make a difference in the world, especially in Ethiopia or South America." Aiden batted his lashes at her, pleading in a melodramatic way.

When she didn't respond, he added, "But if you're set on becoming a famous cardiologist, there's no one better to work for than *old* Dr. Addington in this part of the country." He lowered his leg to the floor before spearing a forkful of pancake and filling his mouth.

Old Dr. Addington. The way Aiden said the word, he had heard the rumors about the man's contrary nature. But how could she marry Aiden when she didn't love him? Joining the mission field would be noble, if she had a relationship with God, but she didn't, and besides that, where would a missionary job land her in twenty years—toiling away in a remote country, lonely? She slipped a tiny bite of pancake into her mouth and chewed on it. Ever since high school, she'd wanted to break free of her boring little farm town and move to the city. And even before her cardiology fellowship, she knew where she wanted to work—the prestigious Addington Complex. But working with society elitists hadn't entered her mind until she attended the Christmas party and witnessed their dress and behavior.

"Okay, so out with it. What are your thoughts?" Aiden leaned his chair back on two legs as he crossed his arms. "Come on, tell me."

Saige swirled her juice glass contents, studying the bits of fiber sticking to the sides. Plenty of things earned top billing as fates worse than spending an entire career with a goofball. Aiden would entertain her, that's for sure. "Your offer is tempting, Aiden, but what about my family, especially Pop and Annie, my younger sis? St. Anne's isn't far from home. I want to be able to see them now and then."

"I get your point. It's family first for you, right?"

Saige nodded. "I can't traipse across the globe and leave them, especially since Mom passed away two years, two months, and nine days ago." She rubbed her bare wrist.

"Ah, right." Aiden stopped eating long enough to look at her. "I see your math skills are plucking at your heartstrings too. Say, did I ever

27

tell you that your heart is one of the best things I love about you?"

She rolled her eyes at him. He forever said the word *love* as though it meant something. But it didn't. Before he latched onto Saige, he'd been madly in love with Darcy for years, until she cheated on him with "the lawyer." Still, Aiden seemed sincere. "Even though my pop is a wonderful father, Annie still needs me in her life."

He patted her hand. "You needn't say more." His sky-blue eyes took on a soft, dreamy look she'd never seen in him. "I've come to know you pretty well during our years in medical school." His fingers worked around her palm until he held her hand firmly in his. "You won't be happy with yourself..." his lips turned down at the corners, "...and you'd probably make me feel more like a louse every day...if you came with me."

"What? Are you calling me moody now?" She'd never badgered anyone in her life. Saige popped her hands on her hips.

Aiden hid a chuckle with his hand. "No way. I'd be nuts to ever call you—that."

"Very funny. I'm sorry to have to let my happy-go-lucky friend down." She hated having to tell him the truth even more. "But you're more like an older brother than—"

"I got that message loud and clear when you ditched me after our only real date to the Comedy Den."

"Maybe it's because you came to my door wearing a fake nose and black mustache. Not to mention the broken arrow cap on your head."

Blushing, Aiden removed his hand from hers. "I'm glad you're honest." He went for his juice, lifted the glass to his lips, then set it down without taking a sip. His eyes bore into hers. "Doesn't the funny guy get the girl?"

"The funny and romantic guy gets the girl."

"Whatever, Saige, I want you to be happy more than anything. And I admire your awesome heart skills. They'd be valuable in the mission field, but I am who I am."

"I'm sorry we wouldn't work out, Aiden." This time Saige touched his hand.

"Yeah, me too." He polished off his last forkful of breakfast, stood, and with a thrust of his leg, kicked back his chair.

Why did she have a feeling she said something wrong? Going with him was out of the question, and that was that. Exhaling an exaggerated breath, she lifted the plates and silverware from the table.

As if capable of reading her mind, Aiden started for the door. "I'm outta here. Can't waste a dismal snowy day gabbing with a pal. Gotta get more shut-eye to make up for lost sleep. See you tomorrow?"

"I guess so. Hey, what about the dishes?" Saige waved a plate at him.

A shrug with raised palms preceded Aiden as he backstepped to the door. Turning on his heels, he exited without so much as a thank you.

Seconds later, the door reopened. His pink lips appeared through the crack. "Oh, I forgot to say, 'my stomach thanks you for the marvelous food.'" With that, the door closed.

Saige quickly bolted the lock before he remembered something else. She placed the dishes in the sink, snatched her cell phone from the kitchen counter, then searched the internet for the cab company that drove her home last night.

When the dispatcher answered her call, Saige gave the woman the information about her driver and cab before inquiring about her bracelet. "Oh, and I gave the driver a false name and had him take me to a friend's house. I'm sorry. I'm a little paranoid about strange men driving me home."

"Not to worry. We hear that all the time." The dispatcher asked more questions before adding, "We'll notify you if we find it." Just as curtly, she ended the call.

Saige rubbed her lip. What should she do now? The obvious thing was to call the mansion. Maybe she could also learn the identity of the charming servant who rescued her.

Again, she searched for a number on the internet. But this time, she checked every lead. Still no luck. How could she contact the home of a famous, wealthy cardiothoracic surgeon with a dreamy servant if the mansion kept an unlisted number?

FIVE

A rap on the study door startled Gray as he reclined in his chair with his feet propped on the desk. He squinted to avoid the sunlight streaming through the room. "Enter, old chap. I could use a cuppa tea or espresso about now."

The valet maneuvered around the partially opened door, juggling a serving tray as he entered. On his left, the crackling fire beneath the mantle's holly branches added a cheerful glow to the room despite the icicles hanging from the eaves outside.

"I believe you could use a change of clothing as well." The valet eyed the tossed suit parts strewn about the room before depositing the tray on the desk. He removed a mug and set the steaming brew before his boss. "It was a fine party last night." He spoke over his shoulder as he crossed the burgundy carpet imprinted with tiny diamond shapes.

"I suppose I missed half of it." Gray removed his bare feet from their perch. The morning sun shot a beam through the window, and it ricocheted off the polished surface into his face. Shielding his eyes with his hands, he swiveled sideways in the leather chair to avoid the glare. "I can't get over the young lady—the one who had that most unfortunate accident—beautiful girl." At least from what he surmised through the mess on her face and the disheveled hair piled on her head. He held his tongue before admitting he had been drawn to her refreshingly kind, yet frank, voice. No need to spark ideas in Fernsby's head.

Squirming as though he wanted to speak but chose to refrain, Fernsby peered at the ceiling.

31

Did his valet know more than he wanted to let on about the mishap? Had he been paying attention when the girl missed the step into the sunken living room, or had he been too busy scouting the room for his archenemy, Lilith?

"Indeed, the lady who fell was lovely." Fernsby's attention shifted to a picture of Lilith and Gray on the bookshelf. A scowl twisted his face into scorn as he scooped cuff links, socks, and a tuxedo tie from the ledge.

Gray noted his valet's contempt, but how could he not when Fernsby made his feelings obvious. "When will you ever get used to Lilith, old boy? She's quite a valuable friend to me." Gray ran his hand through his wavy hair before raising the frothy vanilla latte to his lips. He inhaled the steam then took a sip. "Hmm, new beans?"

"Adele ordered them from Italy." A sigh escaped Fernsby as he pocketed the clothing items from his hand and readjusted the drapes to temper the sun's rays. He walked to the desk.

"What say we make a daily habit of this new brew?" Gray took a longer sip, hoping to savor the smooth taste long after it left his tongue.

Fernsby delivered a respectful nod before adding, "Will there be anything else this morning?"

Pointing the mug at his valet, Gray stifled a chuckle. "For starters, there's a remnant of white paint under your jawline." He unclamped his little finger from the vessel and extended it toward Fernsby's chin. "But you did a marvelous job last night, old chap." He enjoyed calling his valet British terms even though Fernsby had been in America for over thirty years and Gray had never left American soil. His parents' as well as his servant's British accents had rubbed off on him.

A blush traveled Fernsby's cheeks.

"The guests played along," Gray added. "Thanks for being a good sport." He handed a tissue from the box on his desk to his valet.

"I suppose you're welcome." Fernsby removed the paint from under his chin and deposited the tissue in the trash receptacle by the desk. "I'm not sure if I'm cut out to be a nutcracker though."

"Don't spoil the merriment, old chap." The whole charade had been rather fun, even though Fernsby protested when asked to don the role.

But Gray wasn't quite sure what the tabloids might report about his party after the mishap. Next time, if there were a next time, he'd remind the valet that guests' needs come first. The so-called nutcracker's code of silence wasn't unbreakable, especially under dire circumstances. "By the way, do you remember what happened to the young lady who fell?"

Fernsby squirmed.

"Well, out with it, man."

After fishing in his meticulously creased pocket, the valet removed a sparkling bracelet. "I found this in the living room by the chair where she landed."

He dropped the object into Gray's hand. Gray turned the piece over, squinting to read the words on the underside: "To my precious gem. You will conquer giants. Love, Mom."

"This could belong to the young lady. Judging by the inscription, her mother certainly loves her." Gray studied the top side. "Did you notice the diamonds? This must have cost a small fortune. See if you can locate the girl." Gray returned the jewelry to Fernsby. He'd never let on, but he'd like to speak with the woman again. Her pleasant demeanor, considering her ordeal, impressed him.

Fernsby clutched the serving tray under his arm and accepted the bracelet with his free hand. "Won't Lilith become jealous if I find the young lady?"

"We're only friends."

"So you say. Is Lilith aware of that?"

"Of course, old chap." Gray nervously checked his watch. Lilith would be calling soon. She always phoned him on Saturday mornings.

Fernsby touched his cheek as if remembering something then placed the bracelet on the bookshelf. "I'll try my best to find the owner."

Right on time, the landline rang. Frowning, Fernsby lifted the receiver and sighed. "Addington mansion. May I help you?"

"Let me speak to Gray!" The demanding voice blasted through the receiver loud enough for Gray to hear from where he sat.

Lilith was a puzzlement. She could be sweeter than marzipan unless she spotted Fernsby or Adele. Then, her icy tone evoked more fear in his servants than the event that sank the Titanic. But if they were to treat her kindly like he did, she'd thaw. Gray was sure of it.

"It's for you." The valet held the phone for his boss with his lips twisted the way they usually did when Lilith called.

Gray frowned at him, but Fernsby dipped his head as his boss accepted the phone.

"Hello, Lilith." Gray shooed Fernsby with his hand. "Don't forget the bracelet, old chap. See if you can learn where she purchased it. Perhaps we'll find the unfortunate young lady who dropped it last night." He winced. Why did he allow that to slip out?

"I'll return for it when my hands are free. I don't want to accidentally toss it in the laundry bin." Continuing his duties, Fernsby picked up Gray's tuxedo jacket from the love seat.

"What did you say, old chap?"

"Nothing, just thinking aloud. I'll leave you to it, sir." Fernsby exited the room, jacket over one arm, pockets filled with clothing items, and the tray in the opposite hand.

Gray repositioned the phone to his ear. "Sorry for the momentary dalliance."

"Darling," Lilith replied, her voice rising in pitch. "Who is the woman you mentioned to Fernsby?"

"No one special."

"Hmm, is that so? Well, darling, I wonder if you'd take me to the Maximillian Theater tomorrow evening for an off-Broadway musical." Lilith's voice cracked as though her words landed on thin ice.

Judging by her tone, she was upset. Was it jealousy of the girl? How was he supposed to handle it? "I'll ask Fernsby to work his magic on the ticket office."

"Oh, and darling, what's this about a bracelet?"

"It's nothing, Lilith. I must let you go now. I'll ask Fernsby about the tickets."

"Gray, you won't—"

He ended the call, rose from his desk, and hurried from the room to stop the valet before the man headed to the servant's quarters.

SIX

Around lunchtime on Sunday, a rhythmic rapping on Saige's apartment door alerted her that her friend was on the other side. He'd never let up. Aiden being Aiden, he'd weasel back into her business. She opened the door with her hand on her hip.

"Say." Aiden leaned against the doorframe as though trying to act debonair. "I'm all out of bread. Come to think of it, I could use some peanut butter too. Oh, and if you have any, some jelly would be awesome." He thwacked his oval wire rims on his nose as though adding a period to the end of his sentence.

So much for his debonair charade. It lasted all of three seconds. Saige walked to the cupboard and prepared to hand him the items but changed her mind and made the snack for him instead. It was easier than restocking her cupboard.

He removed his fleece-lined jacket and draped it over a kitchen chair back before propping his hip against a maple cabinet. Hovering over the speckled laminate countertop, he inspected every stroke of her butter knife. "Make sure you spread the peanut butter all the way to the crust." He aimed his finger at the sandwich edges.

"Aiden Littlefield, just be happy I'm making it for you."

"Okay, okay. I'll take what I can get." He removed his leather headband and repositioned it across his temples so the tarnished peace symbol landed smack in the center of his forehead. Saige eyed his clothing. "You're looking groovy." Wasn't that what hippies used to say?

"Right on." Aiden held up his thumbs before plunking his bottom

35

into a chair at the table. His usual man bun plus his long-sleeved, tie-dyed tee over patched jeans completed his nostalgic hippie look.

Saige placed the top slice on his peanut butter and jelly then handed it to him as she slid onto the wobbly mismatched chair opposite his at the thrift shop table.

"If you had cut this diagonally, it would've been the best sandwich in the world." Aiden licked his lips and took another bite.

Saige rolled her eyes.

He swallowed. "Just saying, that's all."

She rose from the table and retrieved the butter knife from the kitchen counter. "Here you go. I probably wouldn't cut it right, either—cause it's not 'heart surgery' you know."

She collected clothes from a laundry basket by the table and began folding the items while Aiden finished his sandwich. As he ate, he dragged the truth out of her about the accident at the Addington mansion. The more details she shared, the more he asked. "Did you call the taxi company about the bracelet?" He shifted sideways as he swung his arm sloppily over his jacket on the back of his chair.

"I did. But they didn't find it." Saige tucked socks together then tossed them to a pile on the table.

"You must've dropped it at the mansion. Hey, I have a radical idea. How about calling the Addingtons?"

Saige sighed. "What makes you think I didn't?"

"Sorry. What'd they say?"

"The phone number is unlisted." She folded a sweatshirt and assigned it to a separate stack. "Any more brilliant ideas?"

Aiden tapped his finger on his temple like a detective contemplating clues. "Let's move on to your second dilemma. How about if we ask God to handle your problems and then make a trip to the Addington Complex? After I see the place, I'll have a better idea whether or not you'll fit in with the blue-bloods." He propped his long legs on the opposite mismatched chair under the table. His holey, stockinged feet stuck out the other side.

Saige lowered herself onto the seat adjacent to his and rested her neck back along the chair's upper edge. "Sorry, but I have plans for this evening."

"Doing what?"

"Well, if you must pry—"

"Oh, I must." A grin wove through Aiden's lips.

Saige shook her head at his attempt at humor. "I've set aside this evening to brood over my problems."

"Say, what? That's not allowed." Aiden spotted a sandwich crust on his plate and tossed it into his mouth. "As my dad would insist, 'We'd better hurry up and leave, so we can hurry up and get back.'"

No one could win an argument with the "King of Persuasion," so Saige didn't bother.

"I still think we should say a prayer first. God always takes care of our problems in ways we'd never imagine."

Saige thought about Aiden's statement for a moment. She didn't see the use in praying, but she wouldn't be rude.

Aiden ignored her silence and bowed his head. "Dear Lord, we're handing you Saige's problems because we know nothing is impossible for you. Would you please give her wisdom about the cardiology job offer and lead her to where she left the bracelet? Thank you for always hearing and answering our prayers. In Jesus' name, amen." He slipped on his sneakers then swooped his jacket off the back of his chair.

"Thank you…I guess. God didn't answer prayers for my mother, so I don't bother talking to Him anymore."

"Wait a minute. Did God not answer them, or did He have other plans for your mother? God's ways are not our ways. What about The Lord's Prayer? Remember the words—'thy kingdom come, thy will be done, on earth as it is in heaven?' Some day in heaven, God will explain why He took your mom when He did. I'm sure you'll be shocked at His answer. And your mom will agree with His decision."

"Yeah, if you say so." Still tired from working ten days in a row at the hospital, she walked like the undead to her bedroom closet. Coat in hand, she returned to the living room, a little shaken from Aiden's explanation and hesitant about his trip idea. "I hope you know this isn't a date, Dr. Aiden."

"Are you talking to me?" He pointed to his chest. Every corner of his face stretched into a display of confusion. Ignoring her declaration, he dusted his hands. "Move along, slowpoke." He waited at the door for her to exit then closed it behind them.

Outside in the parking lot, snow blanketed the windows of his hippie-era Volkswagen. The psychedelic "Bug" sported every color under the sun mixed with the '60s and '70s sayings—Do your own thing. Groovy. Peace. Right On! Far Out! Let's Boogie! I'm Okay, You're Okay, and others—perfect examples of Aiden's nutty comedic sense, or maybe, his quest for attention. As a friend, he was a hoot, and so was his wild car.

Saige cleaned the Bug's windows with a snow scraper while he chipped away at the solid ice claiming squatter's rights on the door handles. After several minutes of work, they climbed into the car, and Aiden rubbed his frozen hands. "Off we go!" He pumped the gas pedal.

Like a senior citizen with achy joints, the vehicle grumbled and rattled before heading down the road. Aiden lovingly patted the dashboard as if the car were his best friend. "Good old Cher, she's got what it takes to keep on truckin'."

The trip to De Gaulle Street through the busy holiday traffic took longer than expected due to cars honking and people giving Aiden a thumbs-up along the way. He waved out the window, his head brushing the clouds like a celebrity garnering attention. "Peace," he hollered, as though someone inside a car with its windows up might hear him. Every few minutes, he'd push a button to pop out an antique cassette tape from the player he installed several years ago. Then he'd shove in another song from the '60s or '70s. This time, "I've Got You Babe" blasted from the speakers. Saige sang along since she knew the words; her mother had often played oldie songs at home.

By 6 p.m., the Bug sputtered to a stop before the Addington Complex in St. Anne's Landing. The sleek building, covered in seamless blue-tint windows, stretched five stories high. Snow surrounded the structure like a satiny sheet.

Aiden peered through the windshield, craning his neck to view the entire complex. "I'm flabbergasted they invited you to work here."

"Yeah, since I'm such a bumbling idiot." Saige crossed her arms. Aiden had some nerve.

"I didn't mean it like that. You graduated top of our medical school class."

"Well, you wouldn't believe the interior of the place. It's ultra-modern with fancy-schmancy everything. I checked it out during my interviews. Do you see why I'm worried? Would my country-girl ways fit in with these rich people?" She waved her hand over her faded jeans and sweatshirt.

Aiden glanced at her with the bright eyes of an optimist. "You know, I have the perfect solution."

Saige pivoted to the windshield, too exhausted to peer into his hopeful face. "I can't, Aiden. Annie comes first. Besides, the mission field isn't my dream. It's yours." She rested her head and closed her eyes. "Be serious, though. Do you think I'd fit in with these people?"

"My vote is no—you wouldn't fit in with these people."

"You didn't have to be that honest."

"Saige, it's only because of the way you are—relaxed, genuine, uncomplicated. But you didn't receive an invite to their cardiology team because of your social standing. It's because of your genius in the field. Fitting in with the wealthy will be a cinch compared to your other accomplishments. Study how they dress and behave. Set your mind to it and do it."

"Thanks. Great pep talk."

"Hey, since we're in St. Anne's, let's eat." He pressed on the gas pedal without waiting for a reply, sending the car into a coughing fit.

Was his stomach deeper than the Grand Canyon? When didn't he want to eat? As long as she didn't have to make decisions, she didn't care. Ahh, she allowed her muscles to relax. The life of a doctor had been a shock to her during internships, but it greatly intensified when she moved into her cardiology fellowship. During the entire year, shifts merged back-to-back, depending on the workload. Thankfully, the fellowship ended two days before the Addington Christmas party.

Aiden turned at the next light then stopped the car at a burger joint for dinner. "My treat. I insist." He removed his wallet from his jeans as they headed into the establishment.

Saige followed him into line. Why hadn't he suggested a nice dinner if he liked her so much? Didn't he know how to win a girl? She slipped her hands in her pockets and contemplated his behavior. As busy as she was in cardiology, she had no time for teaching him life skills. During her fellowship, he had joined a family practice clinic near the university. She massaged her droopy eyelids. He couldn't be as worn-out as she was or use fast-food as an excuse to avoid a nice restaurant.

A few minutes later, Aiden accepted their order, found them seats in a booth, and handed Saige her burger. As he unwrapped his food, his expression changed. He reached over and took her hand in his.

She braced herself. What did he have in mind?

"Saige, I've wanted to ask you something." He peered into her eyes with the same dreamy look he'd used when she made him pancakes.

She didn't move. How many times did she have to turn him down before he'd take a hint?

"Would you please, please…" The muscles in his jaw tightened. He squeezed her fingers.

"Aiden, I can't. I just can't."

"I didn't even ask yet."

Saige's shoulders stiffened as she squirmed in her seat. What did he want? "We've been through this before—"

He let go of her fingers and latched onto her forearms to hold her still. "Listen to me. I have a favor to ask." He sucked a deep breath then blurted his request. "Would you please volunteer at the St. Anne's Inner City Free Clinic with me for the next two weeks?"

"Huh?" Her hands flew to her chest. Wasn't he asking her to marry him? "Wh-what did you say?" Her tight neck and shoulder muscles instantly relaxed.

"I said, I'm hoping you'll volunteer with me at the free clinic in St. Anne's Landing. In exchange, I'll teach you how to dress and behave around wealthy socialites. The clinic opens tomorrow morning at 10:00 if you're willing. The place treats children with simple problems—wounds, sore throats, colds. You can save your cardiology expertise for the Addington Complex. Without medical volunteers, the free clinic would have to close its doors."

How could Aiden possibly help her learn social graces? He and his holey socks knew less about the wealthy than she did. His idea of a fancy meal was to open a can of beans in his impeccably organized apartment when he invited Darcy and her over for dinner. "See, the pork provides meat, and the beans are a vegetable," he had explained.

Saige didn't dare correct him about the beans because he nearly passed out from excitement while dumping the contents into a pan. Despite his useless credentials, Saige needed any help she could get for fitting in at the Addington Complex. But she had to answer his question about working at the clinic first, and she adored children.

"So, I'd be donating my Christmas vacation to sick little ones?"

"That's about it. Is there anything better than that?" Aiden's face glowed.

"How about sleep?"

He raised his hands. "What's that?"

"Never mind. Let me think about it." Growls tormented Saige's stomach, forcing her to bite into her burger.

Aiden downed an extra-long drink through his straw before setting his cup aside. "Can I ask you another question?"

Was this the dreaded one? "You only get one a day." Saige bit her lip to keep her nerves from unraveling.

"How about taking in a movie with me while we're on a date?" He crossed his ankle over his knee then chomped down on his burger, avoiding eye contact with her.

"A date? Aiden, this isn't a date." Saige's voice rose a few octaves. How many times did she have to remind him? Was he misinterpreting her need for a friend because Darcy was out of town, or did he have a seriously hard head? She took a quick sip of her caffeinated soda, hoping to rev up her waning energy.

Aiden shrugged. "Just trying to rile you."

Sitting across from her with his oval wire-rims suggesting brains and his wispy hair strands escaping from his man bun suggesting an unkempt hippie scholar, he polished off his messy burger. Good, sweet, naïve Aiden. When would he learn how to romance a woman? And how could he possibly teach her about the world of the wealthy?

"You'll be happy to know that our next stop is the Addington mansion," Aiden announced. "You can march right up to the door and ask them about your bracelet."

"What? You're kidding me, right? I can't show up in jeans and a sweatshirt!"

SEVEN

On his way downstairs that evening, a tempting scent lured Gray to the manor kitchen. Umm. Cranberry pork roast— one of Cook's specialties during the Christmas season. As he entered the room, a blazing wood fire in the massive stone fireplace welcomed him to stay a while and enjoy the tantalizing aromas. Adele closed the oven door. She greeted him with a smile before removing her floppy mitts and tossing them on the marble island.

Now was the perfect opportunity to discuss Lilith with her since Fernsby wasn't there to make faces. During Gray's childhood, Adele had been the one who suggested he go by his shortened middle name after kids in grade school bullied him. He recalled her erupting like Mt. Vesuvius. "Hold your head high." She told him. "Someday people will admire your name." How could Miss Dell, as he called her, then, have known he'd become a famous surgeon?

She and Fernsby had been more like parents to him than his own. The only times he conversed with the senior Dr. Addington and his mother involved the evening dinner. In the afternoons, Miss Dell, with Gray in tow, assisted Chef Dubois in the kitchen. And most evenings, she or Fernsby had read him bedtime stories and tucked him under the covers. But after he went off to the university, Chef Dubois retired and Adele permanently hung her apron in the kitchen as their cook. What would Gray have done if she'd left the mansion? He didn't want to consider it.

"How about adding this morning's coffee to your daily menu, Dell? It was amazing." Gray strolled to an apple pie cooling on the marble countertop. He used his hand to waft the fumes to his nose. "Ahh. You make the best pastries."

"Thank you, Gray." She removed a pen from her pocket and jotted something on a notepad.

Gray settled down on his favorite worn stool at the kitchen island. He'd spent many lively hours laughing with Miss Dell as he helped her roll out pie crusts and cookie dough on the counter. But mostly, he cherished the irresistible smells. His childhood memories came alive in the warm room.

Peering over her reading glasses, Adele raised her brows. "Do you have something on your mind?" She slipped the pen through her stylish silver hair, then selected a utensil from a drawer and plucked a potato from a bowl on the counter. She began carving it with determination.

"Never mind me. It appears you're upset with that potato. What's going on?"

She set down the tuber, now whittled to the size of a chestnut. Biting her lip, she removed a plain chef's apron from a drawer and tossed it to Gray. "Cover your clothes." She nodded at his pressed shirt and creased pants. "I've wanted to discuss Lilith." She let loose a whoosh of air as though she'd been holding the words inside.

"What about her?" Gray slipped the apron over his head. Now that Adele had opened the closet on their mutual problem, his jaw muscles relaxed.

"If your parents were here, I'd stay out of it, but since they're vacationing with relatives in England—well, sometimes others see things in a person we might overlook." Adele wiped her hands on her apron.

"Do they now? What do you see in my friend that I don't? She's gorgeous. She's my right-hand gal. I don't know what I'd do without her." He selected a potato and a paring knife.

"There's more to a person than beauty. What about her character— the way she orders you around or the way she speaks to you as though she has you snagged with her fake fingernails. Not to mention the way she speaks to Fernsby and me as if we were—"

"Servants?" A sheepish grin tugged the corners of Gray's mouth.

Adele's neck muscles tensed. She snatched another potato from the bowl and began skinning it as though vying for "the fastest potato peeler" in The Guinness Book of World Records. While she pared, she clenched her teeth, but words seeped through anyway. "If she speaks to her staff that way, well, I-I-pity them, that's all."

"Are you planning on serving potato chips for dinner?" Gray had to calm her down, or she'd have no spuds left. "I've noticed how Fernsby feels about her." How could he not with his valet's eye-rolling and grimacing? "Could the two of you be overly scrutinizing her? She's merely my friend. Give her a chance. That's all I ask." He expected the same level of kindness from himself. Looking at his cherished cook with pleading eyes, he added, "Try to see Lilith from a different perspective. That's what I do. She's used to many servants because her father's a shipping magnate. Even friendships take time. That's what Mother taught me when Lilith and I met."

"Hmph. Did your mother teach you relationship skills during your thirty-minute evening meals?" The cook wiped both hands on her apron before placing one on each side of his face. "I used to adore your chubby little cheeks. Now they're finely chiseled, and you're a handsome young man. No doubt every girl in St. Anne's Landing would love to place her arm in yours. Beware of those who weasel their way into your life." Furrowing the spot above her nose, Adele removed her hands and changed her tone. "Be careful dear heart. The way a girl treats you now might torment you later."

Gray touched Adele's arm to make her pause. "I'll remember, Dell. Besides, I don't plan on marrying her." His parents had encouraged his friendship with her because she was at ease in their social world. Gray wasn't. "Lilith will nudge me out of my intellectual shell. She's a social snob, not a brainiac."

Adele stopped peeling. "Does your father know she isn't bright?"

"Of course not. He approves of Lilith. Who am I to set him straight? Conflict doesn't fit into our family dynamics." Life never changed in the Addington household. Except when his parents made trips to England, and Adele and Fernsby carried the torch, so to speak, for his upbringing.

"I understand your family dynamics more than you give me credit." Adele scooped the potato peels into the trashcan under the island. "By the way, Gray, when Fernsby prepared your tray this morning, he mentioned something about a mishap at the party last night. He said the poor girl handled herself remarkably well. She charmed him if that sort of thing is possible with the old coot."

Gray chuckled at her remark. Fernsby indeed possessed a curmudgeon streak. "I have to agree with him on this one. The young lady is special."

Gray placed his paring knife in the sink. The girl's casual manner and honesty without airs had charmed him as well. But how could he find her again? He stood at the sink, looking out the window at the dark tree-lined backyard. He'd ask Fernsby to check every jewelry store in St. Anne's Landing and St. James, if necessary, to uncover the owner of the bracelet. With any luck, one of them might know her name. The inscription was quite unique. Gray would apologize to the lady for her unfortunate accident in his home, then he'd return her possession—perhaps over a cozy dinner. Yes, a romantic—er, cozy dinner would be the perfect way to show his remorse.

"I'll see you later, Dell."

On his way from the kitchen, he scouted for Fernsby. In addition to wondering if his valet obtained the theater tickets, Gray wanted him to begin researching the bracelet—today.

As Gray passed the grand staircase, a shadowy figure crossed the study room hallway and headed to the servants' wing. Gray increased his pace. "Fernsby! Is that you, old chap?"

EIGHT

The sun had set by the time Cher arrived at the stately Addington mansion that was guarded by a gatehouse before an iron gate. Decorative lampposts beyond the metal bars showcased the sprawling snow-covered property.

Saige pleaded with Aiden to keep driving, but he slowed the VW Bug. "I'm doing this for your sake, Saige. You want your bracelet back, don't you?"

"Yes, but I'm not dressed for this. Please, turn around!" She waved her arms at him, showing him to circle back, but instead of heeding her squawking pleas and gestures, he shifted into park, parallel with the gatehouse.

"Pipe down, Miss Peacock. I'm going to alert them we're here."

His reference to her favorite Clue character usually made her laugh, but not this time. He rolled down his window and pushed a button on the gatehouse. "Anyone in there?"

She wanted to kill him. She'd do it with a candlestick in the conservatory and blame it on Miss Scarlett. No one would know. But joking aside, he was the most exasperating man she'd ever known.

A screeching of metal announced the intercom had activated, and a woman's business-like voice came over the loudspeaker. "How may I help you?"

Aiden swept his right hand across his waist with his forefinger aimed at the gatehouse, prompting Saige to speak to the lady. Saige pinched her face and bunched her sweatshirt, trying to show him she didn't want to answer. Why wouldn't he take the hint? Did he want the Addingtons to see her in everyday clothes and no makeup?

"Is anyone there?" The woman had no clue Saige and Aiden were caught up in charades.

Aiden poked Saige and pointed again to the gatehouse. He forced his back against his seat, tucking in his chin so she had a clear path to the intercom.

Infuriated by his refusal to leave, Saige leaned across him, as far as possible, while avoiding the gear shifter in the cramped Bug. "I'm sorry to bother you, but I lost my bracelet when I fell at the Christmas party."

"We haven't found a bracelet, ma'am. Good day now."

"Wa-wa-wait! Don't go yet! Will you please tell me the name of the servant who carried me to the study? I'd like to thank him. He was tall, wavy dark brown hair, muscular build."

"Doesn't sound like Fernsby. Sorry. We have no servant with that description."

"But he rescued me. He might know the whereabouts of my bracelet."

"Sorry, miss. I must return to work."

Within hearing distance of the intercom, a manly British voice boomed his annoyance. "Is someone bothering you, Claire?"

"Yes, sir."

That voice. Saige had heard it before.

The British man continued. "I'm sorry, but Claire has work to do. Good day." Silence came over the speaker.

"Aiden, that was the man who saved me! He must not have recognized my voice." Much as Saige strained to see between the gate's iron bars, the mansion had no activity in the illuminated driveway. Had her Prince Charming forgotten her?

"It probably wasn't him at all. Can't hear well over that speaker. Everyone sounds the same." Aiden contorted his neck to look out the window. "Want me to push the button again? I bet they'll let me drive you right up to the doorstep."

Was he seriously trying to help her or deliberately trying to show her she'd never fit in with the elite? "Don't you understand? What if they see me this way?" She tugged at her jeans.

"What way? You look like you always do."

"I'm never going to speak to you again."

"Okay. Time for some rest and relaxation." Aiden shifted into reverse, turned Cher around, and pointed the Bug toward the city. "A drive through downtown St. Anne's might lift your spirits. The Christmas lights and decorations are wild. After that we'll make a trip to the movie theater. We need to get your mind off your troubles." Aiden glanced at her. "Try to chill, Saige. I mean it. You've worked yourself into a frenzy."

Easy for him to say; he wasn't looking for a bracelet or a charming hero. She slumped back in her seat. He'd left her no other choice but to forget about the servant for today, if that was even possible.

As Aiden drove through the busy city, bright decorations lit up the streets and coaxed her into the Christmas spirit—well, those plus the Christmas music Aiden found on his radio. She and Aiden oohed and ahhed at the gorgeously decorated storefronts and homes. By 7:30, he pointed Cher toward the cinema.

With no more than minutes to spare before the movie started, he drove to the adjacent parking garage, accepted a parking ticket, then ushered Saige to the cinema doors. Filled with disappointment, she hurried into the theater with him on her heels. Seeing the place lightened her frame of mind. Because of her rigorous schedule, she'd rarely attended a show in the last twelve years. Playing a board game with Aiden and Darcy late on a Friday night was about the only relaxation she had.

A massive Christmas tree dotted with colorful ornaments and strands of bright bulbs lit the first-floor foyer of the building. Evergreen needles scented the air. Near the tree, Christmas carolers the size of middle schoolers sang, "Rudolf the Red-Nosed Reindeer."

Medical school had engulfed Saige in a time warp. What happened to the old days when a theater simply showed movies? Finishing her schooling had been like awakening from years of hibernation.

Aiden aimed his finger at a sign near the escalator: "Theater, second floor." They hopped aboard the fast-moving steps and rode them to a floor bustling with lines leading to various destinations. A buttery popcorn aroma flooded Saige with warm memories of Saturday afternoon matinees with her mom and Annie. Lord of the Rings and Harry Potter movies had been their favorites.

An older man in the ticket line ahead of Saige scratched his cottony head as he studied the movie options on an overhead sign. His creased pants and stiff collared shirt, not to mention his expensive, unbuttoned knee-length coat, pegged him as a man of wealth.

A familiar scent drifted under Saige's nose. Mint—liniment. The man must have arthritis. She recalled another person who reeked of medicine—the nutcracker. The memory sent her dwelling again on the Christmas party, Dr. Addington, her dreamy hero, and her bracelet. She rubbed her empty wrist.

An opened palm waved up and down before her face. "Saige? Anyone home in there?"

She blinked to clear her thoughts. "Yeah, sorry, Aiden."

"Are you still contemplating taking the job with Addington?"

"Thinking about it gives me a headache. Either way, I have to move from my apartment by the end of December."

"You'll have plenty of time to pack. I'll help you find an apartment in St. Anne's Landing if that's your plan. Besides, the St. Anne's Clinic provides room and board while we volunteer."

"You've thought of everything."

"Be prepared. That's my motto. I learned that somewhere."

The older man ahead of Saige purchased two tickets with manners befitting the King of England. He regally accepted them then handed one to the trim, silver-haired lady by his side. "Do you mind if we sit in the back?" Saige detected a faint British accent.

The older woman, clad in an unbuttoned fancy coat over a knee-length dress, shook her head. "Whatever you say, Fernsby. I'm merely along for the ride." Her British accent matched his as though they were two dignitaries from the same town.

The man steered the stately woman by the elbow, away from the counter and toward the theaters.

British accents seemed to abound in St. Anne's Landing. Saige chuckled before focusing on the white-haired man whose uptight behavior rang a bell. Yet, she couldn't place him. Where had she seen him? The accent reminded her of the servant who carried her to the mansion study, but that hunky guy didn't have white hair or wrinkles detectable in the dim study light.

"Aiden, the man who stood in front of us—he looked familiar." Saige nodded in the older man's direction. "Have you seen him before?"

Aiden squinched his nose and shook his head. "Not me."

The man peered over his shoulder, narrowing his eyes for a few seconds as though trying to remember Saige. Then he moved on with the silver-haired lady at his side.

Saige and Aiden purchased their tickets and strolled into the darkened theater behind moviegoers who scrambled for good seats. A family of teens filed down two aisles and claimed leather recliner chairs nearest the screen. Since the prime viewing spots filled quickly, Aiden selected regular seats behind the safety rail in time for them to see the previews. Saige folded her coat on her lap and propped her feet on the metal bars.

Two hours later the show ended, and Saige wiped her eyes. Aiden had been right. Laughter soothed the soul. The comedy made her chuckle out loud. As the closing credits rolled, she slicked her hair into a neck-hugging ponytail. "Let's hurry and beat the crowd." She poked Aiden in the side. "You with me?"

"Of course." Shoving his arms into his jacket, he watched the cast credits scroll down the screen.

"Hurry! We're going to get stuck behind the crowd." Saige nudged him in the back, pushing him up the aisle.

As they neared the back, the same distinguished older man, who stood ahead of her in the ticket line, rose from his seat. He gazed at Saige for a few long seconds. As he adjusted his coat, a minty liniment scent wafted to the aisle. The smell reminded Saige of someone, somewhere. She returned the elderly man's stare as Aiden took the lead and dragged her up the aisle. "Aiden, stop." She played tug-of-war with his hand. "I think I know him—the man who's staring at me."

"Plenty of men look at you." Aiden gave her one last concentrated tug. "Who wouldn't?" He pulled her in the direction of the exit.

Saige lost her balance and toppled toward him. He wrapped his hand securely around her waist then picked up the pace through the theater lounge and out the door to the parking garage. "We don't have time to stop. Trust me. We'll be lucky to make it home by midnight."

"Won't be any worse than pulling all-nighters while studying for exams." The memory of his funny mnemonics made her smile for a brief second which is all the time she had with him dragging her along. When they reached his rusted Bug, she ran around to the passenger door and gripped the door handle. "I hope your clunker makes it home."

"I'll kiss the ground like I always do if it does." Aiden patted the roof of the car before climbing into the driver's side. He stretched across the seats, unlocked her door, and waited for her to get inside.

Rumbling erupted from the engine as he pressed on the gas pedal. Then he steered the Bug down the ramps, paid for his parking, and turned the wheel to pass the theater.

As they drove by the movie posters in the building's glass windows, Saige spotted the same older man in his knee-length button-down coat standing by the door with the beautiful lady. She recalled seeing white hair tufts poking out from under a coal-black hat and hooded crystal-blue eyes twinkling above cherry-red cheek paint. If she was right, the older man had been the nutcracker—the very one who allowed her to fall and make a fool of herself before ordering a taxi to take her home. Now, there he stood, probably waiting for a cab himself. Was he watching her? He didn't look away.

The seat buckle jammed. Saige wrestled with it. "Aagh!" She looked back again, but the Bug was farther down the road. The older man, hand raised, gestured for them to return.

"Turn around, Aiden!" This might be her last chance to learn her hero's identity and, more importantly, to find her bracelet. "Hurry, Aiden. I remember that man."

The VW Bug chortled as Aiden pumped the brakes before the light turned red. "Sorry, Cher doesn't accelerate well." Aiden glanced at her before focusing on the road.

Saige slapped the sides of her face in disbelief. "Since when do you not hurry to beat a red light?" Why was he acting like a jerk? She couldn't believe his behavior. She huffed as she crossed her arms.

"Time for lesson one on social manners, Saige. Remember, you're a wealthy St. Anne's socialite. Mind your manners. Check your makeup or something. Make small talk. No ranting or raving like a madwoman."

"Ugh!" Of course, he'd throw manners in her face at a time like this. Knowing Aiden, he'd prefer anything but a heated conversation about the guy who rescued her at the party, or about the nutcracker, because Aiden wanted her for himself.

By the time Cher reached the theater curb, the older man and the silver-haired lady with him had disappeared.

NINE

After leaving the musical at the Maximillian Theater, Gray drove down a side street, scouting for a parking space as Lilith rummaged through her purse in the passenger seat. He glanced over at her. "I wonder where we should go for coffee?"

She flipped down the visor and inspected her reflection before applying more lipstick. Gray studied her silhouette. Any woman would envy her pouty lips, and any man would desire them. They were supermodel gorgeous. Surely Fernsby and Dell were mistaken about her personality. They didn't know Lilith as well as he did.

"How about the Pie Factory, darling? I've heard it's a nice place." Lilith dropped her lipstick in the purse then rearranged her silky auburn hair over her shoulders.

"The Pie Factory it is." Gray enjoyed the friendly atmosphere. He and Fernsby ate lunch there now and then on the weekends.

A rusty multi-colored VW Bug painted in sayings from the 1960s and '70s drove past them as Gray turned into the restaurant's parking garage. The girl in the Bug's side seat squinted at him. His memory stirred. Who did he know who drove around in an outdated, hippie-era automobile? If his acquaintances owned one, they would have restored it to its original solid color. Still, something about the girl's high cheekbones and slender nose reminded him of someone he'd seen before.

"Pay attention to the road, Gray!" Lilith jostled his arm. "Stop watching that old jalopy, or you'll get us killed."

Gray's tires screeched as he veered the other direction. "Sorry."

Where had he seen the girl in the Volkswagen? Gray racked his brain as he parked his BMW and escorted Lilith to the restaurant through the parking garage elevator. Inside the fancy establishment, evergreen boughs laced with holly and bright hurricane candles circled with red-velvet bows adorned the counters and walls.

A host, dressed in black except for a red Santa hat lined in white fur, escorted Gray and Lilith into the dining room. "White Christmas" played in the background, enhancing the holiday spirit.

The smiling host led them past an enormous glass display counter filled with slices of delectable pies. The many varieties didn't faze Gray. Adele baked the most delicious pastries in the world, especially her Dutch apple topped with brown sugar. Gray's mouth watered. With enough money, she could start a bakeshop and sell an array of tempting desserts.

After reaching their appointed booth, he and Lilith slid into opposite sides. The young host promptly placed menus on the table as they situated themselves. "A server will see to you shortly." He rubbed his smooth-shaven jawline before turning on his heels to attend to others forming a line near the door.

"What are you craving, Lilith?" Gray opened his menu and perused it, taking his time to consider each dessert entry.

"I'll have a cup of coffee, for starters. And maybe a slice of strawberry pie." Lilith folded her menu.

"I think I'll try their coconut creme."

"It's too fattening, darling. You're a heart surgeon, for pity's sake."

As a curly-headed server arrived at their table, Lilith bypassed Gray and ordered strawberry pie for them.

The busy server never batted an eye as she scooped up their menus, but Gray studied the expensive flooring, the glossy tabletop, and the elegant quilted walls, while trying to calm down from Lilith's rudeness. He needed a change of topic to divert his anger over her making his decision for him. "Did you like the musical?" The question should steer them to a pleasant conversation. Who wouldn't love *Wicked*? The live show had everything—unique costumes, great singing, humor.

"I must admit, it was clever. But not really to my fancy." Lilith placed her fingertips over her mouth, turned her head, and gave the tiniest of coughs.

The muscles in Gray's jaw tightened like violin strings threatening to pop. "I'm quite sorry you didn't enjoy it." What was going on with her? He'd never seen her quite so brazen.

The server returned to their table with cups and a coffee pot. "Would either of you care for cream and sugar?"

"No, thank you." Lilith raised her palm to keep the lady from depositing the condiments on the table.

Had blinders fallen from Gray's eyes? His friend behaved like a tyrant. He'd operated on hundreds of blocked arteries in his short career. He didn't plan on clogging his own. Low-fat cream paired with Stevia rounded out the daily fat-allotment he allowed himself.

Was this what Dell and Fernsby meant by controlling? Now that his servants opened his eyes, he witnessed things he hadn't noticed before.

"Your desserts will be ready in a minute." The server filled their coffee cups before leaving the table. She stopped at the booth ahead of theirs to offer refills before hurrying away.

Lilith brought her cup to her lips and took a polite sip, then she massaged her polished fingernails which were dotted with snowflakes. The emerald and diamond rings on her fingers accented their beauty. As Gray tapped his feet under the table, steam brewed under his collar. "I rather enjoyed the musical."

"I suppose a few people would, but I'm not one of them. I'd prefer *Phantom of the Opera* or *Les Misérables*."

"Indeed, because you are miserable," Gray mumbled under his breath. Why had he never noticed her behavior before? He winced as he took a sip of the acidy black brew in his cup.

"What was that, darling?" Lilith slipped her hand from Gray's to smooth her hair behind her shoulder. "Is it just me, or is it chilly in here?"

"Oh, it's definitely chilly in here." Gray removed his suit jacket and wrapped it around her shoulders.

The server arrived with their dessert in record time, allowing Gray a reprieve from Lilith's frosty conversation. Lilith ate in tiny bites while Gray polished off his slice rather quickly. But he washed down the berries with the coffee, cringing again at its bitterness in the same way that Lilith reacted to *Wicked*.

"I guess we'll have to agree to disagree on the musical." Gray was proud that he stood his ground by sharing his feelings about the show every few minutes. He could and would make his own decisions.

The music in the background stopped. Unexpectedly, the chatter throughout the establishment softened. Oblivious to the sudden quiet, Lilith shouted, "What's gotten into you? You've never disagreed with me."

Customers peered at her in the silent interlude.

"Because I liked *Wicked*?" Embarrassed, Gray's mouth twitched as the surrounding patrons ducked behind their menus or shifted their eyes.

"Silent Night" began playing overhead.

"You're not the same. When I took on this—" Lilith glanced around the room as though she'd said something that might hit the newspapers.

"Finish your sentence, Lilith. When you took on what?"

"I've got a headache. Please take me home."

"I have to know something first. Did you exit my house yesterday around noon—through the study hallway by the servants' quarters?"

Lilith's crossed legs became jumpy, hitting the underside of the tabletop. "Of course not. In case you haven't noticed, I'm not a servant." The skin on her neck reddened. She folded her arms over her waist and tilted her head at an angle. "Furthermore, I spent the day with my mother. Ask her. Wait a minute. Are you accusing me of something?"

Gray raised his hand for the server. "Check, please."

After paying the bill, he walked behind Lilith past the dessert display on their way to the door. What did Lilith mean by her unfinished sentence? Should he be concerned?

TEN

Early Monday morning, Saige's digital alarm buzzed, arousing her from the longest sleep she'd had in years, six hours, unhindered by patient problems, consults, and blood chemistries. She hit the alarm button. Why had she agreed to work at the St. Anne's Free Clinic instead of sleeping in? She shivered from the chilly apartment air as she donned her jeans and sweatshirt.

Droopy-eyed, she washed her face and brushed her teeth before applying a thin layer of foundation. A smidgeon of lip gloss and an elastic scrunchie around her ponytail completed her morning routine.

A pounding knock on the door startled her. Did Aiden think she was deaf?

"You ready for our drive?" he shouted from the hallway.

Saige released the lock and opened the door. "As ready as I'll ever be."

Sporting his usual man bun, Aiden stepped into her apartment dressed for the winter cold. He reminded her of Brad Pitt in a younger *Legends*, less *Troy*, sort of way—meaning more hair, fewer muscles. Too bad his behavior wasn't more like that of a leading man. She squinted at his thin knapsack. "Didn't you say we'd be staying in St. Anne's Landing for two weeks?"

"That I did. Got your things packed?"

A little puzzled by his meager belongings, Saige tossed her backpack over her shoulder, swiped a folded flannel blanket off the sofa, and turned around. "You mean these?"

"Perfect. Let's head out."

59

In the parking lot, Aiden reached the V-dub first. He pried his frozen car door open then walked around to the passenger side and chipped ice on the door handle for Saige. The seat nearly froze her behind as she sat on the icy vinyl. "I'm looking forward to purchasing a car with heated seats someday. That's my short-term goal." She tugged her safety belt a few times before it loosened enough for her to buckle it across her waist.

"Yeah, and a heated steering wheel." Aiden pulled a maroon knit cap with an attached mud-brown beard over his head and face. "This might not look cool, Saige, but it sure keeps my face warm."

Why did he have to wear that ridiculous lumberjack get-up? It topped her list of the worst sight gags in Aiden's toolkit. "As long as you don't wear it in public." She cringed as she slumped in her seat.

He swung sideways at her. His lips puckered through the mouth hole in the wool beard. But at the last second, he swerved to the glove compartment and opened it instead. Saige coughed in annoyance. No sense asking him to grow up. It was too late.

After retrieving gloves, Aiden attempted to shove the stiff leather fingers over his own. "Even these are frozen. Whoo!" His body jerked as he tucked them under his thighs.

The car groaned and complained as he pressed on the gas pedal, but minutes later, he steered it from the parking lot. While Saige waited for the heater to bathe the interior of the car, she shivered in chilly silence. But as the car warmed, so did Aiden. "Have you ever considered having kids?" He peered at her from the corner of his eye.

Saige pointed to her chest. "Are you asking me, the worn-out cardiologist?"

Aiden nodded.

"What brought that up?"

"Just wondering because I've considered it a lot." An SUV attempted to pass the Bug on the busy highway, and Aiden slowed down to allow the vehicle to move around his junkheap. The SUV driver honked and gave a thumbs up.

"How does a family medicine doctor have time to think about

kids?" Saige tightened the coat collar around her neck.

A sedan filled with older folks waved at Aiden's Bug. He returned the gesture then glanced over at Saige. "I'm not talking about wanting them now, while I'm beginning my practice, mind you, but maybe later, after my life smooths out."

Saige refused to look at him. He was trying to get under her skin—trying to make her like him. "I think I'll take a nap. Wake me when we're there."

"Right. Anyway, I'm glad you'll be working at the clinic. Thanks for coming."

She wriggled for a comfortable position in her seat but gave up. "No problem. Besides, I enjoy helping sick kids."

Aiden reached into the backseat and produced the blanket she brought along. He motioned for her to tuck it under her head.

She had forgotten about it. The wadded flannel made a comfy pillow against the passenger window. Okay, he was a nice guy. And he was super bright—she knew that from studying with him. If she were honest, she even enjoyed his funny antics, but was he the man for her?

She popped a cassette in the tape player then closed her eyes. Ahh. The oldie but goodie Paul Simon tune, "The Sounds of Silence," streamed through the speakers. Maybe, if she was lucky, Aiden would take a hint.

ELEVEN

By 9:30 a.m. finding a parking space near the clinic, where vehicle parts were ripe for pinching, was far more difficult than finding a fancy ring in a corn bin. Saige bit her lip. Would she regret volunteering, or worse yet, would she live to tell the story?

Driving down one street after another, Aiden scouted for available spots. Much to Saige's chagrin, he found one after several times around the block. "Do you think it's safe to park in front of a tattoo parlor?" She eyed the barred windows on the seedy shop.

"There aren't any other spaces. Besides, if someone wants my rusted Bug with its bald tires, they can be my guest. Might do me a favor."

"I was thinking about our lives." Saige's voice quivered as she clutched her door handle. "I've never been in this part of the city."

"It's not all bad. Plenty of wonderful people live here." Aiden held his breath as a man carrying a bottle wrapped in a paper bag stepped off the curb in front of them. Head down, the man staggered across the street. Aiden exhaled before glancing at Saige. "There's a local church a few streets east of here that pleads for missionaries every summer. My youth group helps for a week. When I was a teen, we played sports with the kids and assisted at their Vacation Bible School." Aiden removed his hat and beard before exiting the car. He hopped to the curb and waited for Saige to creak open her door. "Not everyone around here is a druggie," he added. "Lots of people live in the area because it's affordable."

Saige unfolded from the car but shuddered as more iron bars came into view on storefronts along the street. Obviously, the shop owners believed as she did about the crime level. On their walk down the side-walk, she glanced over her shoulder often.

A few doors before the clinic, two men covered in tattered clothes and alcohol fumes sat on the cement outside of a liquor store with boarded windows. The man with wiry gray hair sucked a cigarette then blew a smoke stream through his lips. "What're yous doin' downtown?"

"Working in the free clinic for kids." Aiden pointed down the street.

"I'll watch yer car fer twenty dolla a day." The man's mouth spread, uncovering a toothless grin.

"If we had twenty dollars, we would've paid for a taxi." Aiden dug his hands deeper in his jacket pockets as he shivered from the cold.

"Ain't no tellin' what you'll find when ya cum back." The man elbowed the other one, who appeared younger. The two guffawed as though privy to an insider's joke.

"There's not much to take." Aiden's laughter rose above the waning chortles of the men. "You'd be lucky if the bald tires don't go flat. Besides, the old clunker is nearing its final ride before junkyard heaven."

The gray-haired man wiped his mouth with a bony finger. "Hmph." He rolled to his side. Stuffing the cigarette stub between his lips with one hand, he guided a piece of cardboard over his head with the other one.

"If you two stop by the free clinic at noon, I'll order you a pizza."

"What fer?"

"So you can eat. Don't forget. Come at noon." Aiden motioned for Saige. "We need to hurry, or we'll be late."

Saige glanced down the street. Would she survive for two weeks?

Aiden hurried them to the rundown building crouched between two empty storefronts at the end of the street. Saige hoped the inside of the clinic fared better than the rundown outside. But she was wrong. Sick children with caregivers filled every chipped, hard plastic chair in the scuffed-up waiting room. A scrawny Christmas tree with six wide-spaced limbs decorated in paper bulbs monopolized a corner of the room. Saige walked across the cracked tiles to reach the counter and desk enclosed by plexiglass. She tapped on the see-through wall to get the occupant's attention. "Is there anyone in there who can help us?"

"Take a number and a seat," came the hoarse reply behind the booth.

"You don't understand." Aiden slung his backpack off his shoulder and dropped it to the floor. "We're here to work."

A vertically challenged dark-haired lady in nursing scrubs strained to see over the counter as though she were standing on her toes. She inspected Saige and Aiden's outerwear, jeans, and backpacks. "That's a different story." No taller than five feet, she hurried around the plexiglass to greet them. "Why didn't you say so in the first place? You must be the volunteers."

"We're Dr. Aiden Littlefield and Dr. Saige Westbrook." Aiden flashed his crooked front teeth at the lady.

"Welcome." She greeted them with elbow taps, obviously because of whatever viruses were now invading the world. "I'm Maria. We use first names here since it takes the uppity out of egos." She checked a clipboard. "Perfect. You're on the list. Someone called early this morning about Saige. Was that you?"

Aiden nodded.

She eyeballed his man bun as though admiring it. "We're grateful for your help. Now, follow me." She gestured for them to come with her through a hallway lined with metal cubicles and chairs.

Near the end of the passageway, she stopped by a room. "Change into your scrubs in there then place your clothes in one of those." She indicated a group of lockers. "Meet me in the physician's lounge when you're done. It's across the hallway."

Saige studied the dents and scratches embedded in the metal lockers. Had someone bashed them in with a sledgehammer?

"Don't mind them." Maria motioned to several small cubicles beside them. "Those ones have locks, so your stuff will be safe. Druggies come in looking for meds, but we ain't got nuttin stronger than aspirin." She tucked her clipboard under her arm. "Now, go on and get busy changing." She crossed the hallway to the physician's lounge, her ample hips swaying side-to-side.

Saige leaned in and whispered to Aiden through clenched teeth, "Are you sure we'll be safe in this place?"

He shook his head while unzipping his backpack. "The thing is—kids here need medical attention, and their parents can't afford it. So, I'm planning to do my best to help them."

Great, she was stuck.

After Aiden finished changing into scrubs, Saige swapped places with him. He had rocks in his head for bringing her here. She met him in the physician's lounge after stashing her clothes in a locker. The cluttered lounge, if it could be called a lounge, wasn't much bigger than a walk-in closet. A mini fridge languished under a countertop that sagged beneath a microwave, coffee pot, and ceramic mugs. A man in scrubs snored on a bench against a wall with an open magazine covering his face.

"Uh, excuse us." Saige tapped his shoe with her hand. "We're here to help at the clinic. Are you the orderly?"

The man whipped the magazine from his face as he jumped to his feet. "My name's Gray. At your service, ma'am."

"Thank you." The guy reminded Saige of the handsome young man who played Superman in the most recent movie version, only this guy had a cute Southern accent and wavy brown hair flipping over his ears in a playful manner.

"Y'all two must be Saige and Aiden. Maria told me about y'all comin' today. We go by first names here." Gray ignored Aiden and focused on Saige, checking out her scrubs.

"So we heard." As Aiden watched Gray studying Saige, she noticed his clenched lips. Was he upset at Gray for looking at her?

Maria swept into the room. "Gray!" she shouted at the dreamy orderly. "Help me swap out that huge bottled water jug in the cooler! We've got a patient needin' a drink. Chop chop!" She pumped alcohol disinfectant into her palms from a dispenser by the door. "Don't forget to wash your hands with this." She eyed Gray, Saige, and Aiden.

"Of course." Gray lathered his hands before following the lady from the lounge while Saige and Aiden sat on the benches and waited for further instructions.

Maria returned a few minutes later. "Follow me. Jon is seeing patients. You'll meet him later." She walked behind the desk to a short hall with rooms. Then, in airplane hostess mode, she waved her arms in different directions. "That exam room and the one over there, they belong to you two. Just don't go fighting over them."

Fight over them? Saige wanted to run out the front door and down the street except she wasn't sure if that course of action might be more dangerous than staying put.

Maria continued her instructions by pointing to alcohol dispensers outside the rooms. "Wash your hands between patients." Finally, she motioned to cupboards inside Room 2. "Take a few minutes to acquaint yourselves with the supplies. I'll bring patients to you, shortly." She turned on her heels and headed to her desk. "Number twelve!" she bellowed into her microphone to the patients in the waiting room.

In the second exam room, Saige opened cabinets and found essential medical supplies. But where had the handsome orderly gone? Maybe she'd need his help doctoring a cut. She could only hope. He was tall, muscular, and about her age. His eyes reminded her of a pair she'd seen before, but her memory failed her. It did that a lot due to her fatigued state of consciousness. A neurologist pal told her it was because she crammed far too many things into her brain too quickly. Her mind shoved out the nonessential data.

"Tayjonte Carter, Room 2," Maria called over the desk speaker.

Saige exited the exam room and checked the number beside the door. I guess that's me.

"Here's the chart." Maria handed it to her after showing the patient and his mother into the room. "We've got to get those in the waiting area seen before five o'clock." Saige noted her brusque manner. The woman probably needed it to keep doctors moving at the clinic. With a quick spin, the nurse headed back to her desk.

Saige opened the chart and read about the patient: Tayjonte Carter. Six-years-old male. Fell from bike into gravel heap. No known allergies.

With any luck, he'll need the wound sutured. She entered the room where the shaggy-haired tyke cuddled on his mother's lap. He sniffled then swiped his sleeve under his nose.

"Hi! You must be Ms. Carter. I'm Saige. Nice to meet you."

Without acknowledging Saige, the woman, drowning in clothes several sizes too big, nodded at the boy. "Uh, he goes by TJ."

Saige's face lit up as she studied the little fellow. "Nice to meet you, TJ. Don't worry; I won't hurt you. I promise." She walked to the counter and drew a smiley face on a wooden tongue depressor and a frowny face on the back. Then she approached the boy. "Here we go. How about taking this stick? If anything hurts, raise the frowny-face side, but if you're okay, turn it to the smiley one. Do we have a deal?"

The little boy nodded while wrapping his fingers around the tongue depressor.

Saige tickled him in the side. "Which one are you now?"

The smiley face inched upward as he giggled. His bedraggled mother joined in. She swept the hair from her face and sighed as though relieved.

"Okay, I'm going to check out your boo-boo. Wait a minute. Where is it? It must be hiding!"

TJ pulled up his torn pant leg. "Here it is—right there!" He sucked up his runny nose, then wiped tears on his jacket and pointed to his shin.

"Of course. I see it now." Saige winked at his mom. "Which stick face will you choose, TJ?"

The smiley face inched upward.

"Fantastic. I'll take a little peek at your leg now." Saige collected a measuring tape and a wrapped cotton-tipped swab from the counter. The wound measured two inches long by half an inch deep. "Looks like I'm going to have to fix it. Are you up for that?"

TJ raised the smiley face.

"I need to talk with your mom. We'll be back in a few minutes." Saige exited the exam room and waited for TJ's mother. "He's going to need several stitches and something for pain. As long as he doesn't have an allergy to it, I suggest acetaminophen."

Mrs. Carter nodded before heading into the exam room to hold her son.

Saige walked to the front desk where Maria was interviewing the next patient's caregiver. "Maria, where's Gray?"

"He's still on break. Check the lounge."

Since when in the history of medicine did orderlies get to take naps? Saige marched to the doctor's lounge where the young man had returned to dozing on the bench with the same magazine over his eyes.

"If you don't mind me interrupting, I'd appreciate some help, please." She hovered over him, unwilling to take "no" for an answer, considering he had time on his hands for a snooze.

After a full-blown startle reflex, Gray removed the magazine, sat upright, and rubbed his eyes. "What the...." He eyeballed Saige and his demeanor changed. "I mean, shore thang. What can I do ta help?"

"For starters, I'd like to give my patient a mild liquid pain medicine before I suture his wound. Then, would you mind cleaning the cut for me while I ready the suture kit?"

A grin started over Gray's lips, but he covered it with his hand. "No problem. Y'all lead the way," he mumbled in his atypical Southern drawl. Saige couldn't pinpoint where he hailed from in the South.

After he handed her a liquid pain reliever from a cupboard in the cramped medication closet, she asked for a cup of juice or flavored water. Gray removed a carton from a miniature fridge. Saige mixed the medicine with the liquid into a one-ounce medicine cup. Upon reaching Room 2, she handed it to TJ. "You must be thirsty after falling off your bike. Here's a drink. Remember to choose a stick after you finish it."

TJ accepted the cup and downed the juice. Then, after looking at his mom for a head nod, he raised the wooden stick with the smiley face.

"Wonderful. I have a surprise for you. My assistant, Mr. Gray, will wash your boo-boo. I bet he's had lots of them in his lifetime. Tell us about your owies, Mr. Gray."

"I fell out of a tree once. Landed on my arm." Gray washed the wound while he talked. "I needed stitches for that one, y'all."

"Did it hurt?" TJ asked.

"Don't remember. Must not o' hurt too much, or I'd recall the whole thang. Dr. Saige, how about if y'all get started doctorin' while I tell TJ another story. This one is about the time I crashed on a motorbike."

TJ's eyes widened. "I wanna know about that one."

"Well, ya see—"

Saige scooted onto on a wheeled stool behind Gray. "I'm going to touch your skin, TJ. It'll feel like a poke with a scratchy stick."

"Compared to falling off a bicycle, ya'll will barely feel a thang." Gray kept between Saige and TJ's other leg, so the little boy had to look away from his injured limb. "One day, when I wuz riding on my motorbike, I hit a pothole in the road. Boom!" Gray raised his arms over his head as though imitating an explosion.

TJ made a face while Saige numbed his wound, but he didn't take his eyes off Gray's animated storytelling.

"I flew off that bike and onto the side o' the road. Landed on the gravel like y'all did, TJ, so I know the feelin'. Had gravel in my leg and my head. A nice doctor removed the mess and washed my wounds just as I did fer you. I had a big bandage on my leg and around my noggin. Right there," Gray pointed to his head. "Here, I'll show ya." He twisted around and swiped a package of gauze from Saige's instrument table. "Hold yer head still." Gray wrapped the gauze around the boy's forehead several times. "After Dr. Saige is finished with your leg, you can look in the mirror."

TJ touched his head. "Cool."

Working quickly, while Gray chattered, Saige sutured the wound then applied a small bandage. "All done." She crumpled the sterile paper draped over the boy's leg. "How do you feel now, TJ?"

Eyes twinkling, the young man raised the wooden smiley face. "I want to see my head!"

"Of course." Saige winked at Gray. "Hey, do we have any lollipops around here?"

"Shore do." Gray reached into a cabinet, pulled out a glass jar, and handed a red one to TJ. "You were a brave young man."

"But I didn't do anything." TJ popped the strawberry sucker into his mouth.

His mom snuggled him under her arm. "You did a great job, son.

Dr. Saige, you and Gray are amazing. Thank you."

"Any time." Gray set the lollipop jar back in the cabinet.

Heat bathed Saige's cheeks. "Glad we could help."

While Gray lifted TJ to look in a small mirror on the wall, Saige read Ms. Carter the aftercare instructions. The mom nodded, put the instruction sheet in her purse, then scooped TJ's hand into hers and left the room.

"One satisfied customer down, and—" Saige glanced at the waiting room. "Tons more to go." She sprayed down the exam table with disinfectant. "Thanks for upstaging me, Gray. TJ never even looked at his leg." She pulled new paper over the exam table and tucked it under the cushion. "Seriously, though, I couldn't have done it without you. You should think about becoming a doctor."

Gray grinned the same way he did earlier, but this time he folded his lips as though holding back a full-on chuckle. As he strolled to the door, Aiden appeared, chart in hand. "Hey, Gray, can you help me in Room 3? I've got a ten-year-old boy with a lacerated hand."

Gray collected another smile from Saige before turning to Aiden. "What's the matter, buddy? Can't y'all take care of him by yourself? Man up." Gray clapped him on the shoulder before returning to the lounge, leaving Aiden speechless.

"Is that what we can expect from orderlies?" Aiden shook his head.

Saige winked at him. "I guess Gray only assists the helpless ladies."

A middle-aged man sporting a stethoscope around his neck exited Room 1. "Orderlies, did you say? That'll be the day. You two must be the new volunteers. Jon, here, family practice. Glad to have you." After introductions made their way around, he pulled a paper cup from the water dispenser and chugged down the entire contents. "If you have any questions, let me know. Acetaminophen and aspirin are fine to prescribe, as long as a patient doesn't have a contraindication. We don't order narcotics." With that, he deposited a chart on the desk and entered the physician's lounge.

"Looks like it's going to be a long day." Saige eyed Aiden before returning to Room 2.

True to his word, Aiden ordered two pizzas at lunch. One for the staff and one for the men who had all but threatened to steal his car. Around noon, the younger man, clad in a hoodie over several layers of clothes, entered the clinic, head down, as though unsure of himself. Aiden met the smelly young man at the counter. "Glad to see you."

The man glanced around as though wondering what to do next. Aiden handed him a pizza box and a worn business card. "Like I said, I'm glad you came." Aiden pointed to the picture on the card. "Please call this number." He moved his finger to a name and phone number. "I'm friends with the pastor. He'll help you and your buddy find a job and a place to stay if you give him a call."

The young man lifted his head. "No kidding?"

"I called him first. But please, treat him with respect; he's a great guy."

The young man and his fumes hurried to the door, pizza in hand. "Thanks, dude." He exited the clinic, lighter on his feet than when he entered.

The rest of the afternoon and early evening, Maria called patients to Rooms 1, 2, 3, and 4. Saige peered down the hallway. Who was the other doctor?

TWELVE

When the last patient exited the clinic, Saige looked up from the desk as Maria made a mad dash to the front door. The nurse was a split-second too late for a well-dressed lady with an air of importance who pushed her way inside.

"Sorry, we're closed now." Saige dropped her last chart in the rack. Why hadn't outspoken Maria stopped the lady?

Bundled in a stylish camel hair coat, the fancy woman barged past Maria to the desk while Saige crossed her arms and prepared to play defense for the vertically challenged office nurse.

The auburn-haired beauty wrapped her coat collar tightly around her neck as though protecting herself from germs. She glanced at the messy room, diamond pendant earrings swinging as she turned.

Magazine pages and crumpled paper cups from the water cooler covered the scuffed-up tiles which hid under more winter slush than earlier in the day. And the chipped and half-busted chairs sprawled around the room had left their appointed spots hours ago.

"This place looks worse than it did last year." The arrogant woman strutted to the desk in her high-heeled leather boots. "Where's Gray? I have the BMW at the curb. We need to hurry before it's stolen."

"Gray, your ride is here!" Maria hollered to the back.

Saige's jaw dropped as the orderly strolled to the front wearing an ebony knee-length coat over creased slacks and a deep lake-blue sweater that accented his crystal-blue eyes.

"I don't know why you give up your winter vacation every year to

73

volunteer here." The lady tilted her nose, looped her arm in his, and dragged him to the door.

What was going on? Saige hurried after them, trying to make sense of the situation. "Wait, Gray, thanks for your help today."

He released his arm from the lady's hand. With each step toward Saige, he infused the air with expensive cologne. "No problem." His polished British accent sounded nothing like his earlier Southern dialect.

"I couldn't have done it without you." Mixed feelings overpowered Saige as Gray's intoxicating cologne stirred her emotions. Why would a rich man become an orderly? And why would an orderly spend his winter vacation in a rundown clinic?

"It's Dr. Edgar Graybourne Addington to you." The lady eyed Saige from head to toe as though Saige had crawled out from a gutter. Her words were barbed and aimed to whittle Saige down to size. "Come on, Gray, we've got Christmas shopping to do." Pushing open the door, she let out a sigh. "Are you coming or not?"

Was Gray the famed Dr. Addington? He wasn't old or grim. Who was the older man in the internet picture then—his father? Of course. His father must be a doctor too—the one who started the Complex. What was Saige supposed to say or do now? Had today been a joke?

Gray tarried behind the fancy woman, his eyes lowered at Saige. Chewing on his bottom lip, he hesitated. "I'm sorry." He spoke with a distinct British accent! "Today, I had the most fun I've had in a long time." Was his accent natural this time or was it as fake as the Southern one?

The lady took his hand and pulled him through the opened door. He glanced one final time at Saige. "Forgive me for the charade," he mouthed.

Unsure of what to say, Saige removed an extra smiley face/sad face tongue depressor from her pocket and wagged the smile at him like a bona fide dork.

Jon strolled to the desk, holding the last chart of the day. He aimed his thumb at the woman towing Gray to his car. "Hmph, she's got nerve, that one."

"They make a good pair then." Aiden had been watching from behind the desk. He tucked wayward hair strands behind his ear before shoving his oval glasses in place. "I can't believe he pulled one over on Saige and me."

Saige stood at the glass door, thoughts catapulting through her mind. Aiden was right. Gray, who was obviously Dr. Edgar Addington, had tricked them. She grinned despite the dastardly situation. His Southern accent had been hilarious.

Goosebumps danced up her arms. Gray, with his wavy brown hair, enchanting eyes, and cute dimpled chin, had to be one of the most handsome doctors she'd ever met. If he were half as charming and romantic as the man who carried her to the study a couple days ago, he might be the man of her dreams. She spun around. Leaning her head against the glass door, she sighed at Aiden. "If Gray thinks he pulled one over on me, wait until he finds out I'm the gal he invited to work at his complex."

♥

As Gray pressed on the gas pedal, he regretted leaving Saige floundering in the clinic. Why had he embellished the charade by using a fake accent after she called him an orderly?

The last time he'd acted without airs was years ago when he chummed with his friends at the all-boys day school while growing up. He'd pulled many pranks with them in middle school and senior high until his parents whisked him off to a university a few years before graduation. Although he was a bit more casual with Fernsby and Dell, he never let down his guard with his parents or Lilith. They demanded proper upper-class behavior at all times.

Joking around today carried him back to a world filled with laughter—a relaxed world he sorely missed. But would he have embellished the charade if Saige hadn't been so gorgeous? Something about her light hazel eyes, long lashes, and milky skin captivated him, but her sweet voice and tenderness with TJ hooked him. He'd never met a person quite as genuine as her, except maybe the girl who fell at the mansion Christmas party. Yet that young lady had worn a great deal of makeup. By using a little deductive reasoning, he surmised that the lady was either a social icon in the community or a candidate for the Addington Complex. Those two groups were the only ones invited to the party. He doubted she was a social icon since she admitted not fitting in. If she were considered for the appointment to the Complex, then she was a top-notch cardiologist, and he'd have a lot in common with her. Would he ever see her again? Probably not, unless Fernsby worked harder at finding the owner of the bracelet.

Still, Gray's little act today gave him a chance to interact with Saige and her big heart for kids. Meeting females had been a challenge for him, probably because of the all-boys school, but even in medical school, where studies consumed his hours, he had no time for the opposite sex.

Thankfully, he had Lilith for a friend.

They met one evening, many years ago, when his father invited the LaRue's to dinner. Gray's father and Mr. Carlton LaRue adjourned to the study after the main course to discuss a business venture while their mothers chose to take their desserts to the sunroom. That left Gray to entertain their only child, young Lilith.

Not knowing what to say or do on their first encounter, Gray fidgeted until Lilith suggested they walk through the backyard gardens. She did all the talking. Months passed before he relaxed in her presence.

Over the years, his father and Mr. LaRue held many business meetings alone in the study. Lilith usually accompanied her father, but after her arrival, she never left Gray's side. Falling in like with her had happened slowly, although he never enjoyed her stiff, prim and proper behavior which she insisted from him as well.

On the other hand, Dr. Saige was kind, funny, and down-to-earth. He'd give anything for someone with her character to work at the Addington Complex. Based on his luck, though, his team probably selected someone older and dour or rigid and pompous. Why couldn't life be fun more often—like today?

THIRTEEN

After disinfecting the chairs, mopping the clinic floors, and cleaning the restrooms, jobs that fell to the volunteers, Saige handed Aiden the directions Maria gave her for the boarding house. "According to Maria, Mrs. Salucci keeps a comfortable home."

"About now, I'd sleep anywhere with a bed. That bench in the lounge looks mighty inviting." Aiden donned his fleece-lined denim jacket and gloves. "We'd better get out of here before I sit down. I'd fall asleep in five minutes."

"Let's hurry. The streets don't look safe out there." Saige zipped her coat to her neck before stepping outside into the wintery downfall. At least four inches of fresh snow lay on the sidewalk.

Saige eyed a man with his head down, hands propped in his coat pockets, as he speed-walked toward them. She scooted to Aiden's opposite side and tried not to stare at the man. The guy headed past them under a lamp post then crossed the street.

"Maria showed me where to park tomorrow." Aiden nodded at a side entrance. "Hey, it wasn't so bad today, was it? I think we helped a lot of kids." His pace accelerated as he steered Saige along the sidewalk.

She got the hint and walked faster. "Yes, and their parents said, 'Thank you.' Not a demanding voice in the crowd." Saige pinched her coat collar under her chin to shield her neck from the cold.

Aiden reached his car and hurried around to the driver's side. His clunker was in one piece. Criminals didn't even want it. Snow continued to pelt their heads and shoulders with wet flakes as Saige helped him sweep the accumulation off the windshields and windows before climbing into the car. Several minutes later, with Aiden behind the wheel, the vehicle sputtered away to Mrs. Salucci's on the outskirts of the city.

"Today blessed my heart, Saige. Can you imagine helping impoverished people overseas who can't afford medical care? Are you sure you won't change your mind and become a missionary with me?"

"You keep forgetting about Annie."

"Sorry. Well, I won't be leaving for a couple years. I have to pay off my school loans first. It'll give you plenty of time to think about it."

"I'll do that, just for you, Aiden." The short ride provided Saige with an opportunity to put aside the hustle and bustle of the busy day. When Aiden arrived at the boarding house, he parked his Bug along the front curb. Saige admired the nineteenth-century architecture with its quaint, white-washed siding and scalloped trim.

About the time they trudged to the porch steps, a lady torpedoed through the front door, her attractive, though plain dress flared as she ran down the steps and smothered them in warm hugs. "You must be Saige and Aiden. I'm Mrs. Salucci. Please come in. I'll show you around."

Oozing joy flavored with minced garlic, Mrs. Salucci wiped strands of layered shoulder-length hair from her face before taking their coats and guiding them on a tour of the downstairs. A stone fireplace with blazing logs offered the floral-themed living room an inviting glow. But the enticing Italian aromas in the kitchen drew Saige through its swinging doors. Comfort and relaxation dominated every corner of the home.

After the downstairs tour, Mrs. Salucci led Saige and Aiden to the stairs. "How about if I show you to your rooms before we eat dinner?" Multiple laugh lines etched her cheerful face.

"Sure. I'm hungry." Aiden headed up the steps behind their hostess with Saige on his heels.

At the top of the staircase and down the hall on the left, Mrs. Salucci opened a door for Aiden. The tidy masculine room held a queen-sized bed covered with a sage-green quilt, a dresser, and an attached bathroom.

"This is perfect. Thank you." Aiden set his backpack on the floor. "If you don't mind, I'll wash up a bit."

"Of course, dear." Mrs. Salucci led Saige to a room on the right. "You'll be staying here, Dr. Saige. If you need anything, let me know. My room is on the other side of yours."

The beautiful ivy-print room included everything Saige needed: a bed nestled under an ivy-design canopy and quilt, a polished antique dresser, nightstand, vanity, and an attached bathroom. Compared to her apartment with its second, or more accurately, third-hand mismatched furniture, this place was luxurious. Saige longed to slip under the covers, curl into a ball, and sleep.

"Come on down for dinner after you've acquainted yourself with the room. I'll have food on the table in an instant." Mrs. Salucci's sweet voice reminded Saige of her mother's. Mom had been her best friend. Saige used to spend hours in the evenings confiding in her and seeking her advice. Why did such a wonderful person have to die so young?

Saige wiped the tears spilling from her eyes. Memories of her mother still ripped open the scars in her heart. She lifted a framed picture from her backpack and set it on the nightstand. Her family meant everything to her.

A knock at the door made her jump. "Are you coming down, Saige? Mrs. Salucci will have dinner ready in a few minutes."

"Sure. Give me a sec." Saige glanced at her mother's smiling face one last time before opening the door and following Aiden.

Downstairs in the kitchen, Saige went directly to the stove where garlicky spaghetti sauce with Italian sausage simmered in a pot next to a bigger one filled with bubbling water.

"I have the table set, but the noodles have to cook a few minutes before we sit down to eat." Mrs. Salucci walked to a flour-dusted cutting board covered in homemade noodles. With a swoop, she gathered the pasta in both hands and dropped it into the boiling water.

The savory smells caused Saige's stomach juices to pirouette with excitement. "Good one." Aiden nodded at her midsection after it made noises yet again.

Saige covered her abdomen. Since breakfast, which consisted of a bagel slathered in cream cheese, she'd only eaten one piece of Aiden's pizza. Tomorrow morning, she'd ask him to stop at a convenience store for bread and peanut butter. They'd need the food to sustain them through another busy clinic day.

The Italian feast, complete with homemade garlic bread, salad, and freshly grated Parmesan and Romano cheeses, filled Saige's empty belly until she had to unsnap the button on her jeans.

"How about if you two sit by the fire while I do the dishes?" Mrs. Salucci began clearing plates from the table.

Aiden stacked the empty spaghetti, bread, and salad bowls in his hands. "We'll help you." He balanced the load in his arms and headed into the kitchen.

Way to go, Aiden. At least he didn't put his hands up and say, "No." Saige's shoulders sagged. Her head desperately needed a pillow, but she gathered the silverware and glasses before depositing them on the kitchen counter.

"Thank you for helping. Now, go and enjoy the fire. I'll bring homemade cookies to you in a little while." Their white-haired hostess shooed them out the swinging kitchen door with a flick of her wrist.

The warm fire didn't make it easy for Saige to keep her eyes open. Aiden sat beside her on the couch, but her head kept nodding toward his shoulder. Every time it landed, she jerked awake.

"Go to bed, Saige. I'll take care of the cookies. Someone has to do it."

On each side of the floral-print sofa, Christmas pillows hugged the corners. Before Aiden could defend himself, Saige pummeled him in the chest with an applique of Rudolf's head complete with felt antlers. "Save me some treats." A lopsided grin tugged her weary face.

A chuckle escaped Aiden as he blocked her next move—a backhanded pillow thrust at his knees. "Will do." He stopped smiling. "Wait, before you leave, can I ask a question?"

Saige tossed the pillow to its appointed spot. "Sure. Let me have it."

"Is Dr. Addington the type of guy you're looking for?"

Did she hear right? "Why would you ask such a question?"

"Something about the way you stared out the door when he left with that uppity woman." Aiden fiddled with Santa's cottony beard on the pillow beside him.

Saige returned to the sofa. She didn't dare tell Aiden her true thoughts. "I don't know. He was handsome. And he was kind while he helped me with my patient. We had fun."

"He was flirting with you."

"Nah."

"I know flirty eyes when I see them." Aiden turned his focus to the fireplace when she didn't answer.

Curled on the sofa with Rudolf for protection, Saige studied Aiden's profile with her finger bracing her temple. What would he look like if he ruffled his hair and stared into her eyes? He had peered into her eyes in her apartment a few mornings ago over breakfast, but that didn't count because he intruded on her sleep to borrow pancake mix, which he didn't have ingredients for in the first place. She stood to go upstairs with the pillow wrapped in her arms. Aiden wasn't the guy for her. She knew it in her gut.

"Think quick!" She lobbed Rudolf to the sofa. The pillow skimmed Aiden's head. Saige pointed at him, her mouth wide, as though she'd beat him at their game. Then, she loped up the stairs.

Aiden laughed. "You better be nice, or Mrs. Salucci will see how you treat me." He paused for a moment. "Hey, this might be the perfect place for you to stay while working in St. Anne's Landing."

Saige stopped on the stairs. Why hadn't she thought of that? Mrs. Salucci's house would make a great place to stay if she had the nerve to accept Dr. Addington's position. But would the job still hold after Gray learned she was the appointee?

FOURTEEN

Early Tuesday morning, the crisp aroma of ginger and molasses floated to the second floor in the Addington mansion. Gray recognized the smell on his way down the grand staircase. Adele made the cookies every Christmas in preparation for the Addington family get-together. For as long as he could remember, his family hosted two parties for the holidays: A formal gala for professionals in the community during the first part of December and an extended family get-together on Christmas Eve.

As much as Gray disliked the professional party, he truly enjoyed the less formal family gathering. Maybe this year, he'd invite Dr. Saige, if she and Aiden weren't an item. Fernsby and Adele would most likely enjoy her sweet nature.

How had he been so wrong about Lilith? She was his first "girl" friend. What with concentrated studies during high school and then medical school, his social life had been nonexistent. He'd been thankful that his parents met hers. One thing led to another, and they joined the Addington's for Thanksgiving dinner. How long ago was that? Too many years for him to recall.

Lilith bossed him around from the first day they met, but as they grew older, she instructed him on which clothes to purchase, taught him how to dress, and showed him how to behave at social functions. Gray frowned. She even told him what to eat and drink at restaurants. If he allowed her, she'd probably tell him what to think. He didn't have to worry about the mundane facts of daily life, though. Instead, he was able to concentrate on his career—his surgeries—his patients.

Come to think of it, he'd taken Lilith for granted. Maybe he unconsciously used her. But perhaps she used him too. What did he have that she might want or need? Her father was a shipping billionaire. They had the most prominent house, most expensive cars, and more servants than anyone in the community. So why did Lilith want to date Gray? Was it the prestige of becoming a doctor's wife? Well, not any doctor's wife—the acclaimed Dr. Edgar Addington's wife. A significant social standing came with that title. What other reason could she possibly have to stay by his side?

Despite the unsavory things about her, Gray had to admit—he was comfortable around her. She had her role down pat—taking care of Gray. And he had his role memorized from day one—do whatever Lilith says. Should he risk ruining any of that?

Life had been simple for him while he attended the all-boys day schools. But he never had a clue about the opposite sex. Lilith made that simple. Maybe he shouldn't mess with a good thing. She'd help him soar in their social circles. Still, she made his servants uncomfortable, and their feelings were important to him.

Saige, on the other hand, was far different from Lilith. She was relaxed and unguarded during conversations. He hated dilemmas. Why did there have to be one? He and Lilith were simply friends, although she did have a jealous streak. No telling how she'd react if he asked Saige on a date. Would she say country-girl Saige wasn't good enough for him?

After descending the stairs, he made his way to the kitchen where Adele, clad in a holiday apron adorned with poinsettias, stood at the kitchen island cutting gingerbread men from dough on a floured pastry sheet. A fire crackled in the stone hearth several yards across from her in the vast kitchen. The room's warmth coupled with the tantalizing aromas of ginger and molasses hugged Gray with childhood memories.

Perched on a stool on the opposite side of the enormous island, Fernsby, in his usual creased pants, starched collared shirt, vest, and tie studied the screen on his iPad while sipping steaming coffee from a mug. He glanced at Gray. "Good morning, young man."

"Morning, old chap." Snooping like a bloodhound, Gray scouted the kitchen for the hot-from-the-oven cookies. "Ah, here they are." He sucked in the tantalizing fumes. "You know, I look forward to these, Dell."

"Yes, indeed, but I have to freeze them for Christmas Eve." Adele slapped his hand when he reached for a cookie.

Gingerbread houses, complete with candy canes, gumdrops, and icing, swam through Gray's memories. Both Adele and Fernsby helped him make them when he was young, but as he grew older, they competed with him to build and decorate the best gingerbread house of the season. One time he made a two-story condo decorated with licorice sticks, lollipops, and homemade stained-glass candy.

"Don't stick your nose so close to the plate, Gray. You'll put germs on those cookies." Adele chided him matter-of-factly. She rarely ever raised her voice at him.

"Just one gingerbread man, please?" Gray poked out his bottom lip because that usually made Adele give him whatever he wanted.

"One for me too." Fernsby tried his best to copy Gray's pleading child stance.

Adele rolled her eyes at Fernsby, but she removed two festive red dessert dishes from a shelf on the wall. Then, after placing decorated gingerbread men on each one, she eyed Fernsby. "Would you care for some milk, too?"

Fernsby nodded like a young boy starving for a treat. Gray suspected he'd never been able to resist her delicious baked goods any more than Gray could. Sometimes Gray would spot a loving spark in Fernsby's eyes when the valet gazed at Adele. Had there been a relationship between the two? They never let on around Gray.

After placing glasses of milk by each plate, Adele wiped flour from her brow with the back of her hand. "Why aren't you in the study to take breakfast, Gray?"

"I'm volunteering at the free clinic for the next two weeks, remember? I'll be eating on the run." Gray bit off the gingerbread man's arm. "These are amazing."

"That's an admirable way to spend your Christmas vacation." Adele

85

handed him a bagged lunch.

"You always look out for me." Gray set the bag by his plate, finished his milk and polished off the gingerbread body. "I'll most likely miss dinner. Tonight is the annual doctor/nurse basketball game at the Y. This year, we'll be the Reindeers vs. the Elves. Kids will love us."

"Have fun. I'll be here baking and freezing cookies all day."

She surveyed the mess on the counter and wiped her hands on her apron. "I need to bake ten dozen cookies a day until Christmas Eve." The oven timer dinged.

"Don't worry, my dear, I'll help you—if you'll go out with me again." Fernsby clicked off his iPad before batting his eyes at her.

"Nice try, Fernsby. I only went to the theater because you dragged me on a mission to visit jewelry stores. You insisted on going to the movie, so I had no choice." Adele scooped a cookie with her spatula and placed it in a glass container.

Not inclined to interrupt their frequent bickering, Gray collected his lunch sack and rounded the island to leave. "Did you learn anything about the bracelet from the jewelry stores, old chap?"

"Not from any of the stores we visited on Saturday, but I think I spotted the girl at the theater on Sunday evening. She might have been the same young lady from the party, although she was with a young man."

"But she resembled the girl who fell?"

"Far as I could tell. This time she was wearing jeans and no makeup, and her hair was down around her shoulders. But after she gathered it into a ponytail, there was no mistaking her heart-shaped face and soft hazel eyes. The resemblance was uncanny. Oh, and—"

"Yes? Tell me everything." Gray leaned in with his chin on his fist and his elbow on the counter, intent on hearing every word.

"She and the young man drove off in an antique VW Bug. Remember those old contraptions? But this car was multicolored like a kaleidoscope."

Gray rubbed his chin. He had seen the jalopy too. How could the girl from his party have been the same one riding around in a car like that? He'd only invited prominent people. But who was the guy with her? "Did you speak to her? Or return the bracelet?"

"She and her boyfriend left before I had the opportunity."

A boyfriend? Gray reeled in his disappointment before adding, "Where's the jewelry?"

"I meant to discuss that with you."

"What do you mean, old chap?"

Fernsby lowered his eyes as though having a difficult time finding words. "I placed it on the bookshelf in the study the morning I showed it to you. But, when I returned for it on Sunday, the bracelet was gone."

"What about the maid or the gardener? Did they come across it?"

"I questioned them, but they admitted they hadn't been in the study."

Gray scratched the side of his jaw. Who might have taken it? Hmm. Someone in dark clothes had hurried down the hallway outside the study around noon on Saturday, but Lilith denied coming to the mansion that day. So, who else could it have been? "Have you searched jewelry stores?"

"I searched brick-and-mortar stores in St. Anne's on Saturday and in St. James on Sunday without any luck."

"How about checking the internet for pictures of diamond bracelets. If you spot the one the girl lost, inquire about the inscription. Maybe the place will have information about the person who requested the engraving."

"Brilliant, I'll do that," Fernsby replied.

"Thank you, old chap. I believe we'll find her yet."

FIFTEEN

Work at the clinic sped by the following day because the flu had unofficially converged on St. Anne's Landing. Rapid testing proved Saige's diagnoses accurate for each child with congestion, fever, and sore throat. Those with flu symptoms sat in a side room to separate them from the others. Saige and her coworkers wore masks for safety. Maria dispensed paper masks to everyone who walked through the door. The line of patients wound outside and down the street, but Saige, Aiden, Gray, and Jon kept them moving along. Nurse Maria did the testing and vital signs while also taking histories and admitting patients into the clinic.

Before noon, Maria divided the lunch shifts into thirty-minute time slots. Aiden and Jon were to eat together, while Saige would eat with Gray. But how could she face him after using him as an orderly the day before? Worse yet, what would he think about her working at his complex? One way or another, she'd gather the courage to share the truth.

Acting more like a field mouse than a courageous cardiologist, she crept into the tiny physician's lounge at lunch time. Gray peered at her from the bench where he had an opened glass bowl on his lap. The aroma from his food drifted through the tiny room, making her hungry.

"By the sounds of your stomach, I'd say you're starving." Using a fresh plastic teaspoon, he scooped several meat chunks on a paper plate for Saige. "Here you go. This cranberry pork should solve the problem."

Saige slipped off her mask then rummaged through the microwave shelf.

"Looking for one of these?" Gray lifted a fork from a box in the cubby behind him.

"Yes. Thanks." After spearing a piece of meat, she dropped the morsel into her mouth. She closed her eyes, savoring every second before swallowing. The bite had tasted deliciously sweet and tangy at the same time. "Meat with cranberry sauce is a first for me. It's amazing."

"My che—I mean, Adele cooks like a pro. Her food melts in my mouth."

"Is she your girlfriend—the one who came for you at the clinic yesterday?" Saige popped another meat chunk into her mouth and sighed while chewing it. "This is far better than restaurant food."

Gray nodded in agreement about the meat. "No, that lady was Lilith. Nothing permanent with our relationship; we've been friends for a long time. But Adele is...I guess she's...it's rather complicated. She's a great friend to me."

"I see." Saige didn't understand but judging by Gray's inability to sit still as he spoke, the subject was delicate. She opened the grocery bag she'd left under the microwave shelf and withdrew the bread loaf, peanut butter, and jelly. "Care for a not-so-gourmet sandwich?"

"Sure. Maybe another time. I just polished off this pork." After returning the empty bowl to his bag, Gray removed a baggie filled with several frosted gingerbread men cookies. "Would you care for any of these?"

"I'd give my right arm for one." Saige held out her palm.

Gray placed two in her hand. As she bit off a spicy ginger and molasses foot, she allowed the flavor to settle on her tongue. "Mmm. You're lucky to have Adele around."

"What about your mom?"

"She passed away from cancer a couple years ago. Life hasn't been the same ever since."

"I'm so sorry to hear that." He glanced at the wall clock. "Looks like we need to get back to work so our colleagues can eat."

Saige followed him from the lounge and waited while he deposited his bowl in his locker. "Oh, uh, Gray, I have something I need to tell you." She had to inform him now about winning the appointment to his complex because the deadline for accepting the invitation was in a few days.

"Wait a minute. I have something important to ask you first."

Fear gripped Saige. Did he already know she was the girl who fell at his party? Had he seen her fall? Humiliation sent blood rushing to her toes. "I need to sit down."

Gray swiped a chair from the hallway and placed it beside her. "What I have to say isn't that important."

Saige slid down onto the seat. Did he want to rescind his offer for the Addington Complex? "Go ahead. Let me have it." She lowered her head and covered her face.

"There's a Christmas basketball game at the YMCA tonight. Doctors vs. nurses, or rather, Reindeer vs. Elves. Maria will be playing on the nurses' team. How about joining us?"

Was that what he wanted to say? The blood returned to Saige's brain. "I used to play basketball in high school. Sounds like fun. Can Aiden play too?"

"I forgot about your boyfriend."

"My boyfriend?" How did Gray get that idea? "He's a friend. But I can only play if he does. He's my ride."

"Really? The way he looks at you, I thought for sure—" Gray walked toward the reception desk.

Saige followed close behind him. "I volunteered to work here because Aiden encouraged me to join him."

If she hadn't volunteered, she might not have met the playful side of Dr. Edgar Graybourne Addington. He certainly wasn't the stuffy, pompous Brit she imagined him to be, even with his charming British accent. But how had she fallen for his terrible fake Southern drawl yesterday? Worse yet, what would he think when he learned she was the recipient of his cardiology offer? She tugged on his sleeve. "Uh, Gray, I've got a confession to make."

He peered down at her. "Well, it's not Sunday, and I'm not a priest. But if you think I'm qualified to hear your confession, go right ahead." He touched his forehead then each shoulder before palming his hands together. "I'm ready." He waggled his eyebrows, fighting the tiniest of grins.

Saige offered a polite cough as she shifted her stance. "The thing is—"

"The two of you are cutting into our lunchtime. The exam rooms are full." Jon walked to the desk then tossed a chart into the rack. He glanced at the waiting room. "I think the line is longer than this morning."

As Aiden exited Room 3, modeling his famous arrow hat, two little boys in the waiting room pointed at him. "Look at that silly doctor!" The younger one with pale skin and a bald scalp slapped his head as he belted a laugh.

"Yeah, there's an arrow on his head!" The other one, about four years old, dove from his chair onto the floor. "Hahahahaha."

"It's broken," the first boy aimed his finger at Aiden's head again. "See!"

Gray walked by the chart rack and clapped Aiden on the shoulder. "Yeah, he's most decidedly silly. Way to go, pal."

"Too bad you're so dignified you can't entertain little ones." Aiden waved at the boys in the waiting room. Three little tykes fell against their chairs giggling. "Those little fellas think I'm funny."

Gray leaned on Maria's desk with his arms crossed. "True. Little preschoolers think you're hilarious." He slipped by Aiden to sidle up to Saige. "Maybe we can go somewhere for dinner after the game?" He winked at her before cocking his head and walking like a runway model back to his appointed room.

Men! Saige lifted the chart from the receptacle by her door.

A teenager with purple-tipped hair waiting on Saige's exam table cupped his hands around his mouth and shouted, "Hey, dude, might wanna lose the dorky arrow hat. Not gonna score you any points with pretty ladies."

Two shades of scarlet flooded Aiden's face before he yanked off the hat and threw it on Maria's desk. "I guess everyone's not a fan." He stormed to the physician's lounge, huffing and puffing as though having a hard time catching his breath.

Saige had never seen him so riled. She bit her lip to keep from making the situation worse. Telling Aiden about the basketball game would have to wait until later, otherwise, she might ruin any chance of him saying "yes." She'd beg and plead with him if she had to because Gray might be her new boss, and more importantly, he might be the man of her dreams, especially since her hero from the mansion had totally forgotten about her.

♥

Maria closed the clinic door at four o' clock, as she reportedly did annually to participate in the basketball game that evening. But Saige had a difficult time persuading Aiden to join the Reindeers. When he finally agreed to play, she had a feeling he had something planned because he wouldn't let her put her keys in his gym bag. He was usually a good sport, but Gray had humiliated him at the clinic. What was it with guys trying to outdo each other?

"Do you want to talk about it?" Saige tugged Aiden's sleeve on their drive to Mrs. Salucci's house, but he clammed up.

"It was nothing." He shifted gears as though the shifter was Gray's head.

But the minute they arrived at Mrs. Salucci's, he ran up the stairs, straight to his room before greeting their hostess and even before eating dinner—a first for Aiden Littlefield, the "Bottomless Pit."

By 6:45 they arrived at the YMCA gym where hundreds of spectators swarmed the place, excited for the game to begin. Maria handed Saige and Aiden their costumes, and they headed to the locker rooms to change until the sports announcer broadcast over the loudspeaker that the game would start at seven p.m. Saige exited her locker room as the spectators shuffled onto the crowded bleachers.

"Ladies and gentlemen, parents and young people, may I have your attention." The announcer paused until the chatter died down. "Let me introduce the teams. First, we have Santa's Elves. Nurses, please take the court."

The crowd clapped and cheered as Maria and her team of men and women ran to the center of the floor, waving their arms at the spectators while dressed as typical shopping mall elves.

"And now, we have their opponents—none other than Santa's Reindeers." The announcer belly laughed as Gray and the doctors on his team joined the Elves center court for a standing ovation by parents and children. Each team member's nose was painted red. Antler headbands topped their heads. Saige had to smile. Kids were cracking up at their funny costumes.

"Now, let me introduce our big surprise for the evening!" The announcer chuckled. "A special visitor has traveled all the way from the North Pole to referee our game!"

A man with a large belly and fluffy white hair and beard entered the gym, clad in a Santa suit with an enormous green bag tossed over his shoulder. The crowd went crazy whistling, clapping, and stomping their feet at his arrival. Santa hauled the bag to one side of the bleachers, reached inside of it, and tossed candy to the children. Then he headed to the other side of the court and did the same. When the giggles and laughter died down, he set his bag on a sideline bench before taking his place center court for the ball toss.

Dressed in the brown scrubs of her teammates, which accented their red noses and antlered headbands, Saige held her arms at the ready to catch the basketball. Adjacent to her, Aiden copped the same stance, but he sported a striped beanie cap with a propeller on top. It sat over his topknot and between his antlers.

So that's what he had been hiding. Saige shook her head. When would he ever learn?

Waiting at the center court, Gray, dreamy as a reindeer with his deep brown hair curling over his ears, prepared for Santa to toss the ball up between he and his opponent, a hairy-armed, big-eared elf, clad in striped socks, green scrubs, and a Santa hat. The tall elf crouched opposite Gray, ready to vie for the ball.

The referee Santa blew his whistle then threw the ball into the air. Both forwards jumped for it, but Gray slapped it from the elf's hands. Saige caught it and dribbled toward their hoop before tossing it to Aiden. Approximately twenty feet from the goal, Aiden leaped and shot the ball overhand through the air. It landed through the hoop.

"Two points!" the referee shouted.

Aiden spun the propeller on his head before raising his arms for more attention as the crowd whistled and cheered.

"Way to go!" Saige jumped up and down, clapping for him.

The nurses had the ball now. Maria dribbled it toward her basket on the elf team, but Gray intercepted it, turned, and shot the ball across the room. The ball landed squarely through the hoop. The crowd went bonkers, screaming for Gray. He raised his hands in a cocky manner as Aiden had done, then took a tiny bow.

"Oh, it's on!" Aiden mumbled under his breath.

"You're on the same team." Saige clenched her teeth. What were he and Gray doing?

During the rest of the quarter, a power struggle erupted between Aiden and Gray. First, Aiden would score, then Gray. None of their team members had a chance to play. On the Elf team, no one touched the ball.

During the first quarter break, Jon planted his feet in front of the Reindeer bench. He propped his hands on his hips and shook his head at Aiden and Gray. "Should both teams take seats and watch you two play for the rest of the game?" He scowled at Gray, then at Aiden. "Cause you two aren't passing the ball to us, and the other team is twiddling their thumbs."

Gray wiped the sweat from his face with a hand towel. "Sorry. I got carried away."

"Me too. You're right. We need to play like a team." Aiden mopped his arm across his forehead.

"Here's a towel." Saige started to hand hers to Aiden, but instead, she dabbed his brow for him.

From the corner of her eye, she caught Gray watching her tend to Aiden. He grimaced at her behavior then threw his monogrammed towel on the floor. Was he jealous?

For the entire second quarter, he and Aiden passed the ball to their team members. But sweat continued to pour from Aiden by the gallon.

By the third quarter, he lumbered over the court, taking rapid, shallow breaths. Saige hadn't seen him winded before, except when he was upset with Gray at the clinic. Did he need an inhaler for asthma? If so, he'd have one in his pocket and know to use it.

In the final quarter, the teams were tied. Aiden stood on the sideline to toss the ball due to a foul. Surprising everyone, he passed it to Gray.

Gray threw the ball to Saige. She dribbled it toward the hoop, but the tall elf nurse slapped the ball from her hands. Aiden raced to block him. He knocked the ball from the nurse as the man raised to shoot a basket.

The ball flew.

Aiden ran backward at high speed to catch it while Gray swooped sideways. Unable to see behind him, Aiden tripped over Gray's foot.

The ball landed on the floor.

Gray scooped it, shot it, and scored while Aiden's head and back hit the court with a reverberating thud. As the air whooshed from his lungs, his eyes begged for help. A second later, his face twisted, and his body went limp.

Saige raced to Aiden's side as the crowd leaped to their feet, cheering for Gray. But Aiden remained motionless. "Are you okay, Aiden? Are you okay?" Saige slapped his face and shook his shoulders. He didn't move. Leaning close to his mouth, she checked his breathing then placed two fingers on his neck, below his jaw. No breathing. No heartbeat. "Someone call 911!" She quickly began chest compressions.

Gray raced to her side and knelt down on the floor. He took over respirations while she breathed for Aiden.

Santa Claus raced across the basketball court with a black box. "We've never used this, but we keep it for emergencies!" He handed Saige the automated defibrillator.

A silence fell over the crowd.

Spectators on the sidelines strained to see, but Santa and the YMCA officials kept them off the court.

Gray continued compressions while Saige peeled the plastic from the defibrillator pads she'd pulled from the black box. "Stand back," she shouted to Gray. She placed the pads on Aiden's chest. "All clear!" she shouted.

Then she pushed the defibrillator button. The machine began assessing Aiden's heart rhythm. A very coarse line appeared on the screen.

"Administer shock," the machine said.

"You didn't need to tell me that," Saige shouted at the defibrilator. "All clear!"

She spread her arms to keep everyone at a distance as she moved away from Aiden after pushing the defibrillator button again. The machine administered another shock. A slow rhythm scrolled across the screen. Aiden sucked a breath. "He's got a heartbeat!" Saige's face beamed as she clutched her hands to her chest.

Maria wrapped her in a huge hug. "Is he going to make it?"

"We can only hope so," Gray replied.

The paramedics arrived within minutes and placed a hard cervical collar around Aiden's neck and a board under his back. A bearded man applied an oxygen mask over his nose and mouth. Another paramedic swapped out the gym's AED with the ambulance's portable cardiac defibrillator, while the third man started an IV. After everything was in place, the second man collected pertinent information from Saige as they jogged behind the other two paramedics who wheeled Aiden by stretcher to their vehicle.

"I'll ride with him," Saige shouted. "I'm his closest family. H-h-he's my best friend." She waited for the paramedics to place Aiden's stretcher inside the ambulance before climbing up the ramp.

Gray looked at Saige through the open door. "I'll follow you to the hospital."

She shook her head at him as the paramedics closed the ambulance doors. Just when she imagined he was her dream guy, Gray pulled a horrible stunt and tripped Aiden. What was he thinking? She never wanted to see his face again.

SIXTEEN

Driving like a madman opposite the blinding headlights of on-coming traffic, Gray zig-zagged around cars to keep up with the ambulance. The paramedics, per routine, informed the ER doctor of Aiden's status en route to the hospital, and Gray conversed with the physician on his hands-free cellular. "Dr. Littlefield's heart is still beating, and the ambulance expects to arrive within minutes."

"Thank you, Murthy." Gray ended the call to concentrate on his driving. One thing he knew for sure—Aiden's situation could change in a split-second. "Hang in there, buddy."

Passing one car after another, Gray spotted the ambulance as he neared Central Sinai Hospital. The paramedics had pulled up to the back emergency room doors. Gray parked and took off on foot. The ambulance was empty. They had already wheeled Aiden into the hospital.

Still wearing antlers, a painted red nose, and brown scrubs under his ebony coat, Gray ran through the double doors, and straight to the Admissions counter.

"Can I help you, Dr. Addington?" A nurse behind the poinsettia on the countertop stopped him with her raised palm.

Gray paused a second to catch his breath. "Yes, I'm here to see a patient—Aiden Littlefield. The paramedics must have brought him inside."

The nurse eyed his outfit, clearly amused at the costume. As she clicked a switch, allowing the double doors to swing open behind her, Gray hurried to pass through them without waiting for further information.

The familiar ER patient area, lined with curtained cubicles, bustled with nurses and doctors.

"He's in number six." The desk nurse following him indicated the curtains at the end of the hallway.

Gray jogged to the cubicle and parted the curtain to find Aiden lying on a stretcher with an oxygen cannula in his nose. Clad in her reindeer outfit and sporting antlers and a red nose, Saige sat by his side with her hand wrapped around his fingers. She glanced up at Gray before removing her headband. "We must look a sight." She pointed at his head.

Gray's cheeks felt hot as he removed his headband. "How're you doing, Aiden?" Monitors attached by wires to his chest and arms displayed his heartbeat, but it was irregular.

Aiden clenched his jaw but didn't respond.

Saige noticed Gray studying the monitors. She stood and gestured for him to follow her. Her demeanor changed when he complied. She marched to the double doors of the ER before turning around. "Aiden's been sedated for pain. It looks like he's had a heart attack. We'll know the particulars after the echocardiogram, but he's having severe pain in his upper spine and neck as well. He might have a fracture." Gray barely recognized Saige's harsh tone.

"I'm sorry, Saige. I hope you don't mind, but I called the ER doctor on my way to the hospital." He spoke softly, remorsefully. "I recommended my partner for Aiden's cardiologist. He's the best in the area. Nothing against you, but I didn't think you had privileges here." Gray rubbed his forehead while he propped his other hand on his hip. What could he say to convince her he didn't mean for the accident to happen?

"You're right. I don't have privileges at this hospital. By all means, have your cardiologist step in." Shifting her weight to one hip, she crossed her arms. "But let's not pretend, Gray. You caused Aiden's fall, and I'll never forgive you for that. His heart shouldn't have stopped from the fall though. He was short of breath during the second half of the game." Rigid as the Statue of Liberty, she focused on his chest instead of looking into his eyes. "He's got something else going on with his heart."

"Saige, you have to believe me, I—"

"You were both aggressive tonight." She spoke like a cardiologist, not like the sweet little doctor at the clinic.

Granted, he and Aiden were showing off, but it was only for her attention. "I'm sorry, Saige. You're right."

"He'll be transferred shortly to the Intensive Care Unit. We should probably let him rest. We have to work tomorrow."

"Look, I'm worried about you finding a ride home this late. Would you mind if I drive you? I'll pick you up in the morning too. The inner city can be unsafe."

"I'd appreciate the transportation, but it doesn't mean I'm letting you off the hook for what happened."

An orderly passed through the double doors singing, "Pa rum pa pum-pum," as he headed to the Nurse's station. Saige moved out of his way, refusing to look at Gray.

A nurse in green scrubs with a Christmas wreath pin on her top hurried around the counter in her scrubs, carrying a chart in one hand and a syringe in the other. "I'll give him some pain medicine for the trip to the second floor." She deposited the chart on the stretcher below his feet then administered medicine via his IV. After unhooking the wall monitors, she placed a portable defibrillator and an oxygen tank beside him while the orderly attached the IV pump to a skinny pole by his head. Aiden's eyes fluttered and closed as the pain medicine kicked in.

The ER doctor entered the cubicle, his grim expression foreshadowing his visit. "Aiden's scan came back. He has two fractured vertebrae. Come to the desk and I'll show you the report. Dr. McGavern will see him tomorrow. He's the best spinal surgeon around."

"Thanks, Murthy." Gray shook the doctor's hand. "I appreciate you taking care of him."

Saige pursed her lips at Gray before thanking the ER doctor. Gray suspected if her looks could kill, he'd be a dead man about now.

She waited until the orderly wheeled Aiden outside the cubicle before going to his side. In her tenderhearted way, she leaned over her friend and stroked his hair. "You're strong, Aiden. Remember what I told you. Hang in there. You can do it." She pecked him on the cheek, but Aiden didn't open his eyes.

"See you tomorrow, buddy." Gray squeezed his arm.

"There's nothing more either of you can do tonight. He'll be asleep soon from the pain medication." The nurse scooted the defibrillator away from the edge of the stretcher. "Since he listed you as family, Saige, we'll give you information if you want to call. His parents plan to drive here tomorrow."

"Thank you." Saige waited while they wheeled Aiden through the double doors before turning to Gray. "Whatever's going on with his heart, for your sake, I hope he makes it."

♥

The dark sky, filled with ominous clouds, threatened a storm as Saige and Gray reached his BMW in the lighted parking lot.

"Hop in, Saige." Gray opened her car door.

She slid onto the passenger seat, but couldn't stop thinking about Aiden. His accident had happened so fast. One minute he was a healthy, busy physician, and the next minute, he was in cardiac arrest. Would he survive? He hadn't been a good historian about his health in the ER. "I'm fine," he repeated until Saige wanted to scream, "Tell them the truth!"

The clouds burst with sleet seconds after Gray opened his door and slid behind the wheel. He quickly stepped on the gas then steered from the parking lot.

Still lost in thought, Saige recalled her friendship with Aiden. She'd known him through four years of college, four years of medical school, and six years of internship, including her fellowship. In all that time, he hadn't been sick except for an occasional virus. His shortness of breath had bothered her though. She'd seen him huffing and puffing on the tennis court in the summer when they played. But he always denied having a problem.

"You must hate me for the accident." Gray glanced over at her, interrupting her thoughts. But she didn't respond.

Instead, she scooted away from him, her eyes focused on the icy slush hitting the windshield. She wanted nothing to do with him. But less than five minutes later, unable to hold her tongue, she broke down and poured out her fears. "I'm worried about Aiden. He has a preexisting heart problem. I'm sure of it."

"Has he ever mentioned one?"

"Never. I'm calling his parents in the morning. Aiden had the nurse give me their phone number. They live in the country near my farm town."

"So, you grew up in the country? That explains why you don't put on airs."

"Probably because my life involved chickens and cows. I spent many mornings before school milking Fanny Mae."

"Great name." Gray chuckled under his breath. "Did you name her after the bank loan?"

"Yeah. That Fanny Mae saved our farm. I'm tired now."

Exhaustion overwhelmed Saige. Rehashing every detail of the accident had given her a pounding headache. Had Gray purposely tripped Aiden to shoot the winning basket for their team? Even though he didn't appear to be the type for violence, he had belittled Aiden at the clinic. And, of course, Aiden didn't take well to the put-down remarks.

The Addington Complex invitation loomed heavily on her heart. How would she ever feel comfortable working for Gray, or more accurately, Dr. Edgar Graybourne Addington after what happened? In the last two months, she received many offers to join practices around the country. The offers were tempting, but they involved moving too far from Pop and Annie. She wouldn't do that. Unfortunately, if she turned down the Addington Complex, not only would she have to sacrifice her dreams of living in St. Anne's Landing and having a prestigious job close to home, but she might also have to settle on another option—setting up practice in her farm town or going with Aiden to a third-world country. She closed her eyes. Those particular worries were too much to think about until the more pressing problems were solved.

The downpour slowed to a drizzle by the time Gray steered to the curb of Mrs. Salucci's Boarding House, the address Saige had given him. "Pick you up after nine a.m. tomorrow?"

Saige opened the passenger door then leaned back into the car. "I appreciate the ride. I'd be grateful for one in the morning. Good night." The iciness of her words rivaled the frigid cold outside.

Could she have treated him with more disdain? She doubted it.

The BMW drove away as she lingered by the curb, chewing on a pound of anger while sleet frizzed her hair. This morning, her heart had fluttered for Gray. He was a nice man—a great doctor too. And despite his fame, he didn't act like a high and mighty snob. But after what happened on the basketball court with Aiden, that concept of him faded. Now, he reminded her of a spoiled egomaniac. Which image represented the real Gray?

SEVENTEEN

On his way home from the boarding house, Gray called Lilith on his car's cellular. "Would you meet me at the mansion, please? I've had a terrible day."

"Do you know what time it is, darling?" Irritation dripped from Lilith's voice.

"I thought night owls never sleep."

"Fine. I'll be there in a few minutes."

Twenty minutes later, reeking of expensive cologne, Lilith plucked lint from her fitted dress before sitting on the loveseat in the study as Gray, down on one knee, kindled a fire in the fireplace. "I'm sorry to have bothered you at this hour, Lilith." He placed the fireplace poker in its stand before walking to the loveseat. "Did you visit a men's cologne factory today?"

Lilith's face drained of color. She folded and refolded the tissue in her hands for a good ten seconds before responding. "I-I-I tested several samples before…um…before, well, I was…a…purchasing something for you for Christmas. Now, you've spoiled your surprise." She clasped and unclasped her hands as she spoke. "Enough about me. What's your horrible problem that couldn't wait until tomorrow, darling?" She crossed her booted legs and pumped her knee faster and faster.

The whole story about the game, the accident, and the emergency room poured from Gray as Lilith listened with her finger propped on her cheek. She nodded every so often as though attentive, but when he finished, she uncrossed her legs and planted both high-heeled boots on the floor. "Wipe your hands of the mess, Gray. It was an accident. Walk away. Don't waste another minute dwelling on it."

Walk away from the mess? How could he do that when Aiden's life lay in the balance because of his moronic notion to score a basket?

Lilith edged closer to Gray on the sofa until one more scoot and she'd fall into his lap. She cupped his chin with her fingers, coaxing his head toward her as she cooed into his ear. "Darling, I feel so bad for you, but it's time to focus on something else."

"Like what?"

"Us…I've been thinking…We've been together for many years, and I've come to realize how much I love you." She came in close and planted a passionate kiss on his lips while he sat there in shock. "We need to think about our future, darling." She used her thumb to wipe lipstick from his mouth.

A rap on the study door startled Gray. He twisted around, breaking her hold. This was an entirely different side of Lilith. They'd kissed many times, but it usually felt like involuntary pecks. Never any passion. But this time, his toes tingled.

"Are you in there, sir?" Fernsby's unmistakable British accent woke Gray from his momentary stupor.

Gray raked the hair from his eyes and smoothed it back to regain some composure before glancing at the door. "Yes. Come in, please."

Lilith bounced her legs again. "Why are you disturbing us this late in the evening, Fernsby?"

"Indeed. What's your purpose, old chap?" Gray stood with such speed Lilith landed on her side in the depression left by his bottom. "I'm discussing my unfortunate day with my *friend*." Gray emphasized the word *friend* to give Lilith a hint that he had to contemplate her sudden behavior change.

"I brought hot chocolate and your favorite butterscotch toffee cookies, fresh from the oven." Fernsby, in his usual starched shirt and tie ensemble, set the steaming drink and the plate on the shiny desk across from the now blazing fire, but he paused to study something on the polished surface. Using an extra napkin, he removed a spot then rubbed the smudge. "I'll return with a cup for Lilith."

"Don't bother." She opened her purse and reapplied lipstick to her puffy bee-stung lips. "Too many calories."

Fernsby's entire body tensed. Was the old fellow trying to refrain from speaking his mind? Even though Gray noticed his valet's self-control, he had no emotional strength left to deal with the feud between his servant and Lilith. "You're working late tonight, old chap." Gray stood from the loveseat and strode to the desk.

"Yes, sir. The smell of butterscotch lured me downstairs. Cook's working late, too, still making cookies for your upcoming party."

"The smell has been driving me crazy as well. Thanks for bringing them. Is there something else I can do for you?" Gray sipped his hot chocolate, waiting for Fernsby to reply.

"There is one thing. Would you consider dining out tomorrow evening? I'd like to take Adele to dinner."

"Wonderful idea. Dell works too hard." Gray appreciated her dedication to him and the entire Addington household. Through the years, she had done a fine job of showing Gray how to treat people. His parents had often remarked on how pleased they were with Gray's upbringing. Adele deserved the credit as his attentive au pair.

Irritated, Lilith rose from the loveseat, purse in hand. "How convenient. I'm sorry, Gray, but I have other plans for tomorrow night. So, if you'll excuse me, I'm going to the powder room. Oh, and wipe that marshmallow mustache off your lip. It looks ridiculous." She waltzed off with her chin up and her eyebrows raised so high, they nearly climbed off her head.

Gray licked the tasty cream from his upper lip. Maybe he'd invite Saige to dine with him. It would allow him to explain Aiden's accident. He dabbed the rest of his mouth with a napkin.

Fernsby walked to the desk and leaned against it. "I rather liked your fake mustache, Gray." The valet's eyes twinkled. "It showed me what you'll look like in thirty or forty years."

Gray poked him in the side. "By the way, what do you really think of Lilith? Come on, be honest." Gray chuckled because Fernsby disliked ribbing.

"I think the more time you spend with her, the more you'll behave like her." The white-haired gentleman pursed his lips in his dignified manner.

Gray hated to admit it, but he and Lilith were two peas in a pod—rich, social icons. He'd fooled himself into thinking Saige might be interested in him. What would a wealthy, famous doctor have in common with a farm-raised country gal? Eventually, Saige would resent him. She already did, as evidenced by her barely speaking to him in the car. But he gravitated to her casual, friendly manner. She had an earthiness he admired—no pretense—fresh-faced, little makeup, jeans, and T-shirts, unlike Lilith, who reapplied makeup to perfection all—day—long. But he screwed up trying to get to know Saige better. Aiden's crash-landing on the gym floor ruined everything. She'd probably not want anything more to do with him.

"Lilith is quite a handful, Gray." Fernsby glanced away from his boss's inquiring eyes and politely cleared his throat.

"She claims to love me. I'm mulling it over." Gray wouldn't have given it a second thought until Saige accused him of causing Aiden's accident. Had he lost any chance of getting to know the young doctor?

Taking longer than usual to reply, Fernsby swirled his tongue around his mouth. "I'm quite speechless, Gray."

"There's a first time for everything, old chap."

Gray took a seat at his desk. Tenting his fingers, he pondered one last thing on his heart—finding the girl who lost the bracelet. But first, he'd have to devise a new plan.

EIGHTEEN

Scrambled eggs, turkey bacon, and biscuits in serving bowls waited on the table for Saige the following morning. She normally filled her plate, but today, she picked at the food, unable to focus, let alone eat. Placing a call to Aiden's father, Dr. Littlefield, plagued her thoughts. How would she explain what happened? Aiden and Gray were horsing around—showing off—trying to outdo one another—rivalry gone too far?

Mrs. Salucci left the table and returned with a travel mug. "Don't worry about breakfast, dear. I'll wrap it for you. Make your phone calls and let me know how Aiden's doing." She poured coffee from the table carafe into the mug. "You'll have privacy upstairs. Here, take this coffee." She secured the lid and handed the mug to Saige.

"I wish I could bottle your kindness and keep it with me all day." Saige accepted the drink and placed her arm around Mrs. Salucci for an appreciative hug. "I'm so worried about Aiden. Thanks for understanding."

She walked to the living room, clutching the silver mug, with Mrs. Salucci close on her heels. Upon reaching the hearth, Saige stopped before the glowing fire to ponder the problems swirling through her mind. The earthy smell of the burning wood brought back farmhouse memories, and the heat from the flames settled over her like a warm electric blanket, providing a calmness she sorely needed. "Aiden's goofy, but he's one of the nicest people on the face of the earth. The world needs his doctoring skills, and kids need his silly antics."

Tears clouded Saige's eyes. Had she taken her friend's comforting shoulder for granted? He always listened to her problems without interrupting, and his solutions involved prayer first then taking her to square one to figure out the best recourse. Their latest excursion had been the trip to the Addington mansion. Even though he didn't want to lose her, he allowed her the space to make the final decision.

She stared into the fire, gleaning strength from the flames. "I need Aiden, Mrs. Salucci. He's the best friend I've ever had. He's helped me through tough times since my mom died. When girls at college excluded me from their Karaoke Club, he hauled me up to the stage, and together, we sang a bang-up rendition of 'I've Got You, Babe.' After that, the girls begged me to sing with them. Somehow, he has a keen sense of how to handle situations, especially when it comes to my feelings. I can't imagine life without him." She plucked a tissue from a box on an end table and wiped tears trailing down her cheeks.

Mrs. Salucci smoothed her apron before placing her arm around Saige's waist and her head on Saige's shoulder. "Aiden is a wonderful friend. But I know someone who's even better at handling problems. Have you talked to God about Aiden? He'll hear your prayers."

Saige pressed her eyelids with her thumb and forefinger to stop the tear bath threatening to drown her face. Mrs. Salucci was wrong. God wouldn't hear her prayers.

"I've been awful to Him for letting Mom die." Saige's trembling turned to gentle sobs. "I stopped attending church and saying prayers. I even said I hated Him."

"Saige, I know for a fact that God still loves you, even when you say things you don't mean. He's a kind, loving, and forgiving Father who wants the best for you. Blame Satan for your mother's death, not Him. Satan's the one who tests people. He tested Job a few thousand years ago by destroying everything and almost everyone the man loved. Satan also gave him horrible diseases that brought him close to death. Satan wanted Job to blame God and turn away from Him. But Job refused. Because of his faithfulness, God restored his entire situation.

"God isn't to blame for bad things that happen in life. Ask Him for forgiveness, He'll throw your sins as far as the east is from the west. And He'll never remember them again."

"You remind me of my mom. She used to teach me about God."

Mrs. Salucci smiled, tilting her head at Saige as she motioned to the stairs. "You'd better, scat. You're wasting valuable time. Call the hospital. Let me know how Aiden's doing."

"Okay, okay!" Saige wiped her eyes and nose one last time then headed up the stairs, eager to learn about Aiden's condition yet dreading more bad news. Inside her room, she sat on the vanity stool and took deep breaths to steady her nerves. Could she handle more bad news?

She fumbled for her cell phone in her pocket before calling the ICU. "Hello, this is Dr. Westbrook, Aiden's close friend. I was wondering how he's doing?"

"Good morning, Dr. Westbrook. I'm Aiden's nurse, Michelle Vanderlaan. His lab work shows he's had a mild heart attack. And the neurosurgeon, Dr. McGavern, examined him this morning. Aiden hasn't been able to move his arms or hands since late last night. The doctor believes it's from swelling along his spine because of the fall. Aiden will have a full day of cardiac and neurological tests. When can he expect you? He's been asking."

"I'm sorry. I need to get a grip for a minute." Saige covered the phone and sobbed into her sleeve. Would Aiden have permanent heart damage and paralysis? She pressed her lips together to keep from crying before placing the phone back to her ear. "I can't wait to see him. I'll be there right after work. Please tell Aiden I'm praying for him."

"I'll do that."

Anger, bitterness, and fear gripped Saige as she ended the call. Her friend's condition was Gray's fault. If Aiden needed encouragement to hang on, she'd forget about the cardiology job and follow him into the mission field. She'd be bored without his craziness anyway. Besides, life wasn't always about getting what she wanted. Her mother once told her, "If a person sets one dream aside, it often makes space for a better one to take its place."

Aiden was a good man. The best. He'd make a good husband and a terrific father—if it came to that. Mrs. Salucci was right; Saige needed to talk to God and tell Him she was sorry.

She bowed her head and considered what to say. After several minutes, she began. "Dear Lord, I've been angry with You for letting Mom die. I want to apologize for turning away from You and for my anger. Job suffered far more, but he refused to hate You. Please, give me faith to trust You in all things. Will You please forgive me for turning away? I love You, and I need You. Also, would You please heal Aiden's heart and his paralysis so he can live a normal life? He's a great guy and my best friend. He'll make a terrific doctor on the mission field. I promise to go with him and even marry him if You'll heal him. And would You please help me to find the bracelet my mother gave me? I hope You'll answer my prayers this time. Thank You for listening. In Jesus' name I pray, amen."

She hadn't meant to say the parts about becoming a missionary and marrying Aiden. They had slipped out in a moment of fear for his life. But she wouldn't back down now. If God would spare him, she'd gladly keep her vows. She loved Aiden—in a sisterly way, but their love would have plenty of time to grow if God healed him.

Now, she had to discuss Aiden's heart attack and paralysis with his father, the senior Dr. Littlefield. Dread scattered her thoughts in a hundred directions. She slipped the phone number from the pocket of yesterday's jeans lying on the nightstand. After another deep breath, she entered the number.

"Dr. Littlefield here."

"Hello, sir. I'm Saige Westbrook. Aiden's close friend. I'm sorry about his accident."

"I learned that you administered CPR and used the defibrillator on him. You saved his life, young lady. His mother and I can't thank you enough."

"I'm glad I was there. Did you know we were playing basketball in a game that got a bit rough?"

"I wasn't aware. What happened?"

"Aiden fell backward over another teammate's foot, but before it happened, he was short of breath. Does he have a history of asthma?"

"No, but he does have a heart problem. A case of rheumatic fever scarred his heart valve when he was eight. The best cardiologist in town warned him not to play sports or engage in rough activity for the rest of his life. Aiden begged me through the years to join sports teams, but I had to put my foot down. I'll call Dr. Bachman and have him fax our son's history to Dr. Alberetti."

"Thank you, but I'm confused. How did Aiden get so good at basketball then? He can make long shots like a pro. I wouldn't have guessed he never played." Saige dabbed her eyes.

"He had a hoop at home—in the driveway. Dunked baskets while standing in place his entire life. Didn't he tell you about it?"

"No. It never came up in conversation. I suppose the ICU informed you he had a mild heart attack at the game and injured his back? He can't move his upper limbs now. Both a neurosurgeon and Dr. Alberetti are running tests."

"Yes, they called us late last night and early this morning. We're quite worried about our son, but he's in God's hands, so we're trusting Him for Aiden's outcome. He's an only child, you know. The wife and I are heading to St. Anne's Landing as we speak. Should be there by ten a.m. Will we see you today?"

"I'm working, but I'll come to the hospital around six tonight."

"We're looking forward to meeting you, Saige."

After the call ended, she placed her elbows on her knees and cupped her head with her hands. Poor Aiden. The truth about the accident suddenly flooded her with uncontrollable chest heaving and silent wailing. She shouldn't have asked Aiden—no begged him—to play in the YMCA basketball game. He had refused, but she wouldn't take no for an answer. If she hadn't pushed him to play, he wouldn't be in the ICU. His injuries were her fault. She was to blame.

NINETEEN

On his drive to Mrs. Salucci's Boarding House the following morning, a thought crossed Gray's mind. He'd been so preoccupied with Aiden's condition this morning he'd forgotten to speak to Fernsby about his new plan.

A song about lost love boomed from his car speakers. He hit the radio button to end his torment. Fighting a sour mood, he clicked the hands-free cellular option on his dashboard.

A few seconds later, Fernsby answered. "Addington mansion, may I help you?"

"I haven't much time, old chap. Did you find the bracelet on the internet?"

"Nothing identical. A few online stores returned my calls yesterday, but not one engraved the words we read on the young lady's bracelet."

"How about this plan—call my office at the Complex. Ask my administrative assistant to prepare two lists: one with the names of those in the community who attended the Christmas party, and the other list with the names of the candidates for the Addington position. When you collect them from my office, talk with someone familiar with the socialites and the candidates. Narrow down the names to ladies with light brown hair. Then, make phone calls, old chap."

"I'll do that."

"Will you get started immediately? I must find the young lady." The connection he experienced with her reminded him of Saige's forthright nature at the clinic. Could the two possibly be related?

He stopped his BMW along the curb at Mrs. Salucci's house. Would Saige be as angry today as she had been the day before? As though she heard his question, Saige exited the house in her jeans and puffy coat. Face grim, head unmoving, she walked to the car. How could he convince her of his innocence? He hurried around to the passenger door and opened it for her.

"Have you heard how Aiden's doing?"

Saige didn't reply.

Gray climbed into the driver's seat, stepped on the gas, and headed to the free clinic.

What was going through her mind? After Gray stopped at the first light, she fiddled with the zipper on her coat. "Aiden is doing worse than we thought. He not only had a mild heart attack, but he's still short of breath, and he also can't move his arms. The neurosurgeon believes fractured vertebrae and swelling in the spine are the cause of the paralysis. Do you remember how hard he hit the floor, head first?" She filled him in on the rest of what Nurse Vanderlaan and Aiden's father had shared.

The traffic light turned green, and Gray pressed on the gas. Aiden was doing worse. The wheels in Gray's mind spun as he contemplated what to say next. After everything that happened, Saige might refuse his offer, but he had to make it. "Would he allow me to operate on his heart valve if necessary?"

"I-I-d-don't know." Saige pulled her puffy coat sleeves over her fingers. "You're not exactly on his friend list or mine either. You gave him a hard time at the clinic. How could we be sure you'd be objective?"

"I'm a surgeon above everything else, Saige. I have to be objective. I've never lost a patient. And I don't plan to start now."

"I've heard you're the best cardiothoracic surgeon in the Midwest, and some even say you're the best in the nation. But would it bother you if Aiden loves me? I've never accepted it before, but he's said it many times."

"I gathered as much since the first day I met him. He sticks by your side like a bull moose protecting his cow. I imagine he has sharp antlers too."

"Are you calling me a cow?"

A feeling of horror replaced Gray's shaky interior. "No, no, no, it's the name for a female moose."

"Okay, as long as we have that straight."

"Anyone can see Aiden loves you." Gray wasn't sure how, but he'd have to balance his words; stress had made Saige overly sensitive. "Children adore Aiden. He proved that at the clinic."

"Yes. He's good with kids, and he's the kindest man I've ever known. I've promised to follow him wherever he's sent as a missionary if God heals him. Missionary work has been Aiden's dream."

Vehicles overtook Gray's car in the lanes surrounding him. He didn't care. He wasn't in a race to arrive at the clinic. "What's your dream, Saige?"

"It doesn't matter at a time like this. All I can think about is Aiden getting better. He's always been there for me when I needed him. It's my turn to be there for him."

Gray controlled his urge to pound the dashboard. How could he make Saige understand he wanted a chance with her? He'd thought about her day and night for the last two days. She was kind, sweet, faithful to her friend, and intelligent. How could he convince her that he was a worthy man and didn't cause the accident on purpose? "I'm not sure what you're doing is best, Saige." An idea raced through his mind. "But maybe what I'm planning to do isn't either."

"What do you mean?"

"I'll ask Lilith to marry me at our annual family Christmas gathering. Then you'll feel comfortable with me performing Aiden's surgery." The words gushed from his mouth before he considered their consequences. What was he thinking? Could he handle living like a robot—saying, "Yes, Lilith, Okay, Lilith"—Every. Single. Day. For fifty or sixty years? Actually, why not? If he couldn't have a woman like Saige, he might as well settle for one who would solidify his social standing in the community.

Saige's brows almost crossed as she studied him after his announcement. "Are you sure you know what you're doing?"

"I'm as sure as you are, Saige."

"I've been praying about marriage too. I'm going to tell Aiden I'll marry him when he's healed."

The world came crashing around Gray in a vast emotional bag of garbage. Why did he tell Saige he'd marry Lilith? It wasn't his plan. What got into him? Was Saige retaliating? "My family Christmas party is next Saturday." He had a week-and-a-half to mourn his decision. "Would you please attend?"

"I don't know, Gray. I'm having a hard time getting past what you did. What were you thinking when you tripped Aiden?"

"That's just it. I wasn't thinking. My only thought was to grab the ball, make a basket, and win." Gray reached the clinic, parked, and climbed from his car.

The shock of what he'd said—that he'd propose to Lilith—twisted his guts, causing a painful reminder that he would spend the rest of his life with a demanding, controlling social climber. He entered the building, dragging behind Saige. As he passed her on his way to Maria's desk, he was sure she mumbled something about a fool under her breath.

He had to stop thinking about his problems and concentrate on the clinic patients. Since they were down one doctor, Maria whisked the patients in and out of exam rooms as fast as the remaining three could diagnose and treat. When the doors closed at 5:00, Maria and Jon volunteered to stay and clean the clinic.

Gray snagged Saige by the sleeve as she exited Exam Room 2. "Ready to visit the hospital?"

Saige squared her shoulders. "Definitely, but I'm afraid of what we'll learn when we get there."

♥

After Saige and Gray changed into their street clothes, Gray drove them to Central Sinai. When they reached the ICU, Saige pushed the wall buzzer. "Dr. Westbrook and Dr. Addington here to see Aiden Littlefield."

A female voice came over the intercom. "Aiden's parents are in the room. I'll have them step out so you two can visit." The doors swung open, and Saige and Gray entered the ICU.

A trim man with gray streaks in his hair eyed Saige as he hurried down the hall in a tie-dyed T-shirt. Clad in an empire-waist paisley shirt, an attractive lady followed in his footsteps. The couple waved. "You must be Saige!" the man shouted.

On reaching Saige and Gray, pony-tailed Dr. Littlefield and the long-haired blonde shook their hands while introducing themselves as Aiden's parents.

"Our boy is in bad shape." Dr. Littlefield choked up. A few seconds later, he continued. "I have an idea about what the cardiologist will suggest, but I'm family medicine, so I'll wait for his expert advice." He hugged his wife's shoulders as though the act comforted him. "We're proud of our son's spirit. Having God to call upon gives him strength. And the IV medication has kept his pain and breathing under control." Dr. Littlefield glanced at his wife. "We're going to dinner in the cafeteria. Can you two keep Aiden from escaping until we return?"

Saige's mood lifted at the comment. "I see where Aiden gets his humor." And his hippie ideology. "I'm proud of him too." She shifted her stance, a little unsure of how to proceed.

Dr. Littlefield wrapped his arm around her and squeezed. "You saved our son, young lady, and I can't thank you enough."

Mrs. Littlefield joined in the hug. "We'll never be able to repay you for acting as quickly as you did. From what we learned, you wasted no time starting CPR and defibrillating his heart. You minimized his heart damage. Thank you so much."

Tears welled in Saige's eyes. She did what any cardiologist would have done, but seeing her friend limp on the floor made the reality of her job hit her hard. "Your son is the best friend I've ever had."

"Thank you, Saige." Dr. Littlefield and his wife held her hands and gave them heartfelt squeezes before heading down the hall to dinner, leaving her and Gray to walk to Aiden's room alone.

Gray fiddled with his key fob. "You did an amazing job, Saige. If my administrative team hadn't already selected someone, I'd hire you on the spot. Not only do you have skills, but you also have a wonderful bedside manner."

"Gray, I wanted to talk to you about that—"

"Doc!" Gray shouted. A big-boned man with flaming red hair nearly flew down the empty corridor at them from the nurse's station.

"Thanks for the referral, boss." The man, clad in a white medical jacket, clapped Gray on the arm with one hand while administering a firm handshake to Saige. "Mr. Littlefield will need surgery scheduled for a leaky mitral valve with tricky scar tissue. There's only one expert I know who can easily handle the case. And I'm looking at him."

"Thanks, Al. I'll discuss it with the Littlefields. We'll have to wait and see how they feel about me taking the case."

"Why wouldn't they want the best cardiothoracic surgeon in the entire Midwest operating on their son?"

"It's complicated, but we'll work it out. Mind if Aiden's friend and I visit him?" Gray tipped his head at Saige.

"Don't overtax him. He's finally comfortable." Dr. Alberetti looked at Gray, and then Saige, as though to confirm that he meant what he said.

"Thanks. I'll read through his chart and test results. If he and his family are satisfied with me, I'll get the ball rolling for surgery."

"Let me know." Dr. Al shoved his hands into his white med coat pockets.

After a courtesy nod to the cardiologist, Gray escorted Saige into Aiden's room. She tiptoed to his bedside and studied his face. His eyes flickered.

"Aiden, I'm here. And Gray is too. Are you feeling okay?" Saige hovered over his bedrail.

"Yeah…fine."

She brushed a few wayward hairs from his forehead then adjusted the oxygen cannula riding sidesaddle in his nose. "Did Dr. Alberetti talk to you about your test results?"

"Yeah."

"You know Gray's the best cardiothoracic surgeon in the area, don't you?"

"Hmm." Aiden squeezed his eyes closed.

Gray wove around the bed to the other side and leaned over him. "Hey, buddy. If you want, I'll do your surgery. I'll have you back to normal, well, I'm not sure I could ever make you normal, but I'll have you better in no time. Let me know what you decide."

"Can I trust you…Gray?" Aiden opened his eyes and peered into Gray's.

"Don't worry about me. I'm planning to marry Lilith." Gray instantly shot a glance at Saige then sheepishly hung his head.

How could he marry someone like Lilith? He'd be miserable his entire life. Saige's eyes filled with tears as Gray spoke. She stiffened and jutted her chin at Aiden as she stroked his hand. "And I'm going to marry you, Aiden. I promised God. Let Gray do your heart surgery. He's the best around."

Aiden's head relaxed on the pillow. "You'll marry me?"

She nodded. She had no other choice. A promise to God was a promise she wouldn't break. He hadn't spared her mom, but He was still God.

A smile ignited Aiden's entire face. He closed his eyes as if saying a quick prayer, then he opened them at Gray. "Awesome. When will you do surgery?"

"I'll schedule it." Gray moved closer to Aiden's ear. "Listen, I want you to know your fall on the basketball court was an accident. I'd never cause such a thing on purpose. Please, believe me. Since my foot led to your fall, I'll pay for all of your hospital expenses."

Saige heard every word. Gray's generous offer would relieve many of Aiden's worries. He was still paying for med school. Gray's noble gesture touched Saige's heart.

"If I die…on…operating table—"

"Not going to happen, Aiden. Stop thinking about it."

"Will you pay funeral expenses?"

"That's not funny." Saige turned her head, but tears clouded her eyes.

Nurse Vanderlaan entered the room, wielding a syringe. "I'm sorry, but his vital signs indicate the visit has been too taxing for his heart.

He's had enough commotion for one day." She administered medication in Aiden's IV while they watched.

Saige kissed Aiden on the cheek after the nurse moved away from the bedside. "Get well. Oh, by the way, were you forbidden from playing tennis too?" She cocked one eyebrow at him and pursed her lips.

Aiden chuckled then winced as though from pain. "Uh…maybe."

"So, you think going against a cardiologist's orders is funny? You were playing Russian roulette with your life. You could have collapsed on the tennis court. Thanks for waiting a few years until I was knowledgeable enough to resuscitate you."

"Sorry."

"There'll be plenty of time for scolding him later." The nurse gave Gray and Saige the evil eye while shooing them with her hands.

"Take care, buddy." Gray tucked Aiden's hospital blanket under his armpits. "Get some rest. If we stay much longer, Nurse Rachett will skin us alive."

Aiden grimaced again. "Nurse Rachett? That's old material. Think of a funny one…next time."

"Oh, I forgot. You're the comedian. I'll definitely have to get tips from you. Rest now. Doctor's orders." Gray nodded at the nurse. "Don't worry; we're leaving."

Saige squeezed Aiden's hand, lingering, reluctant to let go. "Hang in there. We're getting married, and when you heal, we'll become missionaries." She swept his hair from his eyes again then kissed his forehead.

The medicine kicked in and Aiden's body went limp.

"I'll be back to see you tomorrow." Saige watched him sleeping for a few seconds before fluffing his pillow one last time.

"We should let him sleep." Gray walked to the door and waited for Saige. As they left the ICU and headed down to the hospital's exit, sweat covered her palms. If Aiden died, she'd never forgive Gray for the rest of his life.

TWENTY

S trong winds mixed with snow shoved Gray and Saige through the hospital's foggy parking lot as they trekked to his car. "I'll brush the windshields," he shouted through the turbulent air.

Bundled in her puffy coat and long winter scarf, Saige nodded. She managed to stay at his side despite the gusts forcing her off balance.

Upon reaching his vehicle, Gray ran around to the passenger side and opened her door before heading to the trunk. Hunger pangs struck as he popped it open and removed the ice scraper. He'd been ignoring his snarling stomach ever since leaving the clinic. Would it be too forward of him to suggest getting a bite to eat? Since he'd roped himself into marrying Lilith, Saige should feel at ease with him.

After wiping at least three inches of slushy snow accumulation from his car windows, he thumped the brush end of the scraper on his gloved hand to remove the excess ice before tossing the tool into the trunk. His teeth chattered from the cold as he slid into the heated driver's seat. "Saige, I'm starving. Would you mind if we stop somewhere? Maybe a place where we can unwind from our busy day."

"I should have stayed at the hospital with Aiden." Saige focused out the window on the passenger side. "I'm not hungry. My stomach clenches when I'm anxious, and right now, it's in knots."

"I understand. The restaurant can box your dinner."

Saige yawned and covered her mouth before nodding. "I forgot about work tomorrow. I'm exhausted."

"Didn't Maria tell you? The clinic runs Monday through Wednesday

123

every week. So, you can sleep in for the next four days." Gray steered the BMW from the parking lot but braked at the first stop sign before looking at Saige for a decision. "Yay or nay on the food?"

"I suppose we have to eat, and Mrs. Salucci attends a Bible study on Wednesday evenings. But I'm tired, let's make it quick. Do you know how many patients we saw today?"

"Too many to count as far as I'm concerned. A place that busy makes me thankful for my practice. Working at the clinic every year helps me put my life into perspective. When I think I'm working too hard—seeing too many patients, or performing too many surgeries, Christmas comes around again, and I volunteer at the free clinic. The rest of the year, I'm grateful for what I have."

"I guess when we feel overworked, someone has it worse." Saige's voice lightened as though she forgot about her anger.

"I hate to be the bearer of bad news, but if you become a missionary, you'll need to prepare for longer lines than the ones we have at the free clinic. No one will ever understand how hard missionary doctors work."

"I know. Aiden gave me websites to research several months ago. I'm not sure I'm cut out for it, but if healing people in underdeveloped nations makes him happy, that's what matters."

Gray turned at the red light. "You and I are similar in a way. We both want to make our long-time friends happy. To do that, we've given up our dreams."

"That makes it sound terrible. I fought against marrying Aiden and following him. But maybe God was steering me in this direction all along."

Gray turned into the parking lot of the Fifth Street Karaoke Bar and turned off the engine. "We'll both feel better after we eat."

One of Neil Diamond's famous songs greeted him when he opened the door for Saige. A lady on a stage at the rear of the room belted out the song over a microphone while patrons at tables sang the chorus. Saige joined in under her breath. "Sweet Caroline. Baum. Baum. Baum."

Relief released the knots in Gray's neck and shoulders. Saige liked to sing. Every day he learned something new about her, something that made him admire her even more. He'd visited the karaoke bar when he was in med school. The lively restaurant had been a nice reprieve after a long week of studies. Laughter, music, and delicious food dominated the casual atmosphere. He appreciated that the music showcased every genre. Saige might feel comfortable here in her jeans and sweater.

The hostess, in a cowboy hat, western boots, denim jeans, and a fringed leather vest, clomped across the room. After showing them to a cozy corner table, she tipped her hat. "Nice to meet y'all. I'm Shonda. Tonight, is Golden Oldies night in case y'all haven't noticed the music."

"I love the old songs. How about you, Saige?" Gray peered at her with a raised brow.

She removed her coat and placed it around her chair back. "I enjoy the old songs. Aiden would have been thrilled to sing karaoke here to-night." Her mouth twisted as she wiped the corner of her eye.

A globe candle flickered on the table, adding a dim light to their part of the room. Before leaving, Shonda removed two menus from a metal stand in the center of the table. "Here ya go. The server will take your orders shortly."

For a few minutes, they checked out the menus.

Gray finished making a selection before studying Saige. Despite the long line of patients at the clinic, a complaint never rolled off her tongue. Would she act differently after a month, a year, twenty years? Lilith was the queen of complaints, and she didn't work outside her home. "How are you doing, Saige? I mean, with Aiden's condition." Gray returned his menu to its stand.

"I'd like to stay at his bedside, but I understand the ICU rules about only two visitors at the bedside. His parents come first. It's hard enough to move around the room to care for a patient when there isn't an emergency. Tripping over guests or trying to steer them from a room in a cardiac arrest is difficult, but you know that. You're probably in the ICU often."

"It's my home away from home." Gray's face sobered. "I'm glad you're handling Aiden's situation rationally."

"Let's remove the elephant from the room, Gray—I can't believe you tripped him. Why would you do such a thing?"

"I've tried to explain, but you haven't listened to me. Yes, I wanted to show off for you, and yes, I wanted to make the winning basket for the team, but I went after the ball in case Aiden missed it. The whole accident was unfortunate, but my foot slipped behind him. How can I make you understand it wasn't my intent to hurt him? I've never done such a thing. I've kicked myself a hundred times since the accident. Why can't you believe me?"

"Maybe because you guys fought for the ball during the first half of the game. Teammates don't do that. They work together."

"I'm sorry. That was an alpha male thing. We were showing off. I apologize."

"Okay, Gray, I believe you, but Aiden's the one in the hospital." Saige crossed her arms, resting her elbows on the table. "I'd like to hold his hand and reassure him everything's going to be okay. But the neurosurgeon doesn't know whether he'll remain paralyzed. He needs surgery to repair his vertebrae. And he can't have it until his heart valve is repaired. I'm scared for him to have heart surgery. What if he dies? I've always thought friends and partners were two separate relationships. But what could be better than marrying your best friend?"

"Are you seriously thinking of marrying him?" Gray interlocked his fingers and rested them against his dimpled chin. "I'm guessing the only thing better than marrying your best friend might be to marry the love of your life. Imagine counting the minutes until your next kiss. Does Aiden do that for you?"

He peered into Saige's eyes, but she shifted her gaze to the stage. "When does the next karaoke song begin?"

"Saige, you're not answering me."

She fooled with a string on her sweater. She'd never kissed Aiden at the hospital. Winding the thread around her little finger, she stared at the table. "Does Lilith do that for you, Gray?"

"No. But we're good friends."

"And you're planning to propose to her."

"She's my first relationship ever. I never had time for dating while studying. Then Lilith came into my life unexpectedly, and she stayed.

Last night, she professed her love to me. I guess, I'm comfortable with her."

"Comfortable isn't fireworks."

"I could say the same thing about you and Aiden. I've seen you at the clinic. You're more like buddies. Aiden hangs on your every word, but you barely give him two seconds of your time. Now, all of a sudden, you're thinking about marrying him? Is that you talking, or is it your incentive for helping him heal? Don't you think he might resent you for it later?"

Saige stopped winding the string. "Maybe it's the bargain I made with God to let him live a normal life. I'll do what I need to do. Let's change the subject."

A server dressed in the same denim and cowboy gear as the hostess arrived at their table. "Excuse me. I'm Skylar. What would y'all like to drink?"

Pushing her sweater sleeves to her elbows, Saige paused for a second. "I'd like a tall glass of…ice-cold water. The taller, the better."

"And I'll take tea on the rocks." Gray scanned the menu again. "Are you ready to order, Saige? I know what I want."

"I'll take a six-ounce filet mignon with a baked potato on the side, please." Saige returned her menu to its stand.

"And I'll have a bowl of turkey chili and a corn muffin."

"Will do." The Brooks & Dunn song, "Boot Scootin' Boogie," started overhead.

Skylar hurried to the center of the room. "Callin' all boot scooters to join us for the boogie. Right here. Right now." She swung around to join six other servers in a line.

"Do you boot scoot?" Gray fought to keep from laughing as he spoke. Every time he'd been in the place, he'd watched the line dancers while sitting at his table.

"Are you kidding me? I can do it with my eyes closed, but I can't enjoy myself while Aiden's life is on the line."

The restaurant hostess announced for the servers to find dancers. Skylar glanced around the room before heading straight for Gray, but he raised his palms. "No, no—no, no, no not me!"

"Follow us. It's not hard." Skylar tucked her thumbs into her jean pockets. "Come on. You can do it." She took Gray's hand.

"Maybe I'll give it a try so my friend here can have a good laugh." He allowed the busty blonde server to drag him into the line.

Several other men and women converged on the center space led by Shonda. Clad in his expensive pants and sweater, Gray didn't fit in with the denim crowd, but he tried to kick up his stiff heels. By the song's second verse, he tapped his heels and swung around without coordination, lassoed the air with his arm raised rigidly like the Statue of Liberty, then stepped backward, out of sync with the music and the other dancers.

"Woo hoo!" a lady shouted. The others in the line joined in with animated hoots.

Embarrassment crept over Gray like a blazing fire. He twirled a pretend lasso over his head one more time then winked at Saige.

Saige doubled over in her seat, gripping her belly and slapping her knee, laughing so hard Gray thought she would split her abs.

When the song ended, he rushed to his table and slid into the chair. "Now, did I make a grand fool of myself?"

Saige wiped her eyes as she nodded. Then, in between fits of laughter, she added, "Okay, I have to admit—you definitely made a fool of yourself." She placed her napkin over her mouth to hide her giggles. "Worst part was, I don't know what dance you were scootin' to." She chuckled again. "You were a good sport, though."

"I could get used to boot-scootin', but I sure need that cold tea about now." He craned his neck, looking for their waitress.

Skylar arrived at their table with a tray of drinks balanced on her shoulder. She deposited their water and iced tea. "Sorry about the interruption. I hope you enjoyed the dance." She winked at Gray before swinging the tray back to her shoulder and hurrying away with the remaining drinks.

Another song started. Gray turned to face the karaoke stage as a slender woman clad in a flared daisy print shirt with puffy sleeves and wide-leg jeans walked to the microphone. Her faded pants had patches on her knees and thighs.

"I'm singing 'Yellow Submarine' by the Beatles." She gripped the mic. The DJ adjusted the sound as the lady belted out the lyrics like a pro. She bounced along to the music as though she had stepped out of the '60s. The diners in the joint sang along with the choruses.

Saige's eyes clouded. "Aiden would have enjoyed hearing this lady sing one of his favorite songs, especially since she's dressed in the era he adores."

"I can see why he's so crazy about you."

"Aiden and I are more alike than I want to admit. I should call the hospital and see how he's doing." Saige's eyes suddenly widened as she tugged her cell phone from her pocket. "L-L-L…"

"What is it, Saige?"

"L-L-L—"

"Calm down."

"I need to use the restroom."

"That's all you had to say."

Saige hurried from her table, craning her neck to find the woman she'd spotted walking into the restaurant. The camel-hair coat, plump lips, and auburn locks were unmistakable. What was Gray's high society girlfriend doing in the karaoke bar? Saige ducked behind a wooden support post several yards from the entrance to snoop.

At the hostess desk, Lilith lingered beside a handsome man who stood so close his nose almost touched her cheek. He definitely wasn't a relative. Saige shifted her position to get a better view.

The gorgeous wavy-haired man removed his coat then helped Lilith out of hers. He leaned in and spoke something by her ear. Lilith laughed before leaning back to press her lips directly on his. Saige couldn't believe what she saw, but to top off the bizarre moment, the couple were dressed in jeans, flannel shirts, and fringed vests similar to the restaurant's wait staff. As though expecting them, a hostess walked to the desk and escorted them to the opposite side of the restaurant.

Conflicting thoughts rattled Saige. She bumped into a table of ladies eating burgers and fries on her way to the restroom. "Excuse me. I'm so sorry." She righted their ketchup bottle then sped to her destination.

Should she tell Gray? Should she confront Lilith? Should she mind her own business? Unless Lilith and her date joined in a line dance, Gray might never see them.

Saige hurried into the bathroom, entered an empty stall, and pressed her back against the door. What if she told Gray that Lilith was cheating on him and he didn't believe her? Would he despise her for being the messenger? In Saige's experience, that's what always happened to the brave soul who shared unfortunate information.

The outer ladies' room door opened.

Exiting her stall, Saige came face-to-face with Lilith, who had donned a cowboy hat. "Excuse me." Saige tried not to look in the woman's eyes while she washed her hands, but the effort was futile because Saige kept bobbing her head to see Lilith up close.

Lilith frowned as though annoyed. She turned to the mirror and opened her purse. "It's crowded in this bathroom."

True, the room was narrow, but they were the only two occupants. Lilith reached into her purse while looking over at Saige in the mirror. "If you don't mind, stop staring at me."

Saige was mesmerized by the bracelet on Lilith's wrist—white gold with diamonds lining the top. Was it the keepsake from her mother? Unable to refrain from staring, Saige washed her hands then threw the paper towel in the trash can. "Sorry. I thought I might know you, but I guess not."

Lilith removed lipstick from her purse—a reddish-brown color. But while she applied it with precision to her lips, Saige slipped out the door.

Would Lilith remember her from the clinic? The day Lilith arrived to pick up Gray, she hadn't given a fig about Saige, never even looked her in the face, so she probably wouldn't recognize her now. But what if Gray spotted his soon-to-be fiancé kissing another man? That might be a blessing since Saige wouldn't have to share the info with him. Gray was a work friend who offered her a ride, nothing more.

Saige quickly called the hospital on her cell phone. Nurse Vanderlaan reported no change in Aiden's condition.

Keeping her head down to prevent Lilith from recognizing her, Saige hurried back to her table. The dim lighting made spotting anyone difficult, so she doubted Lilith would see Gray, but she stopped by his chair to be safe. "Would you mind if I sit here and you sit over there—on the other side? It's drafty in my spot."

"Sure, no problem." Gray placed his hand under the overhead vent. He shrugged as though he didn't have a clue what she meant, but he walked to the other side of the table.

Humming the current karaoke song, the server arrived with their food. She dealt the plates to their proper places then tipped her finger upside her western hat. "Enjoy." Picking up where she left off with the song, she danced away, tray tucked firmly under her arm.

"They're busy in here. We should probably hurry up and leave so others can dine." Saige glanced at her cell phone. "Besides, it's getting late."

"My mom didn't say I have to be home by a certain hour." Gray took a bite of his cornbread.

"Very funny, Gray. I'll have to remember that line." Saige rolled her eyes at him. What if he ran into Lilith with the other man? What would it take to spare him from getting hurt? The longer the two of them stayed, the more likely it would happen. What if Gray wanted to dance the next line dance, and Lilith and her date joined them in the center of the room?

"I'm sorry to be unkind," Saige peered around for their server, "but I'm exhausted. Would you mind asking for to-go boxes?"

131

TWENTY-ONE

For several minutes after they left the restaurant, Gray wondered what had gotten into Saige. They were having a great time. Did she see something? Or did her call to the ICU about Aiden not go well? Whatever it was, something upset her. He made a mental note to ring the ICU after dropping her off.

Worried about her behavior, he drove in silence to Mrs. Salucci's Boarding House. As he parked along the curb, streetlights highlighted the cleared sidewalks. Someone had shoveled the path to the quaint old house. "Looks like Mrs. Salucci has been busy."

"She's an amazing lady."

"Can I open your car door for you?" Gray held his breath, hoping against all odds that Saige would say yes. He wasn't ready to leave her yet.

"I don't think it's necessary, but sure—if you'd like."

Gray exited the car and opened her door. "I'm glad you agreed. There's something I'd like to talk to you about."

"There's something I need to talk to you about too." Saige stepped from the BMW to the curb.

"Can I go first?"

She nodded.

"If you don't mind, I'm going to get to the point. I've never had a crush on a girl. Lilith came into my life by accident, but she and I became constant friends as we aged. When I asked you about Aiden at the clinic yesterday, you said he wasn't your boyfriend—he was only a

133

friend. I can't help but wonder if you're marrying him based on fear for his life and not because of true love."

"People marry for many reasons—some do it out of necessity. Why should I be any different? Aiden's a great guy. He's a character, but I can adapt to that. I think he'll mellow out with age. We're compatible on almost every other level." Saige leaned back on the BMW's closed passenger door.

"Saige, be honest with yourself. Do you dream about him? Do you wake up eager to see him first thing in the morning? Could you be around him day and night forever?"

"Wha-a-at?" Saige chuckled. "I do need a rest from him sometimes." She peered at her feet as though peering into Gray's eyes might influence her words.

Gray stroked her cheek with his thumb, guiding her face toward his. "Then, Saige, he's not the man for you."

"I'm not sure I know what true love is anymore."

A war raged in Gray's soul. He struggled with his inner emotions—tell her how you feel—that you've finally found out what love is. Let her know you think about her from the moment you wake up until you fall asleep, and even then, your dreams are dominated by her face. Tell her she's the one for you, and you don't want to lose her. He shoved his hands into his coat pockets, balling his fists to refrain from shouting his feelings. Saige would never forgive him if he tried to steal her away from Aiden, especially while her friend was in critical condition.

Gray gazed dreamily into Saige's eyes. She didn't move. While she pressed against the door, he placed his hand against the car, beside her shoulder, to prop himself. Now was the time to kiss her. He was halfway there. A few inches closer and his lips would brush hers. Should he attempt it? Aiden's face loomed before him—Aiden, who might have died and still could. Gray leaned in anyway and kissed her on the forehead.

How could he justify stealing her away from a man suffering in a hospital bed because of his thoughtless behavior on the basketball court? He'd forever be a jerk—an opportunist—in her eyes. "What did you want to tell me, Saige?"

She wiped her cheek. In the dim light, he spotted another tear rolling down her face. "Nothing. It can wait. I'm tired. I need to sleep. Thanks for bringing me home." She pushed her back away from the car.

A lump formed in Gray's throat. So she didn't want to say how she truly felt. He couldn't force her to share her feelings or drag them out of her. He'd have to remain nonchalant while Aiden's life was on the line. "No problem. Let me know if there's anything I can do to help."

He glanced at the boarding house. A light in the living room highlighted a figure standing at the picture window. Mrs. Salucci had been watching him.

While Saige walked to the door, he climbed into his BMW. As he floored the gas pedal, his wheels slid from the curb. He couldn't resist glancing in the rearview mirror. Saige stood by the doorstep until he drove away. Had he done the right thing? Or had she wanted the kiss as much as he did?

After arriving home, Gray entered the Addington mansion and crossed the foyer. Even though his staff had decorated the estate for the holidays, the place sat empty—the way he felt. He glanced into the living room. Without his parents at home, the Christmas tree lights and fancy bulbs were mostly ignored. Usually, during the holidays, his parents entertained guests in the evenings, and their mansion came to life. One more week, on the day of the family Christmas party, his father and mother would return. He'd welcome their arrival. The massive estate was cold and lonely for three people—Gray, Adele, and Fernsby. Their maid, Claire, and their gardener, Roger, lived on the city's outskirts with families of their own.

Gray took his time walking to the study. Fernsby had left a fire blazing for him. He sat down in his reclining desk chair and gazed out the window. Why had he opened his big mouth and told Saige he planned to marry Lilith? She asked him if it was out of spite. He'd said no, but she was right, of course. He'd said it to get back at her for agreeing to follow Aiden into the mission field.

What would his life be like if he married someone like Saige? He loved how her long hair accented her heart-shaped face, how she put one side behind her ear, and how she wore little makeup except for pear-scented lip gloss. She didn't need makeup. Her creamy pale complexion was beautiful without it. He grinned thinking about Monday— only two days ago—when she'd innocently called him an orderly. Yet, she'd treated him like an equal. He had fun helping her with little TJ.

A gentle knock startled Gray. "Come in, old chap."

Still dressed in perfectly creased attire, Fernsby rounded the door with a small tray of steaming hot cocoa paired with a plate of cookies. "Would you care for a late-night snack?"

"Thank you. I could use one about now." Gray accepted the mug and brought it to his lips. "Adele makes the most delicious hot chocolate. And she always places exactly eight mini marshmallows on top, the way I like it."

"That she does. It seems as though she remembers many things that make you happy. These frosted sugar cookies are from her final batch for the day." Fernsby removed the dish from the silver tray before turning to leave.

"Stay awhile, old chap. I'm rather lonesome tonight. Here, help yourself to the cookies."

As though pleased at the invitation, Fernsby walked to the desk. He picked up a napkin along with a frosted Christmas tree with red hots for bulbs. "I'm rather fond of these cinnamon candies coupled with the crunchy cookie." He planted his bottom on the chair across from Gray.

Gray selected a snowflake cookie with decorator coconut. He swirled it in his mouth for a time while contemplating whether to confide in his valet. He desired Fernsby's counsel, but given the man's distaste for Lilith, would he offer unbiased advice?

"Seems like you have a lot on your mind tonight." Fernsby bit into his cookie then wiped crumbs from his lips with his thumb.

"I do. May I ask you a question?"

Fernsby nodded. "Feel free to unburden your heart. I have a good listening ear."

"That you do, old chap. You've heard my problems for many years. But now, I've got one I'm not sure you'll want to weigh in on."

Fernsby reclined in his chair with his hands laced over his chest and his legs crossed at the ankles. "Try me, sir."

A frown wove over Gray's lips. "I'm not quite sure what to do about Lilith."

"Oh?" Fernsby choked on the cookie crumb remnants still in his mouth. He hunched over, quickly covered his mouth with his napkin, and coughed.

"The thing is, old chap, I get your concerns about her. You and Adele are right; she orders me around. I never noticed it until a couple nights ago. But here's my question: Can a man and a woman live in a relationship for a lifetime without true love? I mean, without the type of love that allows a partner to dance freely without the other person condemning them? The type of love where you offer your true love the last chocolate-covered strawberry on earth because it will make her eyes light up?"

"Many people live in relationships like you described. It depends on the couple and what they want out of life."

"What about you, Fernsby? Have you ever had a relationship with a woman?"

Fernsby rested his chin on his chest. "Many years ago, I loved a certain someone more than life itself. I made a terrible mistake, though. I gave her bad advice. After that, I lost her for good."

"I'm sorry. To love like that and lose it. I can only imagine your pain."

"I did a very terrible thing. I can barely forgive myself, let alone ask the woman to forgive me."

"Did you try?"

"I did. But she was bitter. Her resentment destroyed us. I suppose I was the one who caused it, though." Fernsby used his napkin to blow his nose. "I'm sorry, I got carried away. Were you speaking of your relationship with Lilith? Do you not see doves flying in the sky when you're around her?"

"Never once. I feel as though Lilith could be my sister. A bossy one at that."

"I see. So, what are you thinking?"

"I'm not sure what to do. I met a young doctor at the free clinic who cares about her patients. She's nothing like Lilith. Saige is down-to-earth, sweet, and quite beautiful, but she's a farm girl. I'm not quite sure she'd feel comfortable in our environment. Besides, I feel like I'd let Lilith down after she devoted her life to me for so many years. Do I owe her anything?"

"You owe Lilith nothing. Not every relationship works out. Lilith acts like she's above you. Move on. Go for it. Find the love of your life."

"It's not that easy, Fernsby. Another guy loves Saige."

"Those things happen, Gray. My advice is: May the best man win."

"But he was injured in the YMCA basketball game. It was, uh, accidentally my fault. Now, he's in the ICU. Saige feels like she has to marry him to encourage his recovery."

"I see. That's a tough one. What's your plan?"

"I'm afraid I'd come across as a heel if I try to win Saige's heart at a time like this."

"Does she love him? That seems to be the most important question."

"I'm not so sure. I believe she's only agreeing to marry him because of his condition."

"What might you do to show her you love her—without saying it?"

"Perfect, Fernsby. Thank you."

"For what?"

"For asking the best question ever."

TWENTY-TWO

Gusty winds whisked heavy snow across the road as it poured from the sky. Saige peered at the dismal scene from Mrs. Salucci's picture window in the living room around ten a.m. "Instead of a white Christmas, I think ours will be a white-out Christmas this year."

"We've already accumulated two feet of snow, but the weatherman predicts another twelve inches today." Mrs. Salucci placed a tray with steaming cups of coffee on the coffee table. "Let's relax and enjoy the fire." She nestled into one of the overstuffed chairs across from Saige who sat with one leg propped under her on the sofa.

"Thank you." Saige poured vanilla creamer into her mug then rested her elbow on the Santa pillow.

Here it was only Thursday, yet it seemed like a year had passed because of everything that happened since she and Aiden arrived in St. Anne's Landing on Monday. After work at the clinic the first day, she'd had a pillow fight with him and the Rudolf pillow. He'd taken her ribbing like a champ—laughing, even though tired from seeing scores of patients at the clinic. He understood and cared about her. She couldn't handle a sensitive guy who took everything personally, like her first boyfriend, Justin Randolph. He mistook her teasing as belittling him. Saige spent more time stroking his ego and feeling sorry for him than enjoying his company. She ended the relationship after six months, vowing to stay away from guys.

Aiden had waltzed into her life by accident. Darcy brought him home one day. "Look what the cat dragged down our hallway."

"Actually, I live across from you." Aiden pointed to the door opposite theirs. "I'm a first-year medical student. How about you two?"

"Same thing, but I've never seen you in lectures." Darcy glanced at Saige, seeking confirmation.

"Nope. I haven't seen him either." Since their classes were so huge, Saige didn't expect to know everyone.

Over time, they all began walking to the university together. At night, they studied around Saige and Darcy's old table, and Aiden devised funny memory aids. They laughed all evening but never forgot the material. Saige still remembered one of the first sayings he concocted for physiology. It had to do with the brain's cerebrum controlling six functions: reading, thinking, learning, speech, emotions, and planned motor movements. Aiden changed their first letters into the saying: rapidly tooting, loud, smelly elves play mini mandolins. Saige rolled with laughter, but she learned brain functions twice as fast while having a great time.

Whenever they studied, though, Aiden had his sights on adorable, doe-eyed Darcy. She believed he was the most fantastic guy since Liam Hemsworth, but Saige insisted he resembled a younger version of Brad Pitt.

The Darcy-Aiden relationship lasted for a few years until Darcy met a handsome lawyer at the Comedy Den where Aiden moonlighted to earn rent money. He cried on Saige's shoulders for months. To ease his anguish, Saige played tennis with him in the university's gym during the winters and on the school's outdoor tennis courts during the warm months. But before long, Aiden took Saige's acts of benevolence as something more. At least once a week, he professed his love for her, even though Saige wasn't interested.

What was Saige supposed to do? Aiden was like a brother. He lifted her spirits when she was down and made her belly laugh when she needed a boost. Now, he lay in a hospital bed with an injured heart muscle, a leaky, scarred heart valve, and broken vertebrae with paralysis—all because she forced him to play basketball. What choice did she have but to live up to her bargain with God? She had to do the right thing.

A sizzling noise brought Saige to the present. Bacon. Mrs. Salucci had gone to the kitchen. The inviting smell drifted through the living room. Several minutes later, Mrs. Salucci appeared in the kitchen doorway carrying two plates laden with egg, bacon, and avocado croissants.

"How's Aiden doing?" Mrs. Salucci replenished their coffee mugs then tucked her skirt before taking a seat in the floral chair across from the sofa.

"I called this morning." Saige stopped to add vanilla creamer to her refill. "His cardiac enzymes are improving, but he's still short of breath. I'm so worried about him. I told him…well, I told him I'd marry him. It's what he's wanted for a long time."

A motherly expression washed over Mrs. Salucci as she set down her coffee. "Is that what you want, Saige? Or are you doing it out of pity?"

"Please don't ask me that. Aiden has been my best friend for years. He tells me he loves me. I can't let him go through this alone. Saying I'll marry him will give him something to live for."

Mrs. Salucci rested her finger alongside her cheek, deep in thought. "You know, I'd hate to see you rush into a mistake."

"Thanks for your advice, but I already discussed this with Aiden. I won't break my promise. I'll be happy with him. I don't doubt it."

"But is he the man of your dreams?" Mrs. Salucci rose from her chair and walked to the wall. "See this picture?"

In the picture, three handsome young men dressed in old-fashioned uniforms leaned against a car. Mrs. Salucci pointed to the man in the middle. "This picture is from Italy. And this rakish fella is Paolo Salucci, the man I married. Always a jokester, but I learned to love him. From the day we wed until the day he died, we worked on our marriage. But he wasn't my first love. His friend there, the one on the left, he was the love of my life.

"Giovanni made my heart sing with joy. I dreamed about him every night, but Paolo asked for my hand in marriage first. My parents insisted that I accept his offer. I begged them to wait for Giovanni to ask, but my father's pockets were threadbare from the war. He didn't have much money to support our large family. What if Giovanni didn't ask for my hand? Then I'd be a starving old maid. I held off for days, but never a word from Giovanni. When the time came for me to give Paolo an answer, I told him yes. We were married within a few days. Two weeks later, Giovanni returned from visiting his family and found me at my father's bakery, where I worked. Confident as though he owned the world, he removed the most beautiful diamond I'd ever seen from his jacket. 'Marry me, Elena,' he pleaded. My lips wouldn't move. More than anything, I wanted to say yes, but it was too late. I had settled on Paolo. Please don't settle, Saige. Choose the man of your dreams. I've seen you with Aiden and with the man who brings you home from the hospital. I know which one owns your heart."

Saige listened intently, but her situation with Aiden was more complicated. She'd made promises to God. "Thank you for sharing your story. It touched my heart, but no matter how I feel, I can't go back on my word."

♥

Gray had so much to tell Saige—no, to show her—if he could only muster up the nerve. He pulled up to the curb at the boarding house an hour early in case she had an inclination to talk. Walking up the icy sidewalk in his expensive leather shoes, he attempted to rehearse his speech. Impossible. Four more steps to the porch, several more to the front door—not enough time to think, let alone remember what he planned to say. Then he paused. Choking back anxiety, he ran through the jumbled words spinning through his mind. Exasperated, he pressed the doorbell.

Within seconds, Saige opened the door. "You're early! Would you like to come inside? I'll be ready in a few minutes."

"Sure, that would be nice." Careful not to act too eager, Gray struggled to control his overly enthusiastic head nod. More nervous than he'd ever been in his life, not counting when he performed his first heart surgery, he stepped into the warm living room where he spotted the boarding house owner kneeling at a stone fireplace. She finished stoking embers before adding another log.

Biting her lip, Saige closed the door and hurried up the stairs located behind him. Why wasn't she joining him in the living room? Would all his practicing and fretting about what to say to her be for nothing?

"You must be Gray." Mrs. Salucci placed her fireplace poker in its stand and met him at the door. "I'm Elena Salucci." Instead of extending her hand, she wrapped him in a gentle hug. "Please, make yourself comfortable, dear."

Her kind embrace and invitation calmed Gray's runaway nerves, and her warm fireplace drew him to its hearth. Rubbing his hands near the growing flames, he heaved a sigh. "This feels wonderful after braving the twenty-degree frost outside."

"Would you care for a cup of coffee or hot chocolate?"

"I'd give my inheritance for a cup of coffee if it wouldn't be too much of a bother."

Mrs. Salucci left the room but quickly reappeared carrying a coffee mug. She poured the steaming brew from a pot sitting on the living room table. "Please, help yourself to the vanilla creamer and sugar."

Gray poured the condiments into his cup, thankful he didn't have to contend with Lilith's disapproval. After taking a sip, he touched his finger to his thumb in the gesture of perfection. "Delicious coffee. Thank you."

"You're welcome. Have you heard any news about Aiden?"

"Not this morning. We'll find out more when we get to the hospital."

Mrs. Salucci fidgeted with the hem of her apron during an awkward silence that followed. It seemed like she wanted to say more but didn't know how to begin. Gray studied the floor while taking one sip after another from his mug.

"Saige mentioned her plan to marry Aiden." Mrs. Salucci blurted the information then quickly spread her hands over her mouth. "I shouldn't have said that. Please forgive me." Mrs. Salucci slumped down into the overstuffed chair across from Gray.

So, sweet little Mrs. Salucci had been carrying a secret. No sense allowing her to squirm. "Saige already told me. I'll admit, the prospect quite saddens me." Gray set his mug on the table then braced his elbows on his knees, bringing his steepled fingers to his lips. "If you don't mind me being blunt, I'm not quite sure she truly loves him."

"Aiden is a fine young man. But I think you're on to something. Who do you suppose she loves?" The lady was fishing for information. Gray recognized the telltale signs—she licked her lips, turned her head while speaking, then stared into Gray's eyes.

Did Saige know her hostess well enough to divulge her innermost feelings? Should he share his thoughts? As the seconds ticked by on the mantle clock, Gray chewed on his thumbnail. "I've only known Saige for four days. I'm hardly in a position to give her advice."

"I knew my first love, Giovanni, for less than a week before my heart told me he was the one. But another man proposed first." Gray listened, captivated, as she shared the story of how she ended up marrying Paolo.

"Don't get me wrong, Gray. Paolo was a wonderful man. We spent thirty great years together before he died. But he wasn't my true love. I settled. And I lost my Giovanni."

"I'm sorry to hear that. I can't imagine your pain." Gray had strong feelings for Saige, but was it love?

Footsteps down the staircase interrupted them. "I'm ready to go whenever you are, Gray."

"How about another cup of decaf before you leave?" Mrs. Salucci lifted the creamer.

"Thanks for the offer, but if you don't mind, I should get to the hospital. Aiden might need me." Saige donned her coat and wrapped the long end of her wool scarf around her neck.

Mrs. Salucci's conversation had been enlightening. Gray let out a sigh as he rose from his seat. "I appreciate the drink and the gracious conversation, Mrs. Salucci. Maybe we'll meet again soon." He buttoned his coat and headed to the door, moving slow enough to give Saige an opportunity to change her mind and stay a while.

Mrs. Salucci followed him, but after Saige stepped outside, she snagged Gray's arm. "Please think about what I shared with you. Sometimes it's wise to speak up—before it's too late."

"Thank you, ma'am. I'm hoping against all odds that there's still time."

TWENTY-THREE

S omewhere in the shiny-tiled ICU hallway, a man's muffled shouts erupted. Monitor alarms blasted, indicating a problem. Aiden? Surely it wasn't him.

Ignoring hospital protocol, Saige ran down the polished tiles, listening at each doorway for the noise. Aiden needed her, she could feel it in her heart. Fearful of what to expect, she reached his room and pushed open the door. Hunched over his bedside, the bearded neurosurgeon raised an opened safety pin.

Anger pounded in Saige's chest until she wanted to explode. Hadn't Aiden already been through more pain than anyone should have to endure? Pin pricks went hand in hand with neurological tests, but how deep did the doctor have to go?

Nurse Vanderlaan motioned for Saige to step aside as she barged into the room like a linebacker. "What's going on in here? Aiden's heart is racing and his oxygen saturation has dropped." She placed two fingers on Aiden's wrist pulse then checked his heart rate on the monitor. "They match. But why is Aiden agitated?" She looked at Dr. McGavern again.

The neurosurgeon pocketed his safety pin as a broad smile stretched his cheeks. "Pain in his fingers. The most welcomed sensation Aiden will ever experience. Our patient will be okay."

The nurse shuffled Saige and Dr. McGavern out of the way before pushing buttons on the monitors to make the irritating clatter stop.

Did Saige dare hope for healing? "Do you mean his spinal swelling is resolving?" She gripped the bed rail, hoping for the best but prepared for the worst.

"Aiden, move your fingers."

Aiden wiggled his digits on command.

"Those shouts were from nerve endings experiencing pain for the first time since his paralysis." The surgeon eyed Nurse Vanderlaan as if to tell her to back off. "Perfectly normal reason for his monitors to alarm when I pricked his fingers."

He removed an iPhone from his med coat and touched the screen. "After our patient is healed from heart valve surgery, I'll repair his vertebrae." He began typing on his phone. "I'll notify his parents too. Your job is to keep still, Aiden, and allow for more healing."

"Aye…aye…doctor."

Dr. McGavern finished examining Aiden's cranial nerves then dropped the gray iPhone back in his pocket and excused himself from the room. Nurse Vanderlaan scrambled after him.

"This is wonderful news, Aiden. God is answering prayers! I meant what I said about marrying you. We'll become missionaries." She gripped his hand as he curled his fingers around hers for the first time since the accident.

"I'm…the," Aiden peered at her with excitement lighting his eyes, "happiest…man…alive."

"You'd make any girl a great husband. But wait a minute—" Most of his dishwater blond hair had fallen from his topknot into a disheveled heap on his pillow. "Let me fix this."

She removed the elastic band hanging from his hair. Rummaging through the nightstand drawer, she found a brush instead. "Success!" Careful not to yank Aiden's scalp, she styled his hair around his face. His naturally thick hair spilled below his shoulders. Saige walked to the end of his bed to study her masterpiece.

Aiden was gorgeous. How had she not noticed it before?

The elastic band had created waves in his hair that accented the curve of his jawline. Today he outdid Brad Pitt in *Legends of the Fall.*

But looks weren't everything; he was still a goofball—then again, so was Dick Van Dyke in *Mary Poppins*, yet billions of people loved him.

The memory of Gray with his cute wavy hair curling over his ears as he leaned in for a kiss last night caught her off-guard. He was dreamy. And he was serious at the perfect times—those times when it mattered. She sighed. The image of Gray and her, arm in arm, burst into miniscule dust particles in her mind.

If Gray was the dreamiest man alive, Aiden was on the other end of the spectrum. Why did everything have to be a joke for him? He didn't have a serious bone in his body, but on the mission field, he would make a difference in the world. His life would be worthwhile, and so would hers. Who needed a passionate marriage? She'd have a happy one.

Seeing Aiden lying in bed with his hair down reminded her of the archangel Gabriel's picture in a stained-glass window. The only thing missing on Aiden was the halo. Regardless of her feelings for Gray, she'd never break her promise to Saint Aiden or to God.

Gray peeked into the room, but Saige noticed him at the door, watching her. Gray shifted his stance a few times before walking to the bed. "Are you ready to leave, Saige? We don't want Aiden to get overly tired."

Why was he pushing her to leave? She hadn't been at the bedside more than a few minutes. Nurse Vanderlaan allowed her to visit because Aiden's parents had retired to their hotel room for a nap. And Gray had headed to the nurse's station to give her alone time with Aiden. She expected to visit for at least an hour.

Disappointed at having to make an early departure, she swooped her coat from an empty chair. "I suppose I'm ready." She pressed her lips on Aiden's cheek, then lingered for a second over his mouth, contemplating a kiss. But they'd never shared a real one before. Her lips quivered as she planted them on his forehead instead. There'd be plenty of time for kissing after he healed. "I'll return tomorrow. Hang in there, buddy." Did she just say buddy? Ugh.

Aiden puckered his lips and made a smooching noise at her before looking at Gray. "Hey, thanks...for bringing...Saige."

"No problem, man. Stay strong."

147

Saige donned her coat as she walked to the door, but before exiting, she glanced back at angelic Aiden one last time. More conflicted than ever about him vs. Gray, she left the room with her emotions in fine knots—like the complicated ones in delicate necklaces that require patience to untangle. Because of her promises, she'd have to settle.

♥

Outside in Central Sinai's snow-plowed parking lot, people hustled about, heading into and out of the hospital as Gray escorted Saige to his car. He could relate to the busy hospital staff inside the building. In three short weeks, he'd return to his surgical duties, repairing the cardiac arteries of those on the path to heart attacks or, worse yet, those already in the throes of the event.

After settling into their seats, Gray turned on the radio to avoid discussing Aiden. He'd seen the look in Saige's eyes when she stared at her beau. With his hair down, Aiden appeared older, perhaps better looking, although Gray wasn't a good judge of male features.

The "Boot Scootin' Boogie" boomed from his radio speakers, lightening Gray's mood. "Who would've thought dancing could be so much fun?" He chuckled at the refrain. "I'm decent at ballroom steps, but boot scootin' is a whole different story. I rather enjoyed it."

"In my town, we'd say it was a 'hoot.'" Saige laughed along with him until her face clouded, and she grew serious. "I've got some good news, Gray."

Good news? He wouldn't have guessed it, judging by her somber expression.

"Aiden can move his fingers now, and he can feel pain. We're one step closer to marriage." Saige focused on the space between them, pressing her knuckle over her lips. "Thanks for your support."

My support? "I haven't done much."

"You've done more than most friends—making yourself available, giving me rides, taking me to dinner."

If she only knew why. Gray wanted to scramble up to the hospital rooftop and shout, "Don't marry Aiden. I'm the man for you!" But he couldn't—wouldn't, not when Saige had made up her mind. Still, he cared about her, and he held out hope for another chance to prove himself.

"Then you'll come to our family Christmas party next Saturday?" He looked at her, his eyes pleading for her to say yes.

"I suppose so. Is it formal?"

"Semi-formal. Probably not what you're used to, growing up on a farm, but it's my world."

Gray wished he'd been raised in Saige's world, wearing jeans, riding horses, milking cows. Notions of jumping in mud puddles and running through green pastures without a care in the world made him envious of those who never had to mind their clothes or their manners. Instead, the only fun he'd encountered in childhood involved adventures in books.

"If you have the time, I mean, since I don't have transportation, would you mind taking me shopping?" Saige almost whispered her request.

"There's no time like the present. I'll take you to my favorite shops right now if you're up for it."

"Sure. I'd be grateful. Besides, maybe you can help me find something so I'll blend in with your crowd. I don't want to look out of place."

"I think you'll enjoy yourself since the guests will include our out-of-town relatives and friends."

Saige rested against her seat as if satisfied with his explanation. She relaxed on the way to the three-story mall on the outskirts of St. Anne's Landing while sharing stories about her family's farm. Gray chuckled at her humorous tales of chasing roosters, having egg fights with her siblings, and milking good old Fanny Mae. The stories about playing hide and seek in the barn, chicken coop, and under the front porch in the afternoons made him envious of her upbringing. He would have given all the money in the world to live on her farm.

When they reached the shopping mall, he hopped on the escalator with Saige and led her to several clothes shops frequented by Lilith. Saige tried on semi-formal dresses selected by the salesladies. After donning them, Saige modeled the best ones for Gray. Nothing suited him. He wanted her to wear a dress that captured her sweetness and down-to-earth nature while being acceptable in a semi-formal world.

"I have one final place to take you." He turned her around to the opposite direction. "I think you'll find something suitable there."

As they walked past store after store, Saige spotted a hat shop. She dragged Gray inside despite him waving his hands in protest. "I don't wear hats. Never have."

"We'll see about that." She plopped a beret on his head. "Try this one."

Gray removed his coat, hooked it over his shoulder with his finger, then narrowed his eyes and pursed his lips like a British spy as he walked away from Saige and back again.

"No, that isn't you." Saige covered her mouth but her hand didn't quite cover her grin.

"Why? Is it because I'm not the spy type or not debonair enough?" Gray removed the hat and tossed it on a hook. "I'm done."

"No, no, no, I tried on dresses, so it's your turn to do some modeling." She selected headwear faster than he could pose. After trying on many, including a safari hat, a sombrero, and a fedora similar to the one Indiana Jones wore in his movies, Saige broke into a knowing grin. "The fedora suits you well, but there's one more I think you'll love." She plunked a cowboy hat on his head. "It's perfect!" She clapped. "You belong in Texas."

Gray pranced around in the black western hat with his shoulders back and his chest puffed. "Do I look like an old cowhand?" He propped his thumbs in his pant pockets and pretended to bow his legs as he sashayed toward the mirror.

"You look more like a dignified British butler with an ostrich neck."

"Whoa, that's a blow to my ego. Wait a minute, I know." He began singing "The Boot Scootin' Boogie" while dancing. He had the lasso gesture down pat.

"You've been practicing!"

"Yee-haw!" He kicked up his heels.

Saige laughed so hard her cheeks turned red. "Stop, Gray! My gut is going to split."

He responded by doing the lasso part a few more times, getting funnier with each performance. "How 'bout joining me, little filly?" He placed a western hat on her head before offering her his hand. Together they sang the song and danced until the saleslady shooed them out of the shop—but not before Gray purchased the hat.

"I didn't know you could loosen up like that." Saige continued giggling.

"Me either, but as you like to say, 'it was a hoot.'"

After a stop for hot chocolate, they reached the clothes shop Gray had in mind. "I think this place will have a dress you'll love." He steered her into the quaint yet fancy store.

Saige examined the clothes on several mannequins and racks. When she'd about lost hope of success, a customer exited a fitting room wearing a silver dress with a lace overlay. The mouth of the lady's companion dropped open. "That's it!" he told the saleslady.

Saige nudged Gray. "I like that one, too."

Gray nodded. "Try it on."

Saige found her size and scooted into an empty fitting room, moving fast to check out the gorgeous dress in the mirror. A saleslady followed her for assistance. "Let me know if you need another size, hon."

After trying it on, Saige slid the fitting room curtain aside. She walked out of the area to show Gray.

The saleslady spotted her from a sales rack where she had been replacing fitting room clothes. She hurried to lead Saige to a three-paneled mirror. "Now, turn around, miss, so that we can assess every angle of the fit." The lady brought her hands to her mouth. "My, it becomes you."

Sitting on a chair provided for those waiting, Gray clutched his chest, pretending Saige had shot an arrow into his heart. "We'll take it!" Saige twirled around in the sleek design.

"This suits me!" She peered over her shoulder to view the back. "But I'm paying for it, Gray."

"Whatever you say." While she removed the dress to change into her jeans and sweater, Gray whispered to the saleslady, "Please put it on the Addington tab."

Once Saige exited the fitting room, he handed her the elegant bag.

"What? You shouldn't have paid for this." She snatched the package from him and marched to the counter. Handing her credit card to the shocked saleslady, she sighed. "Thanks, but I'm paying for my dress."

Gray waited for her, feeling a little surprised at her defiance. But she had a mind and a pocketbook of her own. He respected her independence. Transaction completed, he swept his hand toward the door. "How about if we stop at a shoe store next?"

Another hour passed looking at shoes until Saige found the perfect pair for her outfit. They were chic with standard heels. Gray had never been fond of stilettos. They were dangerous as evidenced by the unfortunate young lady's fall at the Christmas party last week. He didn't want Saige to become a victim as well.

On their way out of the shop, Gray tucked her packages under his arm. "I guess the only thing remaining is to head to dinner."

"Gray, you've been kind today. I appreciate your help."

"Does this mean you'll forgive me for the accident?"

"I didn't say that. I wish you hadn't brought it up. Here I am, having a good time while Aiden is suffering. Can we return to the hospital?"

"Of course, Saige. Anything for you." He meant it from the bottom of his heart.

TWENTY-FOUR

Mentally exhausted by ten p.m., Gray stood before the enormous lighted wreath Fernsby had recently placed on the mansion door. Had Gray imagined it, or had Saige shown signs of indecision about Aiden? What made her like him in the first place? And how could Gray capture that reason and apply it to his own life? He didn't want just any love. He wanted deep, faithful, unyielding love like the kind Saige had for Aiden.

The normally quiet mansion bristled with commotion as Gray opened the door. The farther he walked into the high-ceilinged home, the louder Lilith's shrill voice echoed with harsh words directed at his servants. Adele wailed about something Gray couldn't see. Phones rang nonstop. Claire, the maid, and Roger, the gardener, who usually left before dinner, ran in different directions over the shiny marble tiles to answer the calls.

"What's going on in here?" Gray headed toward the grand staircase.

The clip-clack, clip-clack of heels and the slap-clack of slick soled shoes rushed to greet him.

"Gray! I'm so glad you're here. There's been terrible news!" Lilith's high-pitched voice electrified his nerve endings. Decked in a mohair sweater and satin pants, she engulfed him in her arms.

Something bad had happened, but what?

Fernsby and Adele caught up with Lilith and moved her aside. "It's not for you to tell him. That's our job." Fernsby came alongside Gray and looped his arm around his boss's elbow.

Lilith edged around Adele to Gray's other side and latched onto his upper arm. "Darling, you'll need courage to hear this."

Gray's face twisted as he imagined the horror. "What? Tell me!"

"It's your parents, sir." Adele clutched her hands to her chest. "We hate to be the bearers of bad news."

"Quit leading him on! Gray, your parents' taxi crashed in England on the way to the airport." Lilith glared at Fernsby and Adele before turning to Gray. "The phone call came an hour ago. We couldn't get a hold of you. Is your cell phone dead?"

"I-I-I don't know. How are my parents doing? I need to fly out to England tonight."

"Gray. I'm so sorry." Adele walked backward in front of Gray, stopping when he came to a halt.

"They didn't make it, sir." Fernsby clutched Gray's arm to keep him from falling. "Both had their passports and other identification on them. There's no need to make a trip to Europe. They'll be flown home after the investigation."

Gray reached the staircase and gripped the railing, then he slid down to the steps. Placing his hands around his head, he sobbed. "I barely knew them, yet to be without them—I don't know how I'll get on."

His parents had cared about him and made sure he had everything he ever needed, yet they rarely had time for him in their busy social world. They had appointed Adele and Fernsby to take him under their wings—to earn an allowance—an allotment larger than any child his age probably ever received. And while doing chores, Gray learned work ethics, manners, and compassion for others.

His prestigious father might have had time for him if he hadn't built the Addington Complex from the ground up. "St. Anne's Landing needs accomplished cardiologists," he had announced. It might have been true, but the project caused him to sacrifice time with Gray. Yet somehow, Gray learned to manage money and to save. He had amassed a small fortune over the years due to his savings account.

But he'd sorely miss his sweet, though prim and proper mother. She wasn't the type to dole out hugs. But through the years, she taught him important life principles, such as how to overlook hardships in life. "People say things they don't mean, Gray, and they forget them just as quickly," she added. "Ignore angry words. Forgive easily, and people will forgive you as well."

Gray admired his mother's kindness, but she wasn't the mothering type. She didn't kiss his scrapes or wipe his tears. Adele did those things. And Adele was the one who offered hugs. Both she and Fernsby played board games with him in the evenings and read to him before bed—though separately, instead of together. Adele always insisted on keeping a distance from Fernsby.

"Let's go to the study, Gray. You'll be more comfortable by the fire." Lilith nudged him to rise from his staircase perch.

Light-headed from disbelief, Gray walked solemnly down the hallway, flanked by Fernsby and Lilith, with Adele close behind.

"I stoked a fire in the study after receiving the phone call, sir, since it's your favorite room in the house." Fernsby placed his arm around Gray's shoulder. "You'll get through this, my boy. I guarantee it. Take it one moment at a time."

Adele slipped between Lilith and Gray, pushing Lilith in front of them. In her motherly manner, she wrapped her hand over Gray's. "Take deep breaths, dear. It'll calm you down. We don't know the particulars of the crash. So, let's not jump to conclusions yet."

"What are you saying?" Lilith turned around to face them as she walked. She shouted at Fernsby and Adele, demanding they believe his parents were dead. "Don't give Gray false hope. What's wrong with you people?" She raised her hands in a wild display of anger as she shouted.

Adele leaned into his side, and wrapping her arm around Gray's waist, hugged him. "Hang in there, my precious one. We'll learn more tomorrow."

Adele hadn't called him "my precious one" since he was ten years old. Her sweetness had helped him through many childhood traumas.

"I need to be alone now, Lilith. Would you mind? I'll call you tomorrow." Gray's eyes pleaded with her to leave.

"Well, I can see where I stand in this house." Lilith snatched her purse and coat from the desk before leaving in a huff.

After she exited the study, Gray collapsed into his reclining desk chair. Fernsby and Adele sat across from him on the loveseat. "How can we make this easier for you?" Adele asked.

"I'm afraid it's not possible."

"I believe you're in shock, sir." Fernsby folded and unfolded his hands then shifted his position on the sofa.

"What am I going to do now? I don't have family nearby. My relatives are scattered in different states. Will I be alone for the rest of my life?"

"That will never happen, sir. Adele and I will always be here for you." Fernsby twisted on the loveseat to face Gray better.

"Fernsby is right, Gray. We'll stay on. You'll never be alone with us here. We've been with you since you were born. And we won't leave you now."

"Thank you, old chap, Dell. I need you two now, more than ever." Gray had a special place in his heart for his faithful servants. They had been like family to him for as long as he could remember.

He had expected his parents to live forever. What child doesn't? Even at thirty-four, he hadn't considered what would happen if they suddenly died. He expected Fernsby and Adele to work for them for many more years. Why would that need to change? The mansion had been handed down from one generation to the next. He wouldn't have a mortgage, and he could well afford to pay his servants' salaries. He had to stop thinking and rest.

♥

After spending hours in the study, Gray's head bobbed on his way to sleep when the phone rang. He opened his eyes and waited while Fernsby answered the call. "Who is it, old chap?"

His valet replaced the receiver. "The British Metropolitan Police." He relayed the information while Gray wiped sleep from his eyes. "It will take weeks for them to have answers after formally investigating the crash," Fernsby added. "Your parents' taxi collided with another car on the way to the airport. There were no survivors."

"I'm sick to my stomach. We should cancel the family Christmas party." Gray covered his mouth to discourage a heave.

"I share in your grief, Gray. Having your extended family around might lessen your suffering." Fernsby's advice comforted him. He appreciated his valet's rational thinking.

"I'll have the party then. Besides, I have an announcement to make about Lilith."

"Lilith?" Fernsby's voice lowered. "What is it, sir?"

"It'll be a surprise for everyone at the event." Gray expected his servants to balk at the news, but without his parents, he needed Lilith more than ever. She understood their social world, its practices, and its expectations, something he never cared about.

He only hoped she wouldn't insist on him giving up the free clinic every Christmas. He'd volunteered there since graduating medical school. The grateful families helped put his fame, career, and life into perspective.

Adele poked her silvery head into the room. "Follow me. I'll fix us a snack." She motioned for Gray and Fernsby to move along.

Inside the kitchen, a blazing fire glowed in the hearth and soft Christmas music played while Gray slid onto his favorite worn stool. Fernsby walked around the marble island to the freezer. After a few seconds, he produced a glass container filled with toffee butterscotch cookies, Gray's favorite. He set them on the island and removed the lid.

"Are you doing okay?" Adele asked Gray.

"I'm doing as well as can be expected after learning my parents died a horrible death, leaving me an orphan."

"Can I make you some hot chocolate, dear?" Adele patted his hand. "I'll make you anything you'd like."

Gray placed his elbows on the counter and rested his head in his hands. "I don't have an appetite."

"Of course, dear." Adele turned to the refrigerator and busied herself, preparing something anyway. "What are your plans for tomorrow?"

"I'm off today. But on Monday, I begin my last three days in the free clinic. After Christmas, I'll have two weeks of rest before I return to the cardiology complex." Gray took the tiniest bite of the cookie on the decorative red plate to keep from offending Adele and Fernsby. "Surgeries are on the schedule for the third week in January. My life will become a constant whirlwind of activity as usual." He wiped crumbs from his lips. "I won't have time to think about my loss."

Adele poured cocoa, semisweet chocolate pieces, sugar, and milk into a pan, turned on the burner, then stirred the ingredients. "But you must grieve, Gray. If you don't, you'll suffer—high blood pressure, depression, anxiety. Grief is one of those things everyone experiences at one time or another. I wish I could take it from you—or grieve for you, but no one can swap places, as much as we'd like to." She continued stirring the drink.

"Dell, why did it have to happen to my parents? They were good people. Charities will miss their benevolent giving. Why did God let such good people die?"

"The truth, Gray, is that everyone since the beginning of time has died or will die. Our deaths are part of a vast plan we know nothing about. We don't like losing loved ones, but we have to understand that God cherishes every hair on their heads." Adele wiped tears from her eyes before taking the boiling mixture off the stove.

"I never thought of it that way."

She added a teaspoon of vanilla extract before pouring the hot cocoa into three clear glass mugs. "Here you go, Gray." She topped his mug with exactly eight marshmallows.

Gray took a sip of the steaming liquid. "I always thought my parents were aloof. They never let me in on their thoughts or feelings."

"I believe there were reasons for that. Someday you'll understand." Adele handed a mug of hot chocolate to Fernsby.

Silence settled over the kitchen as the three of them sipped the creamy brew and nibbled on cookies.

Fernsby downed his cocoa then carried his mug to the sink. "It's been a long night. How about if we retire to our rooms? Sleep will help us to cope tomorrow."

"I agree. This evening has drained me. Gray, please know this. You're not alone in this world. You'll learn things in the next few days that I hope won't be too shocking." Adele's eyes darted to Fernsby.

"What do you mean? Tell me now!" Gray pushed his empty mug aside.

"I can't. But please be prepared for the truth." Her strained face displayed wrinkles Gray had never seen before. Her unblemished, porcelain skin made her appear younger than a woman in her sixties.

Adele joined Fernsby at the door. Somberly, they exited the room.

Gray rubbed his aching temples. What could possibly be shocking enough that he had to prepare himself? Did his parents have skeletons in their closets? They had always exhibited perfect behavior and perfect morals. Gray had never heard the slightest impropriety about them. Would the truth Adele mentioned shatter their perfect images? An acidy taste rose in his throat. She had told him to be prepared for the truth—but what if he couldn't handle it?

TWENTY-FIVE

Dark and debilitating sadness filled Gray with inconsolable grief as he parked his car along Mrs. Salucci's snow-piled curb. Every conceivable direction in his life led to misfortune right now—his parents' deaths, Saige's rejection, Aiden's near-death, Lilith's character deception—the list had no end. If he hadn't offered Saige a ride to the clinic this morning, he would've considered notifying Maria of his inability to work. How much more sorrow could he endure?

The sidewalk, buried under two feet of packed white fluff, no longer displayed a path. Wearing expensive shoes, Gray trampled the snow as he slogged to the steps. Mrs. Salucci hadn't shoveled yet. Before he reached the porch, the door opened.

The agitated greeter clung to the doorknob, her hand covered by her sweater sleeve. "When I didn't hear from you all weekend, I—" She chewed on her lip.

"Saige..."

She crossed her arms. "I called a cab."

"Saige, let me expl—"

"Did you change your mind about me attending your family Christmas party too?"

"Saige, if you'd let me explain ..."

"Never mind, Gray, you don't owe me an explanation."

"Listen, Saige...my parents died."

"What? Are you trying to get sympathy because you screwed up?" She knuckled her wool-covered hands on her jean-clad hips.

161

"No. My parents' taxi crashed on the way to the airport in England. I've had a hard time dealing with my grief. To make matters worse, I also had to tend to an unstable patient at the hospital."

The bags under his eyes should have given her a clue, but she wasn't as sympathetic as he expected. Maybe he was a poor judge of character, after all, he hadn't recognized Lilith's telltale signs of controlling his life.

A look of horror crossed Saige's face. "Gray, I-I-I'm so sorry. I'm used to Aiden's pranks. But, but, I forgot you're not like him. Please, come in."

A solemn mood clung to Gray as he trudged into the home head down, bundled in his ebony coat and wool scarf. He couldn't look her in the face—not after she made fun of his horrible announcement. "If you'll find me a shovel, I'll take care of the snow."

Mrs. Salucci appeared from the kitchen dressed in an oversized quilted coat, work boots, and gloves with a wide snow shovel in her hands. "I'm heading out front."

"I've got it." Gray dodged her refusals and plucked the long-handled tool from her hands in a gesture of gentlemanly concern.

On returning to the sidewalk, he plowed through the packed ice, slinging it to the side as though ridding himself of anger with each thrust of the blade. After finishing the job in record time, he tromped back to the porch, set the shovel against the siding, then opened the door. "Are you ready to leave, Saige?"

"Would you come in for a rest first?"

Gray stepped inside the home, his face and hands reddened and chafed from the cold. She motioned for him to remove his coat and slip off his wet shoes. Taking his hand, she steered him to the sofa in front of the fireplace.

The radiating heat brought him little warmth. He'd been sick to his stomach ever since the news about his parents. Nothing, not even the crackling fires at home, helped to melt the wretched feeling in his heart. Saige slid down beside him on the floral sofa and wrapped her hands around his. "You're freezing."

"Nothing helps."

"I understand, Gray. It's as if the world has stopped moving." She removed a soft fleece blanket from the armchair across from them. After tucking it around Gray, she sat beside him. "Have you been able to eat?"

"Not hungry."

"You'll need some nutrition, no matter how small. It was the first hurdle I had to conquer after my mother passed. Weight poured off me until my father feared he'd lose a daughter too. I don't want to lose you, Gray."

"You don't? Even though we're only friends?" Gray lifted his eyes. Could he and Saige exist as friends? The whole situation was more complicated than he had the strength to unravel.

"We can be forever-friends. We're similar, you and me." Saige's words caught him off guard. They were similar—how?

She continued. "We've had fun this week. I believe you about Aiden's accident—you didn't mean for it to happen." She walked to the hearth, collected two logs then placed them on the fire. "Tell me about your parents, Gray." She returned to his side. "I want to know everything about them."

A car beeped. Twisting around, she raised to her knees on the sofa cushion and peered outside. "That's my cab. Are you planning to work today?"

"Yes. I need the distraction." How could he say no to her when he soaked up every drop of her compassion like soil craving water? "We can go together if you'd like."

Saige jumped to her feet. "I'll be back." She hurried outside, paid the driver, then sent him on his way.

Gray watched her actions from the window. The taxi driver would consider her a valuable customer for compensating him. He folded the blanket, stood, and met her at the door. "Sorry about your wasted money. We'd better head out, so we're not late."

Mrs. Salucci hurried from the dining room carrying two paper bags and travel mugs with lids. "I overheard you talking, Gray. I hope you don't mind, but I've made two breakfasts to go. Eat what you can."

"Thank you." Even though he had no desire to eat, he wouldn't offend his hostess.

He donned his coat then fidgeted with its buttons. Mrs. Salucci handed them the wrapped items before enveloping Gray in a sincere hug. "I'm so sorry about your parents, dear. No one should live through an experience like this at your age. Please allow me to make dinner for you and Saige tonight. I'm cooking pure Italian comfort food—authentic lasagna."

Gray felt as though someone should pinch him to prove he was awake. He'd never met anyone as kind as Mrs. Salucci, except for Adele. "Thank you. I'd appreciate it." Without realizing it, Mrs. Salucci had arranged a date for him and Saige—or did she do it on purpose?

Their hostess beamed with excitement as she folded her hands at her trim waist. "Why don't we say, around eight o' clock? It'll give you both time to close the clinic, visit Aiden, and make it back here for dinner."

"That sounds perfect." A soft glow spread over Saige's face. Almost dancing, she swung around to don her coat. "You're the best." She picked up the to-go items she'd set on the stairway.

Gray opened the door for Saige and peered outside. Rays of sunshine parted the clouds, filling his heart with happiness for the first time since he'd learned the horrible news about his mother and father. He tipped his head at the amazing older woman whose selfless act had lifted the gloom permeating his soul. "We'll see you tonight, Mrs. Salucci." The woman deserved a crown of jewels.

On the way to his car, Gray recalled the fun he had with Saige when they went shopping. She'd made the task he usually abhorred into one brimming with laughter. The more he came to know her, the more he desired her in his life. Would tonight provide him with the opportunity to show her his feelings? He had to stop fretting about how she'd respond. If he didn't open up tonight, he might not get another chance.

A sudden thought dampened his excitement. Adele's news. What life changing information was coming any day now? The only thing Fernsby divulged was that his parents' lawyer would present the information after ironing out the details. Gray shuddered. How would the news change his life—for the better or…for the worse?

At the end of the clinic workday, Saige retrieved her coat and backpack from her dented locker while Gray brought his BMW around to the sidewalk. He opened the clinic door for her to exit. After she walked outside, he opened the passenger door to his car and closed it while she applied her seatbelt.

"Didn't Aiden have a car in the parking lot out back?"

"Yes, but Mrs. Salucci asked a friend of hers to tow his clunker behind the boarding house after the YMCA game. You've been right—it's too risky for me to drive alone in the inner city." Saige was brave, but not that brave.

"I understand. But why doesn't Aiden purchase a nice car? He's a family practice doctor, isn't he?"

"Debt bothers Aiden. He's paying off his medical school loans before making major purchases." She shivered from the frigid cold and looped her scarf around her neck. "Did you know he still lives across the hall from me in our apartment building? He even wears the same holey socks and faded jeans he's worn since our undergraduate days. According to him, he'll put his money to good use after he pays off his loans. I learned a thing or two from him though. He's the reason why I've been concentrating on paying off my loans too."

"I respect you for that, Saige." Gray's car purred when he turned the key, in stark contrast to the usual coughing and hacking of Aiden's rusted junk heap. In some ways, Saige missed the annoying clatter—maybe because it reminded her of her best friend. A sudden thought struck her. She never called Aiden her fiancé. Why did the word sound so strange on her tongue?

For the first time since Gray had been driving her, he turned down St. Francis Street, the quickest route to the hospital, instead of taking the longer trip. She admired him for working today, despite his grief, but he needed to open up about his sorrow. After her mother passed, she clammed up, and her grief worsened until it showed itself in angry outbursts. Her heart didn't begin to heal until a motherly friend urged her to open up about her grief.

What could she do to help Gray relax and pour out his feelings? An idea came to her. A trip to her family's farm. It might be a catalyst to allow healing.

As Gray turned his vehicle into the hospital parking lot, she asked him about making a visit to her farm, but his cell phone rang. She walked to the ICU in silence while he talked on his phone.

On reaching the ICU room, she found Aiden covered in his usual wires and IVs but resting quietly. Gray appeared in the doorway. "Hey, buddy, your oxygen level is holding steady." He glanced at Saige, who met his gaze with confusion. "Dr. Alberetti called me about Aiden over the weekend. He had a bout with congestive heart failure. I'm afraid his scarred heart valve is worn out. I ordered medication and discussed his cardiac test results with him. Your surgery is set for Thursday, Aiden, but I'll perform an emergency valve replacement sooner if necessary."

Aiden gave a slight nod.

"Why didn't you tell me?" A sick feeling washed over Saige. Aiden was the person Gray had tended to over the weekend.

"I had too much on my mind—my parents' death and the whirlwind of activity at the mansion. Then amidst the commotion, Aiden's breathing worsened. I hurried over to the hospital and met with Dr. Alberetti." Gray leaned over Aiden's siderail. "We're keeping our eyes on you."

Aiden held up his thumbs.

"We'll get you back to doctoring patients soon." Gray studied Aiden's vital signs and data on the wall-mounted monitor screens above his bed. "I'm glad you're moving your hands and arms."

"This was…my last…week at the…clinic."

"You'll have many more years, pal." Gray patted his leg through the cotton-weave hospital blanket.

A nurse, focused on business, charged into the room. "Time for visitors to leave. We can't overtax Aiden's heart."

Saige squeezed between Gray and Aiden. "I—" The word *love* refused to leave her tongue. She administered a kiss on his cheek. "Try to rest."

True to Mrs. Salucci's promise, she had a candlelight dinner on the table by eight p.m. Soft symphonic Christmas music—"Have Yourself a Merry Little Christmas"—played in the background. Garlic and sausage aromas lured Saige to the dining room as soon as she and Gray walked through the front door. "Your house smells like an Italian restaurant."

"I aim to please. Wash your hands then make yourselves comfortable at the table." Mrs. Salucci gave them each a quick hug. "I've been working all day—made everything from scratch—the bread, the lasagna noodles, and the tomato sauce. The fresh cheese is from the farmer's market downtown." She refastened the ties on her ruffled Christmas apron.

In Gray's charming way, he pulled Saige's chair back for her at the table. His manners were something she loved about him. He made her feel cherished, even if they were only friends.

The Italian feast on the table was a sight for Saige's weary eyes. "This is wonderful." She inhaled the smells that mingled together.

"I'm so glad you could come, Gray." Mrs. Salucci poured water into the glass beside his plate.

"I should be home with my relatives from out of town, but Adele and Fernsby told me they'd keep them occupied tonight."

Mrs. Salucci gazed at Gray as she sat down. "Would you like to say grace?"

"I'm not schooled in saying prayers. Dell used to take me to church when I was young, but I gave it up when I grew older. I'm not sure why."

"I'd be delighted to say it then." Mrs. Salucci folded her hands on the table. "Dear Lord, we're grateful for Your love and care for us. Please comfort Gray and his family as they mourn his parents' loss and prepare Aiden for his upcoming surgeries. Protect him while he's in the hospital and watch over him, dear Lord. Thank You for providing this meal. In Jesus' name, amen."

"Thank you." Gray unfolded his hands. "My chef, Dell, prayed with me last night."

So, Dell was his chef? Saige had suspected it all along. Gray had a humble side to him. He didn't boast or make his wealth apparent.

"Now, who wants lasagna?" Mrs. Salucci rose from her chair before cutting the casserole into squares in the baking dish. With melted cheese strings dangling from the serving spoon, she dished portions onto Saige's and Gray's plates. "Pass the salad and garlic bread. Don't be shy. Help yourselves."

Her cell phone rang. "Who would call me at this late hour?" She placed the phone to her ear. "Yes, yes." She covered the receiver with her hand. "A friend from Italy. I'm going to my bedroom for privacy. Please enjoy your meal." As she hurried from the room, her skirt swished under her apron, and her voice brimmed with excitement.

Saige glanced at the beautiful wine-red tablecloth displaying gold ornaments, placemats, and emerald green drinking glasses. Tiny white candles flickered in clear crystal globes on the center of the table. Their glow spread a romantic ambiance over the room. But where was Mrs. Salucci's place setting? Had she planned the candlelight dinner for two all along?

Saige lifted a garlic bread wedge from her plate. She took a nibble and closed her eyes. "This is the best I've ever tasted. Mrs. Salucci used fresh garlic. Have a taste."

"I'll get myself a slice."

"No, no, no, here, have a bite of mine." Saige turned her piece around to the uneaten side and brought it to his mouth.

He took a bite and closed his eyes. "Ahh. This is possibly the best garlic bread I've ever eaten. I believe I need another bite to make sure, though."

Saige brought the bread to his lips again. He took a bite, then another, and another until his lips touched her fingers. He gently kissed them. "Yes, indeed. This garlic bread is delicious. But I recommend we try a bite of lasagna to see if the entire meal is authentic Italian." He cut through his lasagna square with his fork then raised the utensil to Saige's mouth.

She parted her lips for him and accepted the cheesy portion from his fork. He used his thumb to wipe the sauce clinging to the side of her mouth. "Mmmm, this is delicious." Saige savored the scrumptious sauce. "Maybe I need another bite."

Gray brought his face so close to hers, his breath blew over her lips like soft feathers, but he didn't budge another millimeter. He held his position, waiting for her to meet him.

She hesitated for a second before brushing her lips across his—then just as quickly, she backed away. "Gray, I'm so sorry, but I can't do this. I promised to marry Aiden."

"I apologize. If you hadn't promised yourself to him, I'd be…well, I'd be…" Gray pounded his fist on the table. "Saige, I have to share something. I'm smitten with you—there, I've said it. Is it possible for a guy to find the woman of his dreams in less than a week?"

"I think we know our soul mate the moment they walk through the door. But it's too late for us, Gray. I made promises to Aiden and to God, and I won't break them. Only Aiden can release me from my oaths, and I won't ask that of him. I'm so sorry. You and I—we aren't meant to be. Please, let's finish our dinner."

"I've never seen you kiss Aiden in a way that proves you love him. Even when you say goodbye, you kiss his cheek. Maybe I'm wrong, but—never mind, I'm overstepping my bounds. Family members are waiting for me at home. I won't bother you anymore, Saige. I hope you'll attend my Christmas party. I'd love for my relatives to meet you. Good night."

Like a disheartened suitor rejected by his forever love, he strode from the dining room, then gathered his coat and dragged it behind him on his way out of the house.

Saige ran after him but reached the door after he pulled it shut. With her hands touching the wood, she laid her head on the panels and lowered her eyes. Had her true love exited the home or her life?

TWENTY-SIX

The following morning, Saige paced the living room, growing more and more worried over the situation. Where was Gray? She'd be late for work at the clinic. Was his no-show a clue that he was over her? She wouldn't blame him. If he hadn't tried to kiss her last night, they'd still be friends.

Just past the point of he's definitely not coming, she phoned a taxi driver. But she'd waited too long, which made her an hour late to the clinic. After the driver dropped her off, she rushed through the clinic's front door and stopped behind the desk. "Sorry, Maria. I had to call a ride."

"Humph. Gray's late too." Maria crooked her neck to peer into the crammed waiting room. "But the patients are on time—as usual."

Dr. Jon exited Exam Room 1, chart in hand, confusion etching lines on his face. "What's going on this morning? Is there something in the air?"

"I'd say. And it ain't none of our business." Maria picked up a chart and hustled it to Exam Room 2. "Are you going to stand there like a downed baby bird, Saige, or are you planning to start work?" She plunked the chart in the door rack then power-walked to her desk.

Heat bathed Saige's face. Maria couldn't possibly know about her relationship, or lack thereof, with Gray. "Sorry," she called to Maria. "I'll get busy." She headed to her exam room, removed the chart from the door, and waited for a patient.

Maria led a sobbing girl and her mother to the exam table. "You might be late, Saige," Maria whispered, "but the patient line won't stop

171

until we treat everyone. Today's gonna be a long one." Maria's hips swung side to side on her return to the desk.

By noon, Gray still hadn't arrived.

Saige ruminated on the previous evening. Had she harmed his ego by embarrassing him at dinner? When he tried to share his feelings for her, she closed him down. Would she ever see him again? Wiping wayward hair strands from her face, she dragged herself into the physician's lounge for peanut butter and jelly on stale bread. It had to suffice. While she chewed, she pondered why she'd forgotten to call the hospital before leaving the house. She'd been preoccupied with Gray—the kiss, his feelings for her, and the way she'd made a fool of him at dinner. She hated herself.

Surely the ICU nurse would have called her if Aiden had a problem. She removed her cell phone from her scrubs then clicked on the screen. It remained dark after she pushed it—no charge whatsoever. What if the hospital had tried to call her?

Trembling, she seized the landline in the physician's lounge and called the ICU number. "This is Dr. Saige Westbrook. How's Aiden Littlefield today?"

"We've tried to reach you. Dr. Addington came in to assess Aiden. He decided to take him to surgery today."

"Oh, my word. My phone was dead. When is the surgery?"

"The orderlies took him downstairs to the OR a while ago."

"I'll be there as soon as I can." In two leaps she reached the charger by the coffee pot and plugged in her cell phone.

Shaking inside, she hurried to the front desk and tried to get a grip. Calm down. Don't act like a crazy person. "Maria, Gray had to take Aiden to emergency surgery. Can you help me? I need to be there."

Maria's face drained of color. "I'm so sorry about Aiden, Saige. I'll start calling doctors on our list." She rifled through papers in a drawer, found the right one, then began pushing buttons on her landline.

Reeling from shock, Saige returned to her exam room. Praying God would help Maria find a replacement over the next half hour, the line in the waiting room grew faster than it dwindled. Maria caught her coming out of Room 2 and stopped her. "I found three retired doctors who're on their way. They'll fill in for you, Aiden, and Gray today and tomorrow. Keep seeing patients until they arrive." She shooed Saige back into her room.

As the minutes passed, fear gripped Saige. Would Gray be steady enough to ensure her friend's survival? Or would his competitive nature take over, the same as it did on the basketball court?

During the taxi trip to the hospital, Saige called Mrs. Salucci on her freshly charged cell phone. "Aiden's in the operating room with Gray. It's a delicate surgery."

"Oh, my! I'll be there shortly." Mrs. Salucci's voice expressed shock and concern, but the fact that she would come to Central Sinai comforted Saige.

Saige grimaced as cars slipped ahead of her taxi driver or slowed down too soon at lights. She had to sit on her hands to keep from lowering her window and shouting, "Move out of our way!"

The driver glanced at her frequently from the rearview mirror, his furrowed brows indicating concern. Saige placed her hands on the plexiglass separating the front seat from the back. "Please hurry."

After entering the hospital grounds, the driver swung around to the patient entrance where Saige paid him before she tore from the car and ran into the building through the front doors, instead of through the doctor's entrance where Gray usually escorted her. She had no privileges at Central Sinai.

At the information desk, she waved her hands at the volunteer. "My boyfriend is in emergency surgery. Which way do I go?" The lady jumped up from her seat and showed Saige the way.

She led Saige down halls to a fancy room decorated with cushioned chairs, a desk, and a small partition. Near the volunteer's desk, she spotted the ponytailed senior Dr. Littlefield with his ankle propped over his knee, drumming his fingers on his shoe while Mrs. Littlefield bounced her knees to the tune of the symphonic Christmas music playing through speakers overhead.

Saige removed her coat, while hurrying toward tthe Littlefields. "Sorry I wasn't here sooner. My phone died, so I didn't receive the call." Her hands trembled as she took a seat.

"Aiden became more short of breath. Since medication wasn't helping, Dr. Addington decided to take him to surgery." Dr. Littlefield's voice quivered. "They went to the OR a little bit ago, but I'm not sure when the procedure began."

Mrs. Salucci entered the waiting area, looking both ways with her coat draped over her arm. Saige ran across the room to greet her.

"Now, now." Mrs. Salucci wrapped Saige in her arms and stroked her hair. "Let's keep our spirits up." She walked with her to where the Littlefields sat, moving their arms and legs every few seconds as though unable to keep still.

"God will take care of Aiden," Mrs. Salucci told them. She introduced herself before taking a seat.

"Indeed He will." The senior Dr. Littlefield nodded for longer than necessary as though still thinking long after he spoke. Judging by his glassy eyes, he was in a frightened daze.

"Excuse me for a few minutes." Mrs. Salucci suddenly stood and hurried out of the room.

Where did she go? Calm down, Saige. Calm down. Pull yourself together and act like a dignified doctor—like a cardiologist. That was the problem. She knew too much. She knew what could go wrong during surgery. Oh, how she wanted to see her fun-loving friend again. Aiden had been a bright light during medical school. She wanted to be a light for him now. But counting on Gray to live up to his word and perform a textbook perfect surgery on Aiden's heart made her nervous. Would he truly be objective? She walked to the small desk. "Can you point me to the hospital chapel?"

"I'll take you there." The lady with curly red hair left her desk and escorted Saige down a corridor. "Here we are. Be quiet when you enter because people are praying."

"Thank you." Saige peeked inside the small room with stained-glass windows along the far wall. Light enhanced the beautiful colors. The plush blue carpet lined with pews led to a small altar with a magnificent golden cross hanging behind it.

In a pew by herself, a lady in wrinkled clothes sat weeping. Had she dashed to the hospital for an emergency like Saige had? At the altar, a woman with shoulder-length white hair bowed her head, saying prayers.

Trying to be quiet, Saige knelt beside Mrs. Salucci, the beautiful white-haired lady. A few minutes later, the Littlefields joined them. The group prayed silently then left the altar one by one to congregate at the back of the chapel.

"Have you heard anything?" Dr. Littlefield whispered to Saige.

Her mouth crooked to the side as she shook her head. "I hoped one of you might know something."

"I wonder how much longer it'll be?" Mrs. Littlefield twisted what remained of the tissue in her hands.

"Heart surgeries are delicate, dear. Dr. Addington is a meticulous surgeon. I'm sure he's taking his time to ensure perfection." Dr. Littlefield drew his petite wife under his arm.

A lady, wiping her face and blowing her nose, slipped into the chapel and walked to the altar. There she knelt and stared at the cross while palming her hands.

"Code Blue in OR Room 2. Code Blue in OR Room 2." The operator spoke loud and clear on the overhead speaker.

"What's a Code Blue?" Mrs. Salucci lowered herself to a seat in a nearby pew.

"It means there's been a cardiac arrest. Someone's heart stopped in the OR, and they need the cardiac team for assistance." Wooziness overcame Saige. Her knees weakened. Holding onto the end of the pew, she slid down beside Mrs. Salucci.

Mrs. Littlefield gripped her husband's arm in an attempt to stand upright. They walked to the pew in front of Saige and Mrs. Salucci before taking seats the bench.

"How about if we pray?" Mrs. Salucci whispered.

Bowing their heads, they all held hands.

"Dear Lord," Mrs. Salucci began, "we know whether we're here on Earth or in heaven that You're with us, and we have nothing to fear. But it's our desire for Aiden to remain on Earth. He has so much left to accomplish in his doctoring world. Please guide Gray's hand so that he repairs Aiden's heart perfectly. Help Aiden to survive and heal, and if he's not the one experiencing the operating room problem, please heal the one who is. In Jesus' name, amen."

The lady at the altar wiped her eyes again.

"Thank you." Mr. Littlefield tipped his head at Mrs. Salucci.

"Have you met her?" Saige asked.

"Yes, we met Elena Salucci when she first arrived at the visitors lounge. Don't you remember?"

"I don't remember much of anything," Saige said.

"If you don't mind, I'll stay in here while you three check on Aiden." Mrs. Salucci walked to the altar and knelt beside the lady blowing her nose.

Dr. Littlefield waited for no one. He headed to the OR waiting area with Saige and his wife in tow. The three of them crowded the desk, waiting for the volunteer to acknowledge them. "Any word on Aiden Littlefield?" Dr. Littlefield peered down at the pleasant lady manning the phone.

The lady scanned a paper on the desk. "He was transported. I'll call you as soon as I know more."

"Thank you." Digging his hands deep in his jean pockets, Dr. Littlefield plodded to where Saige and his wife stood. "Where was Aiden transported? Not knowing anything is maddening. Where's Dr. Addington?"

"I'm behind you." Eyes peering at the floor, Gray walked toward Dr. Littlefield as the man finished ranting. "Let's go somewhere private." With his OR hat still on his head and his mask hanging from one ear, Gray led them to the enclosed partition at the rear of the room.

A sickening feeling gripped Saige. Her stomach churned. Was Aiden transported to—the morgue? Receptionists in the waiting area usually state where the patient was transported. But the lady didn't tell them. Why would Gray need to talk with them privately? To keep their wailing sounds to a minimum when he told them about Aiden's death? The short walk to the tiny room took forever. Her heart raced. Profuse sweat poured from her brow. The room spun. At the point where her wobbly legs moved like gel, she realized she was going down.

The next thing she remembered was Gray carrying her to a chair.

The waiting room receptionist entered the room and placed a cup to her lips. "Have some water."

Saige took a sip before looking up at Gray. "Tell us the truth, please. Don't sugarcoat it."

"Okay, I'm going to give it to you straight. Are you prepared?" Gray removed his paper operating room hat and wrung it with both hands.

"We're prepared as much as we can be." Mrs. Littlefield clutched her husband's leather jacket, and he covered her hands with his.

"You probably heard the Code Blue alert overhead." Gray smoothed his hair from his forehead.

Saige couldn't wait another second for the news. "Tell us! What happened?"

"That Code Blue was for a patient in another operating room. Aiden's surgery was textbook perfect."

"Will he pull through?" Mrs. Littlefield asked.

"That's up to Aiden. His damaged heart valve caused too much blood to back up, which caused his shortness of breath and congestive heart failure. His heart should function well now."

Dr. Littlefield clapped Gray on the shoulder. "I wish he'd listened to his cardiologist after he left home."

"It must have been difficult not participating in sports. I don't fault him for having the desire." Gray was professional, but he made little eye contact with Saige. Why would he? She'd assured him she was marrying Aiden. And he was marrying Lilith. End of story.

"Can we see him?" Mrs. Littlefield pleaded with Gray, desperate to see her son as any mother would be after surgery.

"He's in the recovery room now. After the nurses settle him in the ICU, one person at a time can stop in to see him for a minute. No longer. Please, allow him to rest tonight. He'll be medicated, so he might not be aware he has company."

"I can't thank you enough for keeping an eye on him over the weekend and getting him into surgery so quickly." Saige squeezed Gray's hand, lingering before releasing it. He'd lived up to his promise to set his feelings aside and perform a meticulous surgery. She wanted to hug him and not let go, but it wasn't an option.

Gray gently rubbed the nape of his neck, his brown hair flipping above his fingers. "I always remember my mission when I go to the OR. Nothing stops me from performing the best surgery possible. Will I see you at the party Saturday night, Saige?"

"If Aiden is stable, I'll be there."

TWENTY-SEVEN

The new jingle on Saige's cell phone repeated several times the following morning while her eyes fluttered open. Lounging under the covers in her boarding house bedroom, she stretched for the phone then checked the screen for the caller. Pop's picture smiled back at her. He'd been calling almost every day. "Hello, Pop."

He asked the usual questions before adding, "Christmas won't be the same without your mother, Saige. Can't you spare a day to come home and celebrate with us?" He usually ended all pleas with a sniffle or two, but this time he added three.

Saige tucked the ivy-print comforter under her chin. With Aiden in the hospital, she had no ride. "I'll try to make it home today, Pop, but I might have to ask Gray for a ride. He's the other doctor I told you about at the clinic. His parents were killed in a car accident a couple days ago. It might do him some good to visit the farm." She stared up at the matching canopy over the bed.

"I'm so sorry about his loss, Saige. We'd be happy for him to visit. Maybe we can comfort him the same way we were comforted after your mom passed."

"That's what I was hoping." She quickly ended the call to avoid reliving her loss, but her focus landed on her wrist. "Please, God, help me find the keepsake from my mother. I can't bear Christmas without it." She rubbed the bare spot, recalling the inner strength she had gathered not to jump to conclusions when Lilith waltzed into the bathroom at the karaoke bar wearing a similar bracelet. The following day, Saige

179

called jewelry stores in the area to learn more about the piece. Millions of women had purchased the white gold, diamond-embedded bracelet around the same time her mother bought hers. There was only one sure way to discover who owned Lilith's bracelet—check the engraving on the underside. But how could Saige make that happen?

She'd have to find the courage to tell Gray about her accident at the party in order to ask him about the bracelet. What would he think of her when he realized she was the selectee invited to work with him at the Addington Complex, and she was also the one and only bumbling idiot—nay, talk of the town—who ruined his fancy Christmas party?

She looked at the time on her cell phone as she rolled to the edge of the bed. The morning was speeding by. She'd spent Tuesday evening and the entire day Wednesday at the hospital, taking turns watching over Aiden while his parents slept. Since he handled the surgery without any complications and Nurse Oswald reported that he was doing well at 5:00 this morning, now seemed to be the perfect opportunity for her to make an overnight trip home for a brief Christmas celebration.

Hmm. What about transportation? Before the dinner fiasco, Gray mentioned he would drive her home if she needed a ride. The fresh air and slow-paced country life might soothe his grief, and her father said he was welcome. But would Gray mind staying overnight on the farm? She had forgotten about that little detail.

If he decided not to take her, she'd have to go by bus. She'd ridden many of them home during medical school. The trip was usually pleasant enough, but it took twice as long to reach her destination. Her only other option would be to take a chance in Aiden's old clunker. But would the Bug make the trip without falling apart? Saige shuddered. Best to remove that option from her list.

She hopped out of bed and selected the other pair of jeans and sweatshirt she'd brought to the boarding house. Since she wore scrubs at the clinic, she hadn't needed many street clothes. Besides, her backpack wouldn't hold one iota more than what she'd crammed inside before she left her apartment.

She donned the clean clothes then checked the bus schedule—no trips to Marysville for four hours. It would take another six hours on the bus to make a three-hour trip. Regardless of the awkwardness involved in riding with him, she'd have to call Gray.

Wait a minute. She didn't have his phone number. She hurried down the stairs in her plaid PJs. Sweeping noises led her to the kitchen where she found Mrs. Salucci, broom in hand, dancing around the room to the tune of "Jingle Bell Rock" on the radio. She startled when Saige pushed through the swinging kitchen door.

"What can I help you with, Saige?" Mrs. Salucci used her wrist to push her bangs out of her eyes. Her wavy, shoulder-length hair created a soft, youthful look around her face despite her age.

"Next week is Christmas, and I haven't been home for a few weeks. Gray offered me a ride, but I don't have his phone number. It's unlisted."

Leaning on the broom handle, Mrs. Salucci paused for a few seconds. I guess you could call the Addington Complex or the free clinic."

"Gray is on vacation from the Complex. They'd never hand out his home number, and the free clinic isn't open on Thursdays." She fished in her back pocket for her cell phone. "Oh brother, why didn't I think of this in the first place. I can call Central Sinai's ICU. They'll have his phone number. He's Aidan's heart surgeon."

Nurse Oswald, who answered the phone, refused to give out the number. She said Saige's reason wasn't appropriate. After much pleading with her, the nurse agreed to call Dr. Gray and give him Saige's phone number with instructions to call her if he desired.

Within ten minutes, Saige's phone rang. "Hello?"

"It's awfully early in the morning. Did you need something?" The charming, though sluggish, British accent was unmistakable.

"Could you possibly give me a ride home today? We'd stay the night and return tomorrow. I haven't seen my family during the entire Christmas season."

"Does this mean you're no longer mad at me?" Gray's sleep-infused voice cleared a little.

"I'm still upset, but we need to talk. We'll have plenty of time on the road."

181

"I remember you had a confession. What is it, Saige? Are you a mass murderer?"

"That's not funny, Gray. Don't joke about something like that. I'm nothing of the kind. There are some things about me you'll want to know, though. Can you pick me up shortly?"

"Sure, no problem. What do I wear?"

"Do you have any jeans and sweatshirts? We don't dress fancy."

"I don't own any. Will my clothes do?"

"Bring your cowboy hat. We'll figure out clothes when we get to the farm."

An hour later, Saige spotted his BMW at the boarding house curb as she peered through her bedroom window. He opened the car door and stepped out, dressed in business clothes under his unbuttoned coat, western hat perched firmly on his head.

Mrs. Salucci let him in downstairs. "Welcome, Gray. Please come in and make yourself comfortable. Saige, your company is here." Her gentle voice traveled up to Saige's room.

Saige grabbed her backpack and hurried down to the living room to find Gray relaxing on one of the overstuffed chairs across from the sofa. The wood fire danced in the fireplace with Christmas stockings hanging on each end of the mantle. Mrs. Salucci had purchased and decorated a real Christmas tree in fake apples, red-plaid bows, and cinnamon sticks while Saige spent time with Aiden at the hospital over the last two days. The apple-pie spices permeated the room.

"Shall I serve coffee and Christmas cookies? I made them early this morning." Mrs. Salucci wiped her hands on her apron.

"Thank you, I'd love to enjoy them, but we need to be going. My family's farm is a three-hour trip."

"Of course, Saige. I understand. Maybe another time." Mrs. Salucci rose from her comfy chair and walked to the door.

Gray lagged behind Saige as she exited, but she turned and spied him hugging Mrs. Salucci. "I'd enjoy having your delicious coffee and Christmas cookies when we return."

Saige dug her hands in her pockets. "Hurry up, Gray, we need to scoot." She hopped down the porch's bottom step.

After Gray opened the passenger door for her, they settled into his BMW, and he stepped on the gas pedal. "Can you tell me what's so important now, Saige? I'm dying to know."

She kindled her hands together for warmth before turning up the heat on her side of the car. "I've been trying to tell you this for more than a week, Gray. Can you look at me for a second?"

Gray shifted his eyes at her. "What is it? Will I think differently about you?"

"That depends."

"On what?" Gray looked back and forth from the road to Saige every few seconds.

"On who you want for a cardiology partner."

A truck passed Gray and nearly sideswiped him. He pulled over to the shoulder of the road and focused on her. "What do you mean? I don't understand."

Saige removed a gold-edged card from her coat pocket. "Recognize this? I received it before I volunteered at the clinic. I won the spot on your cardiology team."

"You're the candidate my team selected?" Gray's face lit up.

"Yes. It's what I was trying to tell you at the free clinic."

Gray lifted the cowboy hat off of his head as he shouted, "Yahoo!" A grin spread over his face. "Did I say that right?"

"You almost got it right. Old-timers say, 'Yippee!' But nowadays people say, Woo-hoo! or Woot, Woot!"

"Saige, your news is beyond wonderful. I couldn't be happier." He slapped the steering wheel in his excitement. "Why didn't you tell me sooner?"

"I've tried. I was nervous about sharing it because I bossed you around after calling you an orderly at the clinic."

"I'll never forget that day as long as I live. You're an amazing doctor. Anyone would be proud to have you on their cardiology team. You treat patients and their family members with kindness and respect, and after Aiden fell, you administered CPR to him more decisively than any doctor I've ever seen. From that day on, I regretted not having a say-so in my team's selection. I'm more than happy they chose you. This is fantastic news."

"Thank you. I'm grateful you're not upset. But I do have one more thing to tell you. After that, you might think differently about me."

Grays forehead wrinkled as his eyes clouded. "What is it, Saige. You can tell me anything."

The phone rang.

"Who would call me today? I don't have any surgeries scheduled for a few weeks, my partner is on call for Aiden, and Lilith already called me earlier." Gray tapped *accept* on his hands-free cellular.

"Is this Dr. Edgar Addington?"

"Speaking."

"Thomas Newman, here—your father's attorney. My office has received official confirmation that it was indeed your parents who lost their lives in the car crash. I'm so sorry, Dr. Addington."

"I…I don't know what to say. The whole accident has been a terrible shock. Thank you for letting me know."

"There's more, sir. Your father updated his will several weeks ago, before he flew to Europe with your mother. He stipulated that if anything happened to them, I was to immediately read the document to you and your servants at the mansion. He prepaid me handsomely to cut through red tape."

"When do you propose we meet?" Gray raised his hand, gesturing an apology to Saige for the interruption.

His news was of utmost importance. She shook her head at him, letting him know to take his time.

The lawyer continued his instructions. "Saturday at noon in the living room if that suits you, sir."

"It's perfect. I'll let my staff know." Gray ended the call but leaned back against his headrest.

Saige ached for him having to deal with the horrible death of his parents. She hoped the trip to her family's farm would not only help his heart to heal but also prepare his head for whatever would come to pass in the will.

For the remainder of the trip to her family farm, Saige sat quietly in the passenger seat until they reached the outskirts of Marysville. But Gray continued pouring out memories about his upbringing with Adele and Fernsby, sharing how his dignified parents had little time for him except at dinner. The sun shone through clear skies as Saige allowed him to vent.

She had needed opportunities to discuss her feelings with anyone who would listen after her mother passed away. Many of her friends had said, "I know you'll want to grieve in private," and "I don't want to bother you while your mother's loss is so fresh in your mind."

Saige had wanted to scream, "Quit shoving me into a dark space and closing the door. I don't want to mourn alone." She would have given anything to share the things she missed most about her mom. Instead of bottling up her feelings and throwing them into the Prince Charles River, she had wanted to talk, talk, talk about them.

Her family doctor had wisely advised her to do so. "If you express your sorrow, you'll sleep better, eat better, and heal from depression." Saige accepted his advice, and she and her family shared events about her mom in the evenings.

Saige was determined to help Gray heal.

"You want to know what I'll remember most about my parents?"

"What, Gray?"

"They were pleasant but always formal, and they were sticklers for manners." A pickup truck passed him on the two-lane highway. "Miss Dell was my au pair until I went to the university. I believe she and Fernsby taught me to be the man I am today. They followed traditions and manners but always made room for breaking them." Gray chuckled.

"What's so funny?"

"Fernsby was a character while I was growing up—but only when he was out of my parents' sight. The things he did made me laugh every day. But when his hair turned white, he seemed to lose a portion of his humor. On some days, he's a downright curmudgeon."

"Turn left down that road. It's our lane." Saige pointed to a dirt road surrounded by snow-covered fields.

Gray seemed lighter in his countenance after he drove the half-mile to Saige's yellow two-story farmhouse. The second he turned off the engine, she hopped from the car. "Come on in, Gray. I want you to meet my family."

She led him up the steps of the wrap-around porch. Despite the snow in the yard, her father or brother had shoveled the porch and sidewalk.

The door flew open.

"Hey, Saige!" Clad in jeans and a pullover sweater, Annie ran down the steps. Intercepting Saige at the bottom, she wrapped her in a hug. "I've got so much to tell you, sis." She peered over Saige's shoulder at Gray. "Is this who I think it is?"

"Yes, he's the surgeon who performed Aiden's surgery." Saige turned to face him, her face beaming with praise. "This is Gray."

"Thanks for saving Aiden. I'm Annie." Gray extended his hand, but Annie pulled him in for a hug like the one she gave Saige.

The door opened again, and a strapping man with mousy brown hair barreled down the steps. "Hey, sis." He caught her under his arm and squeezed, lifting her off the ground, but his eyes were on Gray. "Is he the man you've told me so much about?"

"It is. Gray runs the Addington Complex with his father, and he performed heart valve surgery on Aiden." Saige pinched Gray's arm through his coat. "He's the best around."

"We'll have to see about that. I believe my sister is the best cardiologist around." Liam administered a playful punch to Gray's arm, then he shoved his bare hands into his jacket pockets. "It's cold out here. Let's head inside."

Pop entered the foyer from the kitchen as Saige walked through the front door. He threw his dishtowel over his shoulder to empty his arms for her. She clung to his pillowy waist, not wanting to let go. "I've been away too long, Pop. Can you forgive me? You can't imagine my workload."

"Darlin', we'll take any Saige time we can get." He squeezed her tighter while eyeing Gray. "And who is this young man?"

"This is the guy I told you about. Since I don't have a car, he brought me home for a visit." She glanced at Gray, sending him an unspoken message to relax. "Gray lost his parents recently. I knew he'd find understanding here."

"You betcha. We know about loss, my boy. Make yourself at home." Pop clapped him on the shoulder. "Yes, sir. Pour out your heart, Gray. We're here for you, son, and we're good listeners."

"I-I don't know what to say." Gray scratched his dimpled chin before angling his head at Saige with raised eyebrows. "But thank you for your kindness," he added.

Liam appeared with two cups of cider. "You don't have to say anything, or you can talk your head off. It's up to you, friend." He handed Gray a mug of the steaming drink before handing one to Saige. "Why don't you make yourselves comfortable in the living room until dinner."

Happiness filled Saige to the point of bursting when she walked into the living room. The place was exactly the way her mother had decorated it for Christmas for as long as she could remember. A real evergreen tree occupied a corner of the room with the same keepsake ornaments commemorating Christmas milestones through the years. Saige and her siblings handmade most of them. As she contemplated her hard work at the university hospital, the clinic, Aiden's accident, and his surgery, her worries faded away. She was home.

TWENTY-EIGHT

Gray barely had time to set his cider on the coffee table before a two-foot-tall Australian sheepdog, wielding sixty-some pounds of hair, bounded into the room, knocking him to the carpet, and slurping his cheeks. "He sure is a friendly dog." Between fits of laughter, Gray wrestled the hound on the floor to stop it from bathing his face. "How do I make him quit?"

"Sit, James." Liam ruffled the dog's black and white fur, but James refused to obey, preferring to lick his owner instead. "No treat." Liam eased into a worn recliner chair, cider in hand.

"James?" Gray pushed up from the floor, wiping the gallon of slime from his face.

"He's named after the father of psychology, William James. Didn't Saige tell you I'm a psychologist?" The dog circled the room, panting, before lying by the recliner.

"We haven't had much time to talk." Gray made himself comfortable in a rocking chair near the sofa where Saige and Annie sat.

Liam, with his ankle propped across his knee, sipped from his cup before narrowing his eyes at Gray. "Now that you've been here for a few minutes, how about sharing your intentions with my sister."

"Whoa! We're just friends, everyone. Stop asking so many questions." Saige flopped her hand on her sister's knees. "Annie, what's your big news?"

The attractive girl, maybe ten years younger than Saige, resembled her sister with fawn-brown hair, hazel eyes, and a heart-shaped face.

189

After tucking a foot under her bottom, Annie scooted sideways on the sofa to face Saige and Gray. "Okay, here's the deal. I've decided to become a nurse. I've already taken the prerequisites during my first two years of college. And I can start the nursing program in January."

Saige wrapped her arms around Annie and squeezed. "That's wonderful news. Mom would be so proud of you. I can't wait to hear every detail when we go to our room tonight."

She eyed Gray then glanced at Liam. "Do you have a pair of jeans and a sweatshirt Gray can borrow, so he'll be comfortable outside?"

"I'd appreciate it." Gray waved his hand over his expensive pants and pullover V-neck sweater. "These might be a little formal for farm work."

"Sure. Follow me." Gray left the room with Liam and returned a short while later clad in jeans and a University of Michigan sweatshirt. "It's my alma mater," Liam told Gray.

"Looks like you two are about the same size." Saige rose from her spot on the sofa. "Pop says dinner will be ready in about an hour. Let's get our winter gear, Gray, and I'll take you on a tour outside."

The land was beautiful, even while blanketed with snow. Saige showed him the chicken coop and the fields where her father planted corn in the spring to sell to local merchants. An enormous family garden lay near the house. Although it was buried in snow, Saige gave Gray the rundown on the various seeds they planted to yield food for their shelves. Down from the house, she showed him an apple orchard devoid of leaves. "These are the sweetest tasting varieties you'll find anywhere. We use them to make pies, apple butter, and cider for the local market. And directly behind the house, in separate areas, we have blueberry, raspberry, and blackberry bushes. My mom used to can everything."

Farm life seemed demanding of time, but Gray marveled at their means of harvesting abundant produce to sustain the family and provide food for the community. Saige's eyes lit up as she spoke about the dense woods that shaded areas of the land in the spring, summer, and part of the fall. She led him on a path through the trees, which included evergreens. "I used to take walks out here when I needed time to think. Imagine being surrounded by peace and quiet after the hustle and bustle of the city."

"It's beautiful. I'd love to visit when everything's in bloom."

"You'd enjoy it, Gray. We could have a picnic." She led him to an area with fallen logs. "Liam cleared this space. I used to bring a basket of food then spread out a blanket and read to Annie for hours under the cool shade trees. We devoured the entire Chronicles of Narnia series one summer."

Gray had seen woods and farms from afar when traveling with his parents or Fernsby, but he'd never visited them. As he listened to Saige share memories, he yearned for the pleasure of growing up on her farm instead of being tormented with strict dos and don'ts while living in a pristine mansion.

Much to his chagrin, Saige ended the serene tour and doubled back on the path. "Let's head to the barn." They trudged through the snow until they reached the enormous reddish-brown building.

"We keep it slightly heated for our animals. It'll be chilly inside, but warmer than it is out here." Saige showed Gray the stalls housing pigs and cows. When she came to a black and white cow in an end stall, she introduced Gray. "Meet Fanny Mae. She's been my personal pet for years. I helped calf her then I bottle-fed the little heifer when her mother died after birth. For several months, I slept with her to keep her company after her loss—did you know that cows cry? It's true. She mourned for her mother. I stroked her head throughout the night. In the mornings Fanny would nudge me awake to take her out to pasture."

The cow placed its large, wet nostrils under Saige's hand. She stroked its black and white hair until Fanny sloshed her tongue at Saige, as though thanking her for the attention.

"I'll show you another place I used to enjoy." Saige climbed a ladder to the loft. "Join me up here, Gray."

She leaned over the rail and waited for him to reach the top. After he stepped into the vast space filled with hay bales, she led him to a cleared spot on the side. "This is where I used to come in the winter to get away from everyone, especially when I was mad or sad. It was my alone space. No one bothered me up here." She sat on a bale and motioned for Gray to sit on the one beside her.

"I can see where it would be fairly private." Gray looked around at the wood floors and walls—nothing but hay and more hay filled the space.

A meow came from behind them. Saige searched between bales for the feline. "Several times over the years, our barn cats have had babies up here. I watched them grow from tiny nuggets to noisy kittens and on to full-grown cats. The circle of life is amazing on a farm." On finding the gray-and-white bundle of fur, Saige scooped it into her arms and cuddled it to her neck.

"The whole farm is wonderful, Saige. I enjoyed the tour, but if you don't mind, can we talk about Aiden?"

TWENTY-NINE

As Gray contemplated how to begin his discussion with Saige, he crossed his legs at the ankles and pulled a piece of hay from the bale beneath him. Attempting to act like a laid-back cowboy, he stuffed the straw between his teeth and used it for a toothpick. He hoped it would make him appear relaxed, but instead, it made him cough and hack. "Listen, Saige. I fully expect Aiden to recover. In a few weeks, he'll have spinal surgery." He cleared his throat again.

"I know, Gray. Things are looking up for him." Saige sat on a scratchy hay bale in her jeans, with her foot under her thigh. "Won't be long until I'm Mrs. Littlefield, or rather, Dr. Littlefield."

"That's what I wanted to discuss."

"We've talked about it until there isn't anything left to discuss. Life doesn't always turn out the way we expect. Even the best-laid plans develop snags." Saige scratched the kitten behind its ears.

"What about Mrs. Salucci's lifelong regret?"

"She settled. So what? We all settle for something."

"We shouldn't settle for love." A mouse scuttled across the floor. Gray watched it scurry under a hay pile and hoped it wouldn't return. "Do you believe we need to use wisdom for our choices? Aiden made you laugh at the clinic. You were comfortable with him. But seriously, I never saw stars in your eyes. I can make you smile too."

"You and Aiden are vastly different. He doesn't have a lick of romance in his veins. And he couldn't be serious if he tried."

"Am I too serious?"

"You're a little more intellectual."

"Is that a bad thing?"

"Not at all. I enjoy that you're serious at the right moments." Saige shifted on her hay bale. "It's fun to watch you loosen up. But will you convert back to Mr. Prim and Proper when you grow older?"

"I think my time with you has changed the way I see life. I'll never be the same again." Gray walked to where she sat and took a seat beside her. "I no longer desire my life the way it's been. It's boring and filled with pretentiousness. People aren't who they seem to be. They create a mask, even a wall, that makes them appear better than others. But I've learned it's all a sham. The happiest people in the world are the people who open up to others and share their souls. People who dress down and not up. The wealthiest individuals I know worry about where their next dollar will come from to keep up appearances—when they can't even seem to be themselves."

"I'm a little confused, Gray. But I know you're being sincere. Have you been pretentious?"

Why did she have to pry? Lilith kept her conversations at surface level, but Saige had to dig down deep and demand that he open his soul. It made him feel uncomfortable, exposed. "I've obeyed my parents' rules. Dr. Addington insisted I learn to save money and learn the social graces. They were rich—we come from wealth handed down through the centuries. I can't say that about Lilith and her parents. Through the years, she's strutted her clothes, cars, and belongings for the world to take notice. Their mansion is the largest and most elaborately decorated in St. Anne's Landing. Gold fixtures, you name it; they have it in spades. I wondered for years why her father often came to the Addington mansion. Shortly after Mr. LaRue would arrive, he and my father would retire to my father's professional study. I wanted to listen at the door, but Mr. LaRue always brought Lilith with him. She monopolized my time."

"You called your father by his surname just now. How come?"

Gray stood and leaned against the loft railing. "It slips out sometimes because people call him Dr. Addington or the senior Dr. Addington. I've never had a loving connection with him. He and my mother were stiff and formal. His motto was: 'Maintain your manners!' I believe what he meant was—maintain your manners at all costs." Gray gripped a rake leaning against the loft railing and used it to redirect loose straw strewn about the floor into orderly piles.

Saige hugged her arms as she shivered. "I'm sorry about your upbringing, Gray, but I'm glad you're looking for a better way."

"What comes to mind when you think of me, Saige?"

"Hair gel, expensive cologne, manners—like you said."

"What about Aiden? What does he bring to mind?"

"Tacos, body fumes, and laughter."

"Is he your guy—the man of your dreams?"

"Gray, I don't know."

"You have to know. You have to be sure."

"Since you're giving me the third-degree, tell me what you love about Lilith."

"Uh, she's beautiful. Her lips are full. She's a pro at social graces."

"Is that all? Because I can think of a good one—she leads you around by the snout like a pig going to slaughter."

"Not fair."

"Isn't it?"

Saige stood, rubbed her hands, and jogged in place, trying to rev up her body heat against the cold. "There ought to be a way we can know for sure if we're making the right choices."

Gray put his hands on her shoulders and stopped her activity. "I know a way. Hold still, Saige. This isn't going to hurt." He leaned in as she stared into his eyes, quirking her brows as though she wondered if he was checking for a splinter, but he made it to her mouth and softly pressed his lips against hers.

She didn't draw away this time. She threw her arms around his neck and kissed him deeply.

"Are you kids in the loft?" Just when they made headway at uncovering true love, Saige's brother, Liam, shouted, "Come on down from there. Dinner's on the table!"

Gray climbed down the ladder behind Saige, and they followed Liam to the two-story farmhouse with the wrap-around porch. The farm and the house put on no airs. Nothing fancy about them, especially not the people on the inside.

In the casual dining room, Mr. Westbrook had covered the oval oak dining table with serving platters and bowls of food. Mouth-watering aromas emanated from breaded pork chops, potatoes with mushroom gravy, potato rolls, and roasted carrots. "This looks delicious." Gray licked his lips on his way to the table.

"Annie and Liam helped me. I can't take the credit." Mr. Westbook took a seat at the head of the table then motioned to the others. "Let's all sit down and dig in."

After he said grace, he passed the food dishes to his left. And keeping in step with Liam, Gray filled his plate to overflowing. The walk in the woods had stirred up his appetite.

With their plates filled, Saige and her family broke into animated conversation. Liam shared about meeting a nice girl he might want to settle down with; Annie gabbed about nursing school; Gray brought them up to the minute about Aiden and how Saige saved his life, then she discussed the work they did at the inner-city clinic, and her pop rounded out the friendly banter by reminiscing about his wife and the meals she used to cook.

"If I can offer one piece of advice, Gray, never stop sharing the good times about your parents. Grief comes from fear that you've lost them, but memories keep them alive. Don't let their lights fizzle, son, share their stories." Mr. Westbrook picked up his pork chop and took a bite.

"Good advice." Gray eyed the man's approach to eating, feeling a little uncomfortable with the idea of using his fingers. But not wanting to offend his host, he set down his fork and knife, lifted his chop to his mouth, and took a bite. Eating meat directly off the bone was more satisfying than he could have imagined. He finished the chop and speared another one from the platter.

Before dessert, Mr. Westbrook and the others cleared the table, then he left the room but returned with a large box and set it on the floor while Liam, Annie, and Saige chattered about their past. Gray enjoyed hearing their stories of sibling rivalry. Teasing a brother or sister was something he could only imagine, but the tales made him laugh out loud.

Mr. Westbrook began dinging his water glass with his knife handle. "May I have your attention, dear family?"

Saige whispered in Gray's ear, "We do this every Christmas."

Unsure of what to expect, Gray eyed the box with suspicion. What did it hold?

Mr. Westbrook rose from his seat. "I usually do the honors, Gray. A few days before Christmas, we share gag gifts to get us into the holiday spirit. The family members sitting around this table placed the gifts in the box."

Pop dug into it and lifted out a package, then he read the card. "This gift is for the person in our group who can't get enough of the old God-father movies. In fact, this person has watched them over fifty times."

Everyone at the table turned to Liam. He raised his hands in surrender. "Guilty as charged. What can I say?" Pop passed him the gift, and Liam tore through the wrapping paper. "This better be good." He lifted the lid and peered inside before laughing like a hyena. "Everyone, close your eyes."

A bit of shuffling took place. "Okay, open them." Liam rose from his seat with a rubber horse head mask over his head. He let out a few whinnies, curled his hands like hooves, and pawed the ground with his foot while the group laughed. "This is the perfect gift."

"Okay, who do you think put this one in the box for you?" His father asked.

Liam studied each person at the table for a few seconds. "I guess it would have to be my co-Godfather enthusiast. None other than—you, Pop."

Everyone had a good laugh. "I wouldn't have known anything about the Godfather if Pop hadn't introduced me to the old 1970s gangster movies." Liam removed the rubber mask from his head. "This is a keeper." He laughed again at the mask's details. "I can't promise someone won't find it in his or her bed if they misbehave."

Gray recognized the reference to an event that happened in the first Godfather movie. It wasn't a pleasant scene, but the gag gift was definitely funny.

"Next!" Pop reached into the carton and pulled out another gift. "This one is for a family member a lonely celebrity approached asking for friendship, not only because he was lonely, but also because he wanted her to invest in his motorcycle company."

Saige covered her face. "No, no!" Her pop and her siblings pointed at her while howling with laughter. Her father tossed her the gift. She groaned as she unwrapped it. "A pillow? This isn't so bad," She wrapped her arms around it.

"You've got to brush the cloth on the front for the celebrity to appear." Annie leaned forward on her elbows and brushed the pillow in a downward direction. Nothing happened.

"Yeah, you have to rub the pillow because he's hiding in there, just like he was hiding on the internet." Liam howled with laughter.

"Huh?" Gray didn't get the joke.

Saige brushed the material in the opposite direction. A face appeared on the pillow. She held it up for everyone to see. "It's Keanu Reeves!" Annie shouted.

"Hoo boy!" Saige covered her face with the pillow.

"Yeah, he even sent her a picture of his fake driver's license to prove he was trustworthy so she'd send him a thousand dollars!"

Saige laughed. "Okay. Okay, you guys got me on that one. I was a hopeless dork. He said he was a lonely movie star, and I fell for it. I'm a sucker for sad sack scammers."

Gray roared with laughter this time. Little by little he was learning about the gullible, soft side of Saige's character.

"Annie bought this one for me, didn't you?" Saige tilted her head with a sideways glance at her sister.

Annie sheepishly nodded. "How could I resist?"

After two more gifts, Pop removed the last one. "The card on this one says it's for a reindeer."

Gray wanted to crawl under the table. What would the gift be—

LOVE CALLS THE SHOTS

antlers, a basketball, handcuffs? Maybe a subpoena to appear in court regarding Aiden's accident?

"The card also says that I'm to carefully hand it to the person. Who's the reindeer in our group?"

Gray lowered his head. Saige nudged him with her elbow. "It's for you, Gray,"

"You shouldn't have, Saige. I mean, really. You. Shouldn't. Have."

"Take it, Gray."

He hesitantly accepted it from her pop then ripped open the candy cane paper with the red bow on top. Reluctantly, he removed the lid. Inside the box were twelve milk chocolate-covered strawberries. He shook his head. "How…w-why? I'm in shock."

"Maria told me about your favorite sweet treat. Are they what you like?"

"They're perfect!" Gray selected one and sunk his teeth into the chocolate and strawberry deliciousness. "Mmm." His most cherished treat in the world.

He recalled what he'd said to Fernsby about one's true love being the person for whom you'd give your last chocolate-covered strawberry. Saige was that girl for him. She just didn't know it yet.

THIRTY

Before breakfast, Saige awoke to find that Liam had asked Gray to help milk cows in the barn. She threw on her clothes and headed out with them until Annie tugged her to the chicken coop. As they gathered eggs, Annie opened up about her hopes and plans for college, nursing, and a career. "Someday, I might even find the man of my dreams." She tossed Saige an egg to set in her basket.

"What's he like—the man of your dreams?" Saige wanted to know for her own sake—to judge if she was on the right track with Aiden and Gray.

"My dream guy will love my quirkiness." Annie picked a feather from an egg and gently placed her find in the basket. "He'll cherish the person I am, despite my faults. I want a man who kisses me last thing before heading out the door in the morning and hurries home to me every evening. A man who understands me more than I understand myself. A soul mate."

Annie's passion was almost palpable. Saige wanted those things, too, but was Aiden that man for her, or was it Gray? Aiden cherished her, but would she enjoy spending her life in an impoverished country? Or would it grow old?

On the other hand, what about Mr. Manners? Gray tried to loosen up over the last few days, that was obvious. But he had no more control over the way he acted than Saige had over her farm girl ways. Could two people from vastly different cultures fall in love—and more importantly, stay in love?

"Thanks for sharing, Annie. I hope you find your man."

Saige scanned the yard for any signs of Gray.

Trudging up the path from the barn in rubber work boots provided by Pop, Gray raised his hand to greet her. "Can you believe I milked a cow?" He held up a metal bucket half-filled with sloshing milk. "Wasn't as difficult as I expected—just time consuming."

Liam bypassed him with two full milk pails, one in each hand. "You did good, buddy, for a first-timer."

"Hey, how about we go inside and eat breakfast?" Annie bounced up the steps, swinging her basket.

Pop opened the door when she reached the porch. "Careful with those eggs!"

"Sure, Pop." Annie led the way into their home with a little less enthusiasm as Saige walked behind her. Liam and Gray circled to the back of the house to remove their boots and wash up in the mud room.

"Breakfast!" Pop hollered.

Within minutes Saige, Gray, and her siblings converged in the dining room, slid into chairs at the table, and began enjoying the feast her pop had prepared—biscuits, sausage, gravy, scrambled eggs, and pancakes. Excited chatter filled the room while Saige, Gray, and her family discussed lives and plans. Gray listened and interjected his thoughts here and there.

After breakfast, each person carried dishes and bowls to the sink, still gabbing about things that mattered. Gray had a look of yearning on his face, as though he would've loved to have grown up in her household. Annie placed the items in the dishwasher like old times while Liam snagged Gray to help him clean the oak table and laminated kitchen countertops.

"I sure miss our family teamwork." Pop swept the last crumbs into a dustpan. "We completed the job in record time."

Much as Saige desired to stay, she had things to do. She hugged Pop then hung her dishtowel on the stove handle. "We've had a great time everyone. Sorry, but we need to be going. Gray has to check on Aiden at the hospital, and I need to pay him a visit. If Gray wouldn't mind stopping by my apartment on the way home first, I'll clear my things out so Darcy's new roomie can move in." She glanced at Gray to judge his reaction.

"No problem, Saige. I'd be happy to help you."

Two hours down the road, Gray followed Saige's directions to her apartment building with taupe siding and white trim. From the apartment they would have a short trip to St. Anne's Landing, but first, Saige would load up her belongings.

After Gray parked, she led him to her place on the second floor. "There's not much in here that belongs to me except for some clothes, shoes, toiletries, and a few books, so we should get in and out in no time."

The interior of her apartment reminded Gray of a TV "tiny" home—cramped but stylish, yet the furnishings appeared ready for the furniture graveyard. That fact didn't faze him as he scooped up a box Saige had quickly filled. "I'll carry this load to my car. Keep them coming."

True to her word, Saige owned very few clothes and shoes compared to Lilith's vast wardrobe. Gray had rarely seen Lilith wear the same outfit twice in a given year. But she always looked beautiful, much like a painted doll in a display case. Saige, on the other hand, wore little to no makeup, but with her creamy pale complexion, pink cheeks, and heart-shaped face, she was gorgeous au naturel.

Gray returned and carried three more loads to his car before taking a seat on a mismatched kitchen chair. "Mind if I rest a minute?"

Saige joined him at the table. "Would you care for a drink?"

"Sure, what do you have?"

She opened her refrigerator, staring at the lack of contents. "Let's see. I have water on the rocks, filtered water, water with a slice of lemon, bottled water, and plain water."

"I wouldn't want you to go to any trouble on my account. How about making it simple?"

Saige removed the filtered water pitcher and poured several ounces into a clear glass. As she worked, Gray observed her movements. She was sure of herself. He liked that about her. She also had a servant's heart. He noticed that by the way she fussed over Aiden at the hospital. What was there not to like about her?

Why had he been so stupid, saying he'd ask Lilith to marry him? Honestly? He did it out of retaliation. Saige promised to become a missionary with Aiden. He wanted to hurt her as badly as she hurt him. Trouble was, she probably didn't even know that her words caused his heart to ache. How could he marry bossy Lilith? Saige was right. Lilith dragged him around by his snout. If he'd had another girlfriend growing up, he might have recognized Lilith's behavior as undesirable, but he was a nerd, an intellectual pinhead. As a young man he had struggled to grow into his height as well as his brain.

Up until he met Lilith, he buried his head in books and a few sports. He never should have allowed her to push him into a relationship. She took advantage of his ignorance in the dating world. Going to an all-boys school hadn't helped his shyness around females either. And now, he pledged to marry the old chain jerker. He told Saige he would ask Lilith at the Addington family Christmas party this coming Saturday. Tomorrow. Did he have the nerve to go through with it? He had little more than twenty-four hours to convince Saige not to marry Aiden. If he couldn't change her mind, he'd concede to hand her over to him and be done with his whole effort to win her heart.

But didn't things in life happen for a reason? Why did he meet Saige? She possessed a fierceness to stand by her promises. He had never met another person with such conviction and fortitude to remain faithful.

She handed him the filled glass then poured one for herself. Saddened by the way things turned out with Saige and Aiden, Gray slumped in his chair, barely wanting to move. "I wonder what would have happened between us if you had volunteered at the free clinic without Aiden, Saige?"

"I wouldn't have known about the free clinic if it weren't for Aiden. He's the reason I volunteered." She sipped her water, slowly, politely.

"I understand. Have you and he always been together?"

She slipped into a chair next to his and folded her arms on the thrift shop table. "We've never truly been together. I always considered him a friend. Aiden was almost engaged to Darcy at one time."

"Really? What happened?"

"The three of us met when we started college back in our freshman year. After Aiden and Darcy hit it off, they dated for several years. I was envious of their relationship for a long time. They rarely went anywhere without each other, and I was usually their tag-a-long dateless friend. But one day, about five years into their relationship, Aiden discovered Darcy cheating on him with an aspiring comedian—a lawyer—at The Comedy Den. It broke Aiden's heart. I've never seen a grown man wail, but Aiden sobbed from the depths of his heart. First, he was in shock—he kept repeating, 'How could Darcy do this to me?' I felt badly for him because there didn't seem to be a reason for Darcy to cheat. But the more I consoled him, the more he leaned on me, and the more that happened, the more he became attached to me."

"Did you ever ask Darcy what happened—why she cheated?" Gray stretched out in his chair with his hands laced behind his head.

"Yeah. I did. She was sorry about it and wished it never happened. Aiden forgave her but wouldn't take her back because of why she did it. She said Aiden wasn't romantic enough. I have to admit, she's right on that front. But Aiden's the nicest guy a girl could ever meet. Is there any man on the face of the earth who has every single quality a girl wants?"

"I guess not. Sorry about Aiden getting burned. Darcy should have told him her desires. How could he know what she expected if she didn't tell him? Men don't read minds, you know."

"I guess they're the same as women then." She downed the rest of her water.

"Would you like to know what I'm thinking, Saige?" Gray cleared his throat and leaned forward in his chair, hoping she'd open up but trying not to intimidate her.

She rose from the table and collected their empty water glasses. After placing them in the sink, she slowly turned to face him. "If I hadn't made a promise to Aiden and God, I'd love to know what you're thinking. But I can't risk having to break my promise."

Gray walked the few steps to the kitchen where Saige leaned against a cabinet. He placed his arms on either side of her, bracing his hands on the countertop. "What about our kiss yesterday? Didn't that mean anything to you?"

Saige turned her eyes from his. He felt her pulling away. "I wanted that kiss as much as you did, Gray. I feel like our hearts are two magnets drawn together from opposite poles. It takes all my strength to push you away, but you have to respect the oath I made to God. He brought Aiden through the heart surgery and healed his paralysis. Now, I have to live up to my end of the bargain. I cannot and will not break my promise to Aiden and especially not to God. Our kiss yesterday shouldn't have happened."

Gray moved away from her, his face downcast, his hands in his pockets. "My heart is broken, but I understand. Can we be friends, though? I'd cherish your friendship."

"As long as you understand—we can never be an item as long as Aiden lives." Saige covered her mouth and left the kitchen, but within minutes, sniffles erupted from her bedroom.

He pressed his thumbs against his eyelids, trying not to allow tears to flow. "I'm going outside for some fresh air."

"There's only one box left," she hollered from the bedroom. "We can head on out as soon as I bring it to your car."

His cell phone rang. He removed it from his pocket and checked the caller ID. Central Sinai Hospital. He only had one patient at the moment—Aiden. He put the call on speaker phone so Saige could hear. "Dr. Addington," he answered.

Saige appeared from the bedroom with a reddened nose. She eased down on the sofa and wrung the hem of her sweater as she listened.

"This is Nurse Oswald, Dr. Addington. We've got a problem."

THIRTY-ONE

Gray swung around to look at Saige, his brow creased as he listened to the nurse. "What's going on? Do I need to come in?" Saige bit her lip, waiting for the nurse to answer.

"Aiden is short of breath again," Nurse Oswald replied.

"The surgery was text-book perfect. Order a nuclear med scan STAT. Turn Aiden on his left side and get an echocardiogram." Gray rattled off a list of blood tests for her to order as well. "I'm heading to the hospital." He ended the call. "We've got to get a move on it, Saige." Lung clots were serious business.

"Thankfully, Central Sinai has excellent nurses."

Gray nodded then called Dr. Alberetti. "Al, this is Gray. Aiden Littlefield is short of breath again. I ordered a nuclear scan. I'm an hour out. Can you run over to the hospital and check on him? And order the blood thinner if the scan is positive. I'll be there as soon as possible."

Gray ended the call. "We've got to go."

Saige grabbed the last box of her belongings, but Gray intercepted her at the stairwell and lifted it from her arms. She peered at him with gratefulness lighting her eyes. He nodded at her before hurrying down the stairwell.

He reached the car first, opened the backseat passenger door, and tossed Saige's box inside. He opened her door, and she scrambled into the front seat. Not missing a step, Gray jumped into his car and stepped on the gas, almost squealing tires from the parking lot.

Dr. Alberetti would beat them to the hospital and tend to Aiden. Since Gray was such a stickler for details, he felt confident that any doctor who worked for him would follow suit.

After a few traffic lights, Gray slammed the brakes and slapped the steering wheel. "We've hit every red light!" He gripped a handful of his hair. "Why can't doctor specialists put sirens on our roofs to bypass lights and traffic like ambulances do?"

"I agree." Saige braced her hands on the dashboard as if preparing for a wild ride.

The light turned green and Gray floored the gas pedal. He'd never lost a patient, but nothing was certain in medicine, especially with surgeries. Problems could erupt out of nowhere from even the simplest of cases; he'd seen firsthand examples.

He made the hour-long drive to the hospital in forty minutes—record time. After parking, he and Saige tore from the car and raced to the ICU through the doctor's entrance. On their arrival, Gray headed to the nurse's station to read test results and talk with the nurse and Dr. Alberetti, while Saige walked double time to Aiden's room.

Aiden was pale but resting quietly as Saige entered the room and walked to his bedside.

"I'm here for you, Aiden. Are you doing okay?"

"I'm fine."

Why did he always say that when he wasn't *fine*? She stroked his arm and studied the monitors and IVs. "This is just a hiccup. Gray and Dr. Alberetti are on top of things. You'll be okay." She eyed his heart rhythm, vital signs, and oxygen level. "I was wondering if I should call Darcy? I think she'd like to know about your accident and surgery."

His eyes filled with tears. "Sure."

"I'll step outside your room for a few minutes and call her." Saige walked to the visitor's lounge on the other side of the ICU door. "Darcy? This is Saige. Are you having a nice vacation?"

"I am, Saige. What's up?"

Talking a mile a minute, Saige filled her in on every detail.

Urgency replaced Darcy's usually calm voice. "I'll be there in a few hours."

Why hadn't Saige called her sooner? Was she that protective of Aiden? Yes, she was. She had tried to spare him from more tears after Darcy's cheating incident, but his heart problem was a life-or-death situation. She hoped Darcy wouldn't fault her for the delay.

Saige returned to Aiden's room and gave him the news. He sobbed like a baby—unless they were tears of utter joy. She insisted on staying at his bedside while Gray drove home to catch up on some much-needed sleep.

The senior Dr. Littlefield and his wife welcomed Saige's offer to allow them an evening to rest as well. Saige didn't bat an eye at the inconvenience—she was used to spending long hours on call.

Just before 5:00, Aiden's door opened. Saige hurried through the threshold and hugged Darcy, who stood there wide-eyed as she scanned the ICU room. Saige filled her in on Aiden's condition then walked with her to the bedside.

Intravenous lines hung from a pole at the top of Aiden's bed. One line infused a heparin drip. An empty antibiotic bag hung piggyback to a larger fluid bag. Oxygen continued through a mask over his nose and monitors flashed his heart rhythm and vital signs. But he looked up when Darcy entered the room. She nodded at Saige before tiptoeing to his side. "I wish I'd known you had surgery, Aiden." She peered down at him with sadness brimming her eyes.

"Everything happened so fast, Darcy. I'm sorry." Saige stepped back, giving her space. "I should have called you."

Without hesitation, Darcy leaned over the bedrail, lifted the oxygen mask, and planted a kiss on Aiden's lips. "I've missed you. I haven't dated a soul since the lawyer. I'll understand if you want me to leave, but if you don't mind, I'd like to stay here until you're better." She lifted his hand to her bosom.

Tears ran down Aiden's face. "Darcy…I…still…love…you."

She lowered the siderail, placed her head against his cheek, and hugged him. "I love you too. I'm so sorry for hurting you. I'll sit here by your side. You don't have to talk now. Just heal."

Aiden squeezed her hand, not letting go. He raised his shoulders at Saige in an "I'm sorry" gesture, and she nodded at him. "I understand."

Darcy repositioned the siderail and lowered herself into the chair by his bed, holding his hand through the rail. "Try to rest, Aiden."

Saige touched Darcy's shoulder. "You two were meant to be." She winked at Aiden then backstepped to the door. But she glanced over her shoulder before leaving the room. Darcy hadn't stopped staring at Aiden, and he hadn't let go of her hand. It had never been about Saige for him. But why had he strung her along? Had it been his retaliation for Darcy's mistake?

Saige had to call Gray. She nearly ran to the visitor's lounge, cell phone at the ready for the most important call of her life. To her amazement the ICU visitor's lounge was empty. She tapped in Gray's phone number.

"Hello, Saige. How's Aiden doing?"

"He's hanging in there. But you aren't going to believe this. I called Darcy to let her know about his condition. She arrived a few minutes ago and plans to stay by his bedside until he heals. She and Aiden had a wonderful reunion. He told her he still loves her, and she told him the same. He's forgiven her. I no longer feel obligated to marry him or follow him into the missionary field."

"I believe the difference between love and friendship is that a friend will be there when needed, but a true love will never leave your side."

Saige thought about Gray's words. She hadn't stayed at Aiden's side the whole time he was in the hospital, but then again, his condition hadn't allowed for him to have much activity or excitement. And she'd never in her life given him a real kiss on the lips. The only thing she'd been to him was a friend—not a girlfriend. Gray noticed it. Aiden must have figured it out as well. He told Darcy he still loved her in front of Saige as though releasing her from her commitments.

Saige didn't mind. She loved Aiden—almost on the same level as she loved her brother Liam. She and Aiden had fourteen years of history behind them as friends, but never a true romantic moment.

She thought she'd have to settle by marrying Aiden when in truth, he was settling to marry her. Darcy had kissed him on the lips as though comfortable with the act. She was Aiden's true love.

Relief washed over Saige.

"Saige? Saige? Are you there?" Gray was still on the phone.

"Yes, I'm so sorry. I was lost in thought for a minute."

"Your news is wonderful. But I wish you'd called me twenty minutes ago. I told Lilith to expect a ring tomorrow night. She's buying a special dress and making elaborate plans. Saige, this is a terrible mess. What can I do now? How do I fix this? If I change my mind with Lilith, she'll make a terrible scene and destroy me in front of my friends. You've never seen her tantrums. Let me come to the hospital and take you to Mrs. Salucci's Boarding House."

Saige cried harder than she'd ever cried before. "Why? Why? Please tell me this is a joke. We finally have the opportunity to be together, and now, you've made a commitment to Lilith?"

"It isn't a joke. I'd never joke about something this serious." Gray's voice choked as he spoke. "I had to tell Lilith. She doesn't like surprises. She has to wear the perfect dress for every occasion. Why didn't you call me twenty minutes ago? Now, I have a disaster on my hands. Wait there for me. I'm coming to the hospital."

Saige sobbed into the back of her fist. "I'll wait for you. But hurry."

Fifteen minutes later Gray dashed into the ICU waiting room. "Saige!"

She had nodded off on one of the comfortable chairs, but Gray's voice startled her awake. "Gray!" She ran into his arms and hugged him with a steel grip, not letting go, not caring if anyone walked into the room. Gray kissed her passionately, and she hoped it would never end. "What are we to do?"

"For now, I must go through with the engagement. Saige, believe me, I'm as distraught as you are."

Saige shook her head. There was nothing either of them could do, but their hug and kiss gave her strength to do what she knew she had to

211

do. "I'll call a cab to take me home, Gray. You sound beyond exhausted. When I get to Mrs. Salucci's, I plan to sleep."

"It's been a long week. I enjoyed visiting your farm and meeting your family though. They're wonderful people." Was Gray's sluggish voice from tiredness or depression?

"I'll get my boxes from your car tomorrow." Saige stepped away from him, afraid if she didn't now, she'd never let him go.

"You won't have to get the boxes. I already dropped them off at Mrs. Salucci's. You're all set. And Mrs. Salucci is pleased you'll be staying with her. Does this mean you'll accept the invitation to work at the Addington Complex?"

"Yes, Gray. It's my dream job. But I'll only work there if we agree to be friends. I won't break up your relationship with Lilith. I do have something to discuss with you tomorrow night though. Then you can decide if you still want me working for you."

"Is it the one last thing you tried to tell me in the car? I apologize for not finishing our conversation after the lawyer called. Whatever you have to say, I can handle it."

"Thanks, Gray. We'll see how you feel about it tomorrow."

THIRTY-TWO

A t precisely noon the following day, Gray took a seat on one of the overstuffed designer chairs in the mansion living room. Fernsby, ever the fastidious valet, ushered the businesslike attorney past the blazing fireplace, the ribbon-laced evergreen boughs on the mantle, and the grand Christmas tree. After escorting the man to a seat beside a makeshift wooden desk, Fernsby walked to the sofa by Adele, who scooted a few feet away from him as he planted his bottom on a cushion beside her.

Claire, the maid, and Roger, the gardener, entered the room and studied the attendees as though trying to pinpoint the reason for their invite. The two servants scooted onto the loveseat while Gray repositioned himself in his chair by the matching one Lilith had chosen. Gray raised his brows at his soon-to-be fiancé. "Why are you here?"

"Mr. Newman notified me to attend, darling. Why else would I be here?" Turning her head and covering her mouth, she gave the tiniest of coughs.

The attorney cleared his throat. All eyes converged on him as he unbuttoned his suit jacket, settled into the leather armchair, and opened his briefcase. Taking his time, he removed a few papers and closed the lid. Then, after pulling reading glasses and a cloth from his inner suit pocket, he wiped the glasses and put them on his face.

Peering down over his narrow-rimmed glasses at the group, he began in a booming voice. "I'm sure you're all quite confused as to the reason behind the expedited reading of this will. And, I might add, for

213

the selection of the required attendees. But all will become apparent soon.

"First, I must tell you that I had many talks with the senior Dr. Addington. It might come as a shock, but due to the worldwide virus more than a year ago, the Addington Complex lost a great deal of money—"

Lilith smirked and crossed her legs. "Excuse me, but is this information necessary in front of the servants?" She placed her elbow on the chair arm then pressed her finger against her high cheekbone.

Mr. Newman gripped his glasses before lowering them to inspect Lilith more closely. "I'm doing exactly as Dr. Edgar Bridgemont Addington instructed."

Lilith whipped her head away from him and tapped her foot on the polished floor.

The attorney readjusted his glasses before continuing. "Now, if I may. The Addington Complex lost a great deal of money due to the shutdown of businesses in our state."

Already in shock from his parents' deaths, Gray's mind went into a tailspin. Was his world about to crash around him?

Mr. Newman studied Gray for a few seconds before softening his demeanor. "I'll get right to the point."

"Prestigious doctors' salaries are exorbitant, and the good doctor had to decide whether to pay out of pocket to retain his specialists or risk losing them to other hospitals and medical venues after the state-mandated isolation. The senior Dr. Addington mortgaged his home to pay for his doctors' salaries during the six-month quarantine."

Gray's jaw tensed as Lilith gasped.

The attorney flipped over the first page. "Now, if you will be so kind, I'll summarize the contents of the will: the senior Dr. Addington used his entire savings to build the magnificent Addington Complex. The business hadn't quite reached the point of making money for him when the virus hit, but he had already depleted most of the money in his bank account to keep the Complex running. Which is why...Dr. Addington died penniless."

Gasps filled the room.

"What will we do? Are we destitute?" Adele scooted to the edge of the sofa.

Gray coughed uncontrollably until Fernsby handed him a glass of water. "This will help, sir."

Gray chugged down the liquid, hoping it might wash away the horrible taste of the unexpected disclosure. How many more calamities could he handle at one time? As an experienced surgeon, the answer was obvious—every one of them and more. "Calm down." He coughed then cleared his throat. "I have a sizable savings account. Plus, I earn enough money as a cardiothoracic surgeon to pay your salaries."

Mr. Newman cleared his throat again. "If Gray were to sell the Complex, he'd eliminate the immediate problems from its revenue loss. And if he were to sell the mansion, he could purchase a wonderful new home, although it might not be as sophisticated as what he's used to."

Lilith jumped up from her designer chair and ran to the lawyer's makeshift desk. Casting her dignity aside, she grappled with him for the paper. "What about me? Am I in there? Will I stop getting a paycheck?" Mr. Newman removed her flying finger from the page.

"I've been paid well for teaching Gray how to blend into society." Lilith fisted her hands on her hips. "Dr. Addington assured me that I'd inherit enough money to keep my father's shipping business afloat if I marry Gray. Without his money, my family will lose our glorious mansion, the one I adore and stand to inherit."

So that's what Lilith meant when she stopped mid-sentence at the Pie Factory. She worked for his father. It all made sense now. Gray, the intellectual nerd, required instructions on manners and how to dress. He was nothing more than a job to Lilith. No wonder she acted so business-like around him—ordering him to do this and demanding he do that. Gray ran to her side and clutched her wrist. "So, you've lied to me? You never loved me?"

Lilith fought to free herself from his grasp. "I love Romano Cortalini, an Italian clothing designer from Italy. I've loved him for years. But I've stayed with you out of a sense of duty."

"Or was it for the paycheck? You're finished, Lilith. There's no more need for you in my life." Gray dusted his hands of her, turning away from her side.

"Humph." Fernsby shook his head. "We've known her and her family for what they are, sir—"

Planting her palm in the air, Adele interrupted him. "She's a money-grubbing, pretentious socialite who wouldn't have two sticks to rub together if it weren't for your father, sir." She punctuated her speech with a dramatic head nod.

"That's right, sir." Fernsby picked up the tale. "Mr. LaRue would have gone out of business years ago except for the constant cash flow from your father. The man mismanages accounts, sir."

"What Fernsby is trying to tactfully say is that Mr. LaRue is a gambler of the highest order." Adele narrowed her eyes at Lilith.

"I couldn't make my father stop." Lilith pointed at Adele and Fernsby. "But I'm not the only one who's carried a secret in this house. What about you two sniveling no-goods?"

Fernsby and Adele lowered their heads without uttering a word.

His most trusted servants? "What's going on?" Gray raised his hands. "Out with it then! Tell me what I don't know!"

Fernsby and Adele studied each other's faces as though deciding who should speak first. Fernsby walked to Adele's side, sat down, and placed his hand on her knees. "I'll do it." He sucked in a deep breath then laced his fingers, taking his time to think.

Unable to stand still, Lilith jumped into the conversation and spewed venom at them. She wagged her finger from one to the other before shouting, "Ask them who your real parents are!"

Gray shoved the hair away from his forehead, clutching it in his hands. "Wh-what? Am I adopted?"

Fernsby cleared his throat and mopped his brow. "I'm sorry, sir, it's my fault. Don't blame your mother."

"My mother?"

"I've wanted to tell you since you were old enough to understand, Gray," Adele began. "Fernsby and I came to America from England with our two children a little more than thirty-four years ago. We journeyed to this country for a better life, hoping to find employment since I was pregnant with our third child. But our pockets were empty. Worse than that, we had no prospects for a job. So Fernsby decided we should knock on mansion doors in St. Anne's Landing."

"Begging for money?" Did he belong to paupers? Gray dropped into a nearby chair, gripping the arms for support.

"No, Gray. To ask for work as a valet and cook—" Adele's voice rose to a pitch that betrayed her raw nerves as she quivered while telling their story.

Fernsby interrupted her. "Mrs. Addington answered the door. She was kind and understanding. When she noticed our British accents, she brought us inside for an interview. But it wasn't until Adele waddled to the study that Mrs. Addington's eyes went to her pregnant belly."

"Let me tell it, Fernsby." Adele continued. "Mrs. Addington shared about her numerous miscarriages—her inability to bear children. Quite flustered, she excused herself to fetch us tea. On her return, she brought her husband. They held hands then dared to speak to us about a plan. 'We've got a brilliant idea,' Dr. Addington said. 'Since you two are penniless, would you allow us to adopt your child at birth? We would give it our family name and inheritance and raise it as our own.'"

"They agreed to hire me as your au pair to oversee your upbringing." Adele wiped the tears streaming down her face with the back of her hand. "They insisted on Fernsby and me learning proper English to erase our lower-class British accents. They brought tutors to the mansion."

Fernsby stopped Adele by touching her shoulder. "Adele didn't want any part of their plan. She begged me to say no. But the Addingtons were our last hope for employment. We would have been beggars on the street at that point. I was fearful that our family would die from starvation. And with no income, how would we feed, clothe, and house an infant?"

"It was hard for me to place my baby in another woman's arms." Adele blew her nose on a tissue supplied by Claire. "They named you. They paid for your entire upbringing. But I changed every one of your nappies, bathed you, and kept you under my wings. We agreed never

217

to speak the truth. If Lilith hadn't opened her mouth just now, it would have remained a secret." Sobbing inconsolably, Adele wrung the hem of her dress.

"I'm not happy about my decision," Fernsby said. "I had to use wisdom to decide the best course for you. Was it better to place you in arms that would sustain you rather than in arms that would bury you? Starvation is an ugly thing. Before we traveled to America, we witnessed deaths on the streets of England."

Gray was unable to speak. He looked at Lilith with narrowed eyes as the shock of her exposing his servants took hold. Unsure of the answer, he hesitated before asking Fernsby, "If I was your third child, where are your other children?" He held his breath, hoping for good news rather than bad.

"They were under the age of ten when we arrived at the mansion. The Addingtons took them in as well—Roger as a young gardener's assistant and Claire as an apprentice to their maid. They lived here in the mansion with Adele and me for more than ten years—until they married and had families of their own. They played with you when you were a lad."

Gray peered at Claire and Roger, who sat uneasily on the loveseat. How had he not seen it before? They had his same wavy brown hair, dimpled chin, and crystal blue eyes. "It must have been difficult to share your parents with me. Weren't you jealous?"

Roger shook his head adamantly as though sure of his response. "Not at all, sir. Mum and Dad gave us every bit as much love as you received until we married and had homes of our own."

"We were happy, sir, but we missed our times together as the years passed. When you became a doctor, you were out of our league." Claire smiled. Was she happy the charade was over?

"Please, don't call me sir. I'm not your boss. I'm your sibling." Then he glanced at Fernsby and Adele. "And you two, please call me Gray."

Lilith rose from the chair, unfastened a bracelet on her wrist, and threw it at Gray. Without waiting for Gray's response, she stomped across the room. "Enjoy your family reunion!"

"Wait, Lilith!" Gray scooped the jewelry from the floor. "You've been wearing this?"

Roger blocked her exit from the sunken living room. "The way I learned it, that's called stealing. Claire, call the police."

"Stop! I wasn't stealing. I've never stolen anything in my life. I borrowed the bracelet to locate the owner before you did, Gray. I wanted to tell her about your father's plan for me to marry you and keep you in your social standing. Your father didn't want anyone ruining it. He only meant well for you. Please believe me. He and Mrs. Addington loved you more than life itself. They used me to accomplish their plans and compensated me well for it. As a result, your adoptive father made you into the man you are today."

"So, you merely pretended to love me?"

"I'm sorry. If you'll think about our time together, I protected you from social blunders. So please don't hate me. I only followed orders."

"No wonder I felt controlled. My father didn't allow me to make decisions or fail. Why didn't you tell me about Lilith, Fernsby?"

"I tried many times, and in many ways, but you refused to heed me. Because of my agreement with your parents, I couldn't say too much. If we ever told the truth, they would have called us liars, ended our employment, and thrown our family out on the streets, keeping you in the bargain."

"So, everything the Addingtons did was because they loved me and couldn't bear anything unfortunate happening to me?" The whole thing was incredulous. He couldn't wrap his head around it.

"That's right, Gray. It's the only thing that's kept me sane." Adele dabbed the corners of her eyes.

Gray studied Lilith. "What would you have done had you found the owner of the bracelet?"

"I did learn who she is, and I planned to tell her there's a far greater plan for your life than falling in love with a farm girl, darling. I had to intervene. Your father paid me to keep you in good social standing, so I decided to return her bracelet and ask her to bow out of your life. You must believe me on this. I've always cared for you. I'm sorry I led you to believe I loved you. That was wrong. But you must understand, I was trying to help my family."

A sudden thought struck Gray—the girl who fell came from a farm. "No need for the police, Claire, Roger. I feel used, but that isn't grounds to jail her." Gray slipped the bracelet into his pocket. "Please leave, Lilith. Find another way to save your father from ruin."

"Perhaps if he stopped gambling, there would be hope for his business." Fernsby walked to Lilith's side, his elbow crooked for her arm, prepared to escort her to the door.

"Perhaps if Dr. Addington hadn't used my father as a bookie to place his own bets, you wouldn't have lost the Addington Complex, Gray." Lilith licked her finger and pressed it against the air as though scoring the winning point. Then she tilted her nose, shunning Fernsby's arm. "Darling, ask your parents to divulge their last name." With that, she strutted out of the room like a proud peacock.

♥

"This was quite an enlightening experience." Thomas Newman packed the briefcase with his paperwork then stood to leave the Addington living room Saturday afternoon. "I left copies of the will on the desk, Gray. Please sign and return them to me at your convenience. There's no money to change hands, but I have the key to the lockbox where your parents placed the deeds to the Complex and the mansion." With a nod, he added, "I'm sure you'll come up with a plan for what to do next."

Gray shook the man's hand before Fernsby ushered him to the door.

Trying to make sense of the many revelations, Gray rose from his seat and paced the floor. The news about his childhood had been hard to swallow, but the little time spent with the Addingtons and their desire for him to learn social graces because of his upbringing with lower-class Fernsby and Adele became all too clear.

As Fernsby returned, Gray stopped pacing. "So, you and Adele are married?" He watched the valet cross the marble tiles.

Fernsby completed his trip to the sofa and resumed his spot beside Adele before answering. "We never divorced, but she's avoided me since the day I forced her to hand you over to the Addingtons." He glanced at Adele. "If it weren't for her distaste for Lilith, she'd still not be talking to me. But after the girl fell at the Christmas party, we joined forces—to find her bracelet, that is. It gave us hope that another girl had captured your heart. The two of us would have done anything to steer you away from Lilith."

"Because she knew too much about my adoption?"

"No, no, no. Because Lilith was using you and your family for money. We've known about Romano. We've seen her around town with him. We also overheard your parents' conversations with Lilith's parents, the LaRues, about Mr. LaRue's failed business deals. After you became a prominent doctor, the LaRues threatened to tell society about your adoption from beggars. To keep it from happening, Dr. Addington paid them hush money. But I had no idea that Mr. LaRue placed bets for your father."

"I'm glad they're out of our lives now." Gray wanted the whole terrible mess to end. But would the surprises never cease? "Lilith said something about me not wanting your last name. I can handle anything at this point. If I may ask, what is your surname?"

Fernsby glanced at Adele then at Claire and Roger. "Our ancestors hailed from Scotland, having moved to England a century ago. He pointed to each member of his family—we're the proud Smellies."

"I'm a Smellie?" Gray scratched his head.

"Indeed, son, you're a Scottish Smellie.

"About what I said a minute ago—I'm not sure I can handle that one."

221

THIRTY-THREE

Early Saturday evening, Saige scooted to the edge of the canopy bed in her room at Mrs. Salucci's and lifted the picture of her family from the nightstand. God must have had an amazing reason for allowing Mom to die, but Saige didn't have to be happy with it. Mom had been the most important person in the world to her. Life had been perfect before she became ill. Pop had grown corn and sold it to the community as well as to major canning companies, and their cows and chickens provided milk, butter, and eggs. She and her siblings had made cheeses while Mom baked loaves of bread and pies to sell at the local market. People in the community picked blueberries and strawberries from their fields. Saige loved growing up on their plush green farmland.

But nothing was the same after Mom developed breast cancer. And to make matters worse, Saige had gone away to medical school, leaving Pop, Annie, and Liam to make do on their own. But they had done it. They made their lives count. Liam had become a psychologist, Annie would soon be entering nursing school, and Pop was still good ol' Pop. The farm hadn't changed, and her family still laughed about everyday things.

Mom would have liked Gray if their relationship had blossomed instead of drowned in tears. He wasn't pompous or stuffy for a wealthy man. Instead, he was down-to-earth, kind, and considerate. She couldn't imagine him wearing a silk smoking jacket at night or saying "old chap" this and "old chap" that. He would make a nice friend.

Now that becoming a missionary with Aiden was no longer part of her equation, Saige needed to pay heed to what her mother had engraved on her bracelet—the one she lost: "To my precious gem: You will conquer giants. Love, Mom."

What had her mother meant? Saige didn't have giants in her life, did she? She thought for a few minutes. If she had one, it was fear—fear of being exposed as a bumpkin and not a socialite. And fear of being labeled a dummy instead of a brilliant cardiologist. But what did any of that matter? As Aiden would have said, she was who she was. And as Gray had told her at the farm, social status didn't matter. Many wealthy people weren't who they appeared to be. As she thought about it more, she should have had the courage to tell Gray about her invitation to work at his complex soon after she met him at the clinic. She also should have told him she fell at his mansion. Those confessions would have eliminated two weeks of worry. And Gray might have known the whereabouts of her bracelet.

If the piece of jewelry on Lilith's wrist belonged to Saige, then Lilith had seen her fall. It was only a matter of time before Lilith exposed her identity. Did Saige care about that anymore? No. She did not. Gray enjoyed visiting her family farm, and he didn't blink an eye when he learned she was the appointee to his cardiology team.

So, she would work at his complex and her dream of becoming a prominent cardiologist would come true. Gray would marry Lilith. And Saige would go home after work to the boarding house and her friend Mrs. Salucci. Saige didn't need to live in the high society world. She was done fretting about social status. Gray liked her as a friend the way she was. But what might he think of her after learning she was the lady who fell at his first Christmas party?

She studied the gorgeous silver lace dress hanging on her doorknob and the practical high heels she had purchased. Her credit card had come in handy, but soon she'd have the income to pay for the items. Now, she had to think about the party. Did she have the nerve to attend the semi-formal event? Of course, she did. Gray had invited her. And she prided herself on keeping promises.

But before dressing for the evening, she wanted to do what Aiden had taught her—pray about everything first. She bowed her head. "Dear Lord, thank You for watching over Aiden and keeping him from harm. I'm so grateful You answered my prayers. And thank You that he and Darcy have reconnected. I would have kept my promise to You, but I'm happy things worked out the way they did. Was that You at work, Lord?

"Tonight, would You help me to have a wonderful time at the mansion and not fall or embarrass myself? And would You please help me find my bracelet and my Prince Charming? Those are the only two things I really want for Christmas. I pray that the man who carried me to the study will be there, and he'll recognize me. And this might sound crazy, Lord, but I hope he's my soul mate, the man I've dreamed about for so many years—my one true love. Will You please help me to find him? Thank You, Lord, for hearing my prayers. In Jesus' name, amen."

She rose from the bed, but as she stepped into the gorgeous dress she removed from the doorknob, a frown tugged at the corners of her mouth. She had lost Gray, the man she thought fulfilled her dreams. Tonight, Lilith would become his fiancé. But did he know about her infidelity? The man at the karaoke bar couldn't have been her brother—not from the way she kissed him. Lilith was all wrong for Gray. He'd spend a wretched lifetime with her. But how could Saige tell him what she saw? Lilith would deny it, and Gray would never believe Saige. He'd probably label her a troublemaker.

In another world or another time, he would have been the perfect man for Saige. He was everything she desired. But in God's vast plan, a relationship with him wasn't meant to be. Even though Aiden released Saige, Gray was still bound to Lilith.

But what did it matter? Once Gray learned the truth about her lack of social graces—the very things his parents despised, he'd likely put Saige out of his life anyway. Tears clouded her eyes. She'd never see Gray's cute, dimpled chin or sexy smile again. Tonight would be her farewell to him and his complex. She had decided to set up a practice in Marysville, her hometown. She opened her bedroom door and listened for Mrs. Salucci. "Are you upstairs?" she hollered.

"I'm down here," Mrs. Salucci called from the bottom stair. "What can I help you with, dear?"

"Would you mind zipping my dress?"

Mrs. Salucci hurried up the steps. "I'd be delighted to help you, dear." Saige twirled sideways for Mrs. Salucci as her hostess reached the landing. "My, you look lovely!" Mrs. Salucci's eyes sparkled, reflecting the shimmering silver dress.

"Thanks. I like the fit. I'm afraid I'll ruin my polished nails by pulling up the zipper, though. Do these stockings match the dress?"

"They're perfect. Let's see what the heels look like."

Saige returned to her bedroom and slipped on the fancy silver shoes. She pranced to the hallway and spun around. "So? What's your verdict?"

"You're stunning, Saige, but there's one more thing to polish your look. I used to be a hairdresser before I retired. Can I fix your hair?"

"That would be wonderful." Eager to look like the women guests from the Christmas party two weeks ago, Saige hurried to the vanity stool in her room.

Mrs. Salucci followed her then studied Saige's face from several angles. "Wait here. I'll collect a few pins and sparklies. You're going to look even more gorgeous than you already are."

After Mrs. Salucci hurried from the room, Saige bunched her hair above her neckline, posing this way and that in the mirror to determine how the upsweep might look.

"Here we are." Mrs. Salucci waltzed into the room like a schoolgirl, her hands filled with hair supplies.

Brushing and twisting several hair sections in the back of Saige's head, Mrs. Salucci created a masterpiece. The updo accented Saige's high cheekbones. Tiny sparkly diamond-like dots adorned her upswept tendrils. "This is much better than I expected. Thank you so much."

"You'll make a lasting impression tonight, my dear. I guarantee it." Mrs. Salucci zipped her dress.

Saige stared into the mirror. Would the impression affect Gray? She wouldn't dare try to steal him away from Lilith. So, it didn't matter. Her appearance tonight was strictly on a friendship level.

226

She checked the time on her cell phone: 6:43. Then she glanced out the bedroom window. The taxi driver hadn't arrived, so she placed another call.

"I'm sorry, ma'am. Christmas Eve and New Year's Eve are the two busiest days of the year. You'll be lucky to make it anywhere by 7:00." The call ended.

What was she supposed to do now—dressed in a gown without a ride? Saige wouldn't give up. The Westbrook stubborn streak ran in her family. She marched down the stairs with a matching purse in her hand and fierce determination in her strut. Throwing open the closet door, she snatched the cashmere coat, the same one she'd worn to the first Addington Christmas party. But a thought crossed her mind. She ran back upstairs. There was more than one way to skin a hog, pluck a chicken, or however rich people would say it.

Returning to the living room, coat buttoned to her shins, she searched for Aiden's car keys. She'd drive his limping junk heap to the party. If she were lucky, no one would spot it in the dark. She'd slip through the mansion gate, park in the darkest area of the front, and slip out again before midnight—the hour she didn't want to be on the road if the psychedelic pumpkin fell apart.

More than her desire to avoid disgrace, she wanted to support Gray on this special night—the night he'd slip a ring on the finger of the wicked witch of the west, and Lilith would slip one in his snout.

"Are you looking for these?" Dangling the keys between her fingers, she walked into the living room, Mrs. Salucci chuckled. "It's getting late, and I figured Aiden's car would be your only recourse tonight. People around here make plans with cab drivers far in advance."

"You always seem to read my mind." Saige donned her wool scarf before accepting the keys. "I'm off!"

"Enjoy yourself, Saige. You deserve a fun evening."

Saige hugged her hostess then headed to the back door. "Don't wait up for me. Who knows what'll happen tonight."

♥

After driving the rattling car past the mansion's gatehouse, Saige clutched the steering wheel. She headed toward a darkened area down from the home's circular driveway. As she stared up at the towering mansion, she experienced déjà vu. Except this time, she wasn't wearing stilettos. Time had whizzed by in a flurry of dilemmas since her last unfortunate visit to the place.

But most of her experiences with Gray had been fun—at the clinic, the karaoke bar, shopping, and visiting her family's farm. She sighed, reminding herself they were friends, but nothing more. Two short weeks ago, she had two men competing for her attention, and now she had none.

She'd make an appearance tonight, watch the engagement, and slip out the door without creating a fuss. Psyching herself with a can-do attitude, she checked her hair and makeup before opening the creaky car door and walking to the mansion steps. Light snow flurries fell on her face, a welcome sight compared to the heavy snowfall in the last few days.

Her heart quivered with remorse at losing Gray as she climbed the steps in her practical heels—the heels Gray had insisted on her purchasing to keep her safe. At the massive front door, she stopped to peek inside. Bright lights shone through the frosted glass side panels as they had the first time she arrived at the mansion. Similarly, a piano rendition of "Deck the Halls" boomed inside the home. It was the same music she'd heard on entering the mansion two weeks ago. But she wouldn't fall this time because she was prepared for the sunken living room. One more sidestep to the door. She checked that her dress wasn't bunched under her coat then lifted the brass door knocker. Three raps. Was that enough?

The door opened.

The elderly nutcracker met her face to face. He clicked his heels, removed his black hat, and swished it across his waist to bid her inside. A minty scent wafted by her nose. The nutcracker's appearance hadn't changed: white mustache, goatee, and hair; ruby-red lips, cheeks, and uniform; and his painted white face.

He helped Saige remove her coat. "You look lovely, miss." A grin widened his face and his eyes sparkled. Was he happy to see her? He disappeared with her coat as he had done before.

While Saige waited for his return, she reacquainted herself with the foyer. It was just as elegant as last time. White candles set in cranberry-red globes decorated a skinny wall table adorned with holly and evergreen boughs.

The nutcracker returned and crooked his arm for Saige. She looped hers in his and walked at his side—past the grand staircase and the piano player on the landing overhead. When the toy soldier reached the sunken living room, he turned to her. "Watch your step, miss."

She raised on her toes and kissed his cheek. "Thank you, sir. I only have one question. Where is the man who carried me to the study on the night I fell?"

"Follow me, miss." The nutcracker had lost his wooden behavior. He was still dignified and soldierly, but he conveyed more feeling as he tightened his elbow to his chest, securing her hand. Together, they stepped down into the sunken living room.

Walking in harmony, they headed for the fireplace, where a man in a designer suit peered at the fire. Even though his backside faced Saige, she recognized the figure. The wavy hair, the muscled frame. Even though his hair was lighter than she imagined because of the dimly lit study, his physique in the suit was unmistakable.

The nutcracker halted and clicked his heels at attention. Then, in the formal manner of a military soldier, he made an announcement. "Excuse me, sir. This young lady would like to meet you."

The man at the hearth turned in slow motion.

Saige peered into his crystal-blue eyes and smiled at his dimpled chin. Gray was the most handsome man she had ever seen. Was he the person who had carried her to the study?

Gray beamed from ear to ear. He cocked his head and squinted, searching beneath her makeup. "Ahh, I know this lady well, Fernsby." A glow spread across his chiseled face. "This is Saige. The young lady I've worked with at the free clinic downtown." He took her hands in his. "I'm so glad you came." His eyes moved over her dress again—the same gown she had worn on her ill-fated evening at the mansion. A hint of recognition sparkled in his eyes.

He must have remembered her. Her plan worked. She had changed into the rose-colored gown at the last minute, hoping the man who carried her to the study would divulge her identity so she woudn't have to. Breathless, she struggled to pull her thoughts together. "Gray, were you the man who rescued me the night I fell—at your first Christmas party?"

"Indeed, it was me."

She peered into his eyes. "I'm sorry for leaving the mansion without saying anything. But since then, every day, I've wanted to thank you for your kindness."

She also wanted to hug him, kiss him, and tell him "thank you" for rescuing her at the party and helping her in the clinic. But hugging him wouldn't be appropriate at his engagement party. She could barely take a breath in the fitted dress, let alone speak.

Gray placed her arm in his. "I believe you've met Fernsby, though not formally. He's my father. Dr. Addington adopted me."

Saige glanced from one man to the other, noticing the same crystal-blue eyes and dimpled chins. "I'll explain later," Gray whispered.

Fernsby puffed out his chest, and his eyes danced with delight at the mention of his relationship with Gray. "Nice to meet you, miss." He shook her hand.

Saige dipped in a slight curtsy. "You were the first person I met at the mansion."

"I apologize for your mishap, miss. I should have been paying attention. I learned a lesson that night."

Gray clapped him on the arm. "You certainly did, old chap."

Saige chuckled under her breath. Did he really just say, "Old chap"?

Taking her hand, Gray escorted her to the overstuffed chair that had trapped her upside-down during her accident. "Would you do me the honor of sitting here, Saige?"

What did he have planned? Was this her prime spot for viewing the formal proposal to his fiancé? Where was Lilith anyway—applying last-minute touches to her makeup? Unsure of Gray's purpose, Saige lowered herself into the comfortable cushion.

He reached into his suit pocket and removed a glistening diamond bracelet. As Saige watched him in disbelief, he gently took her hand and snapped the jewelry around her wrist. The keepsake from her mother! God had answered her prayers again. And her mother had been right. She had conquered her giant—her fear of the unknown. If Gray weren't marrying Lilith, she would have eagerly worked at the Addington Complex with all of its prestige.

"Where did you find my bracelet?"

"I had Fernsby scour the city to learn where it was purchased. He spotted you once—at a movie theater, but you got away before he could speak with you."

"Aiden and I returned to the cinema, but Fernsby and the lady at his side had already left."

"I've got to ask. Does Aiden drive a multi-colored Volkswagen Bug?"

Saige wished she didn't have to answer. "Yes, that partially describes his car."

"I saw it the night you went to the theater. It passed by Lilith and me on our way to a restaurant. To think, I was so close to meeting you."

"Where did you find the bracelet? And how did you know it belonged to me?"

"It's a long story. Let's just say, Lilith found it and gave it to me today."

"Where is your soon to be fiancé? Is she preparing for your announcement?"

"Forget about Lilith." Gray got down on one knee.

What was he doing? His behavior didn't make sense. "Gray?"

"Saige, since the moment you called me an orderly, you captured my heart. I've thought about you day and night—your smile, your laughter, and your kindness for others. I want to spend candlelight dinners and trips around the world with you. Would you please fulfill my dreams?" His starry eyes ignited her soul with hopes of love.

He handed her a small box that might hold jewelry. But it couldn't possibly be what she thought it was, could it? If so, it would be the biggest diamond ring she'd ever seen. Bigger than the Hope Diamond. She braced herself not to faint. Ever so carefully, she peeled off the silky ribbon and the beautiful velvet wrapping paper. Then she opened it. Inside the box lay a chocolate-covered strawberry. What was she supposed to do with it? Eat it? She tilted her head, wondering what to say.

"Do you remember giving me twelve chocolate-covered strawberries at your family Christmas gathering? They're my favorite treat in the world. I once told Fernsby that I'd know when I found my true love because I'd be willing to give her the last chocolate-covered strawberry on Earth. This is the last strawberry from the box. You're that person, Saige."

She peered back into his dreamy eyes then removed the strawberry from the box. "Thank you, Gray. And I'd know my true love because I'd eat it—even though I'm allergic to them." She brought the berry to her lips.

"Stop, Saige!" With a look of horror, Gray removed the chocolate treat from her hand and tossed it to Fernsby, then he smiled as he wrapped her in his arms and bestowed upon her lips the most charming, the most romantic kiss she'd ever imagined.

Did you enjoy *Love Calls the Shots?*
Would you please spread the fun by taking a pic of the book or ebook and share it with a few words on FB, Twitter, TikTok, and Instagram? And give a shout out in a brief review on:
Amazon: https://www.amazon.com/Love-Calls-Shots-sweet-romance/dp/1936501686
and at www.crossrivermedia.com?

~Thank you sweet friend! May God bless your heart~
Deb Gardner Allard

Love Calls the Shots
www.debgardnerallard

Love Calls the Shots
www.debgardnerallard.com

ABOUT THE AUTHOR

Deb Allard has been a follower of Christ for more than forty-five years. Since becoming a Christian, she cherishes the joy and peace that come from having handed the reins of her heart and home to the Lord.

After growing up a Navy brat, she continued in her father's footsteps and spent two-and-a-half years in the Navy as a Corps Wave. She was even awarded the American Spirit of Honor Medal in boot camp. It was in the Navy that she met, and then married, the love of her life—Brian Allard, a fellow Navy man. Throughout Brian's twenty-year shore duty stints from Key West, Florida to Seattle, Washington, to California, and many states in between, they explored the sights, cultures, and traditions of different parts of the country with their three children.

During those years, Deb earned a BS degree in psychology and a second degree in registered nursing. She retired from nursing in 2010. Since then, she has taken numerous writing courses and workshops and attended many writing conferences. Deb has also read a plethora of books on the writing craft. A couple years ago she studied freelance editing and proofreading with The Christian Pen Institute and has taken the Writer's Digest copyediting course. Editing is Deb's passion.

She has a children's picture book under her belt and has won several writing contests and had two short stories published in anthologies.

When Deb isn't writing, reading about writing, editing, hiking, or playing with her eight bubbly grandchildren, she enjoys vegging out while watching Hallmark movies, chic flicks, HGTV, and PBS. Deb also enjoys encouraging other writers on their writing journeys.

Visit Deb at her website, debgardnerallard.com and friend her on two Facebook sites: Deb Allard and Deb Gardner Allard, author. She is also on Instagram and Twitter.

ACKNOWLEDGMENTS

Call it a village or call it a team, it takes many people to write a book. The author is merely the center of a vast hub. I have many people to thank. First, comes *my beta readers* who not only read my story but cheered me on to the finish line—getting the book published. If it weren't for these people, I might have given up on my dream. Thank you for your valuable feedback *Catherine Brakefield, Vie Stallings Herlocker, Susan Sloan, Bettie Boswell, Patsy Reiter, Lindsay Allard, Brenda Garver, Beverly Robertson, Dorothy Schwemmer, Ruth McGlothlin, Carol Williams, Barbara Thompson, Donna Vernon, Marlene Stuart Townend, GeAnn Powers, Judy Wilson, Brenda Hopma, Linda Crothers, Mary Jo Thayer,* and *Brian Allard.* I can't thank you enough for your time and your wonderful comments.

In addition to my beta readers, I owe a huge thanks to those who offered their opinions on the title of my book. Thank you for taking the time to give your suggestions. The winner of the drawing was my delightful new FB friend, *Deborah S. DeSantis.* Thanks, Deb!

I also owe much appreciation to CrossRiver Media Publishing. Thank you for taking a chance on my book. Thank you for teaching me the things I need to know about book marketing. I am forever grateful to you, ladies. May God bless your every endeavor.

And lastly, I'd like to thank all the readers out there who love romance books. Thank you for making writing these books pure joy. I hope and pray that you like *Love Calls the Shots* and will be eager to read the sequel.

Books that build battle-ready faith.

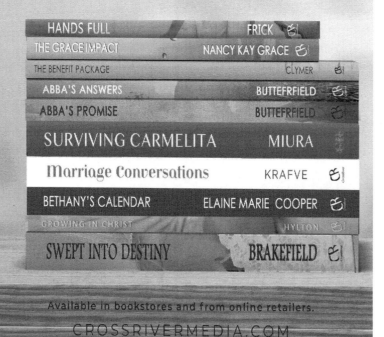

HANDS FULL	FRICK
THE GRACE IMPACT	NANCY KAY GRACE
THE BENEFIT PACKAGE	CLYMER
ABBA'S ANSWERS	BUTTEFRFIELD
ABBA'S PROMISE	BUTTEFRFIELD
SURVIVING CARMELITA	MIURA
Marriage Conversations	KRAFVE
BETHANY'S CALENDAR	ELAINE MARIE COOPER
GROWING IN CHRIST	HYLTON
SWEPT INTO DESTINY	BRAKEFIELD

Available in bookstores and from online retailers.

CROSSRIVERMEDIA.COM

Discover more great books at
CrossRiverMedia.com

CLAIMING HER INHERITANCE

A shooting, a stampede, a snakebite...Sally Clark has received an inheritance of a lifetime, but first she has to survive living on the ranch in Montana. Chase Reynolds is astounded that his father has willed one-third of their ranch to a total stranger. Who is this woman and what hold did she have over his dad? What Sally and Chase discover is beyond their imagination and wields far greater consequences than the inheritance.

OBEDIENT UNTO DEATH

Sinister forces are at work to destroy the fledgling Christian faith in Ephesus, and Sabina is in their way. A young scribe is murdered during a covert Christian worship service. Sabina, a member of this outlawed religion, can't believe a member of this new faith could be the killer. But when her Roman magistrate father arrests the church bishop for murder, she reluctantly admits all is not brotherly love and harmony among the faithful. Will she discover the truth in time, or will she be thrown in prison herself for her faith in Christ?

LOTTIE'S GIFT

She's a little girl with a big gift. Lottie Braun has enjoyed a happy childhood in rural Iowa with her father and older sister. But the quiet, nearly idyllic life she enjoyed as a child ended with tragedy and a secret that tore the two sisters apart. Forty years later, Lottie is a world-class pianist with a celebrated career and an empty personal life. One sleepless night, she allows herself to remember, and she discovers that memories, once allowed, are difficult to suppress. Will she ever find her way home?

Surviving Carmelita

When Josie's world implodes
there is only one place to go.

Available in bookstores and from online retailers.

 CrossRiver Media
www.crossrivermedia.com

If you enjoyed this book, will you consider sharing it with others?

- Please mention the book on Facebook, Instagram, Pinterest, or another social media site.

- Recommend this book to your small group, book club, and workplace.

- Head over to Facebook.com/CrossRiverMedia, 'Like' the page and post a comment as to what you enjoyed the most.

- Pick up a copy for someone you know who would be challenged or encouraged by this message.

- Write a review on your favorite ebook platform.

- To learn about our latest releases subscribe to our newsletter at CrossRiverMedia.com.

Made in the USA
Columbia, SC
18 September 2022

67468706R00130